The Cowboy Who Saved Christmas

Books by Jodi Thomas

Novels

Honey Creek series

Breakfast at the Honey Creek Café

Picnic in Someday Valley

Dinner on Primrose Hill

Beneath the Texas Sky

Novellas

One Night at the St. Nicholas

The Valentine's Curse

One Wish

Anthologies

A Texas Kind of Christmas

One Texas Night

Give Me a Cowboy

Give Me a Texas Ranger

Give Me a Texas Outlaw

A Texas Christmas

Be My Texas Valentine

Give Me a Texan

Books by Sharla Lovelace

Charmed in Texas series

A Charmed Little Lie

Lucky Charmed

Once a Charmer

Charmed at First Sight

A Charm Like You

The Cottage on Pumpkin and Vine

Books by Linda Broday

Anthologies

Give Me a Texan

Give Me a Cowboy

Give Me a Texas Ranger

Give Me a Texas Outlaw

A Texas Christmas

Be My Texas Valentine

JODI THOMAS
SHARLA LOVELACE
LINDA BRODAY

The Cowboy Who Saved Christmas

ZEBRA BOOKS
Kensington Publishing Corp.
www.kensingtonbooks.com

ZEBRA BOOKS are published by

Kensington Publishing Corp.
119 West 40th Street
New York, NY 10018

First Kensington Books Trade Paperback Printing: November 2020
First Zebra Books Mass-Market Paperback Printing: October 2021
ISBN-13: 978-1-4201-4993-7
ISBN-13: 978-1-4201-4994-4 (eBook)

10 9 8 7 6 5 4 3 2 1

Printed in the United States of America

Contents

Father Goose

Jodi Thomas

Chapter 1

Time: December 1867
Location: Jefferson, Texas

Trapper Hawkins rode into the settlement of Jefferson, Texas, at dusk, just as he had the day before. Late sunshine flickered off Big Cypress Bayou like diamonds on new-formed ice.

The wind was cold, promising rain that might change to snow by midnight. The temperature didn't matter. He'd been cold to the bone so long he wasn't sure he was alive. Now and then he thought if someone cut out his heart, he'd still function.

Memories drifted in his mind like sand on the wind. He'd been seventeen when he'd signed up to fight for his state, Tennessee, in a war he didn't understand between states. But his three big brothers were excited to go, and

Trapper didn't want to be left home on the farm with his father.

The old man blamed Trapper for his mother's death. His father never looked at his youngest and left Trapper's raising to his older sons. One of his first memories was being locked out of the cabin for forgetting to do something. He'd been four and the night was cold. He lay on the ground without cover and pretended he didn't feel the cold. Pretending became his first defense.

Trapper grinned to himself. His bad luck might have started at birth, but he chose to remember his childhood as easy, not the hard reality it had been. Maybe that was how he made it through the war. Maybe that was why playing the part of a gambler at night fitted him well. No one knew him, so he could be whoever he wanted to be.

As he moved down the main street of Jefferson, Trapper saw two soldiers walking toward him. The war had been over for two years, yet he still came to full alert when he saw Yankee blue.

He leaned forward, patting Midnight's neck so the soldiers couldn't see his face. "Easy now, boy," he whispered as he had a thousand times during the war. The horse seemed to understand to remain still and not make a sound.

Trapper never wore a uniform in the war. He'd first been assigned as a dispatcher. He rode from camp to camp delivering messages. He was tall and lean at seventeen. Young enough, or maybe dumb enough, to think it fun to tease danger. He'd cross the lines, play the part of a farmer when he was questioned, and set traps so that anyone following him would be sorry.

Often the traps caught game, and as the war lingered

on, the fresh meat was much needed. That was when the men began to call him Trapper. By the end of the war, he barely remembered his given name or the life he'd once had.

"Hello, mister," one of the soldiers yelled, drawing Trapper's attention. "Mind telling us why you're out so late? Shouldn't you be home having dinner?"

Trapper had no idea if this town had a curfew. When the soldiers came in after the war, they set all kinds of rules. Jailed people for pretty much any reason. Most of the Yankees were just doing their job, but a few, who came south to make a fortune, liked to cause trouble.

Trapper kept his hat low. Few could identify him from the war, but if someone did, he was a dead man. He'd been a spy many times. He'd traveled through northern states, picking up information. Men who crossed the lines were sometimes called gray shadows. They were the only Southerners not pardoned.

"I ain't got no wife." Trapper made a Southern accent drip from every word. "I'm heading to the saloon for my dinner. Heard it's only two bits."

One soldier moved closer. "Did you serve in the war?"

"I did." Trapper straightened. "I was one of the cooks for General Lee. They call me Trapper 'cause I can trap a rat, roast it with onions and greens, and you'll think you're eating at your mother's table."

Both men laughed. "My mother never cooked rat," one answered.

The other soldier waved him off.

Neither one questioned Trapper's lie. He'd figured out the more elaborate the lie, the easier it was believed.

As he neared the saloon, he smiled. Maybe, if his luck

held a few hours, he'd make enough money to buy a ticket on the westbound stage. Following the sun was his only goal.

When he'd gone home two years ago, he'd learned his brothers were dead, the farm had been sold for taxes, and his pa had disappeared. That night he'd slept in the trees near town and realized there was no home to go back to or memories to keep.

Trapper grew up during the war. All he'd learned was to fight, and he'd had enough of that for a lifetime. The only skill he'd developed was passing unnoticed through towns and open country. He could shoot and track any animal or man. He could live off the land, but he didn't know how to live with people.

Ever since the South surrendered, he'd watched people, never getting too close to anyone. You make friends, they get to know your secrets, and then they're not secrets anymore. In his case, one secret could end his life.

Saloons seemed to be the easiest place to find a cheap meal and disappear among strangers. He'd learned to play poker well during the war and followed three rules from the first day he walked into a saloon: One: Never step away from a table broke. Two: Never cheat. Three: Never sleep with one of the soiled doves who leaned on his shoulders from time to time.

They were the only women he met. A respectable woman wouldn't talk to a drifter or a gambler. Which left him with no midnight life, even though he left the tables with money in his pocket.

As the months rolled by, he kept moving west until he finally crossed into Texas. Here, there was less of a stain on the earth from war. The people might be poor, but they were still dreaming, not like most he'd seen. Yankees and

Rebels even talked over a drink now and then. Texas had more to worry about than scratching at old wounds. The state was still untamed, with most saloons little more than tents with dirt floors. If the storms and the rivers didn't kill you, outlaws and Apaches would.

Folks said half the men who survived the war were broken, but it seemed the ones in Texas were also downright crazy.

Trapper thought there must be good people in the world—settlers, farmers, traders—but the men he saw at the gaming tables often had dead eyes. They'd given up on life even though they still walked the earth. Others had become hunters looking for their next prey, be it animal or man. But here, in the Lone Star State, he'd found dreamers. And dreamers will always take a chance on the turn of the cards.

He managed to avoid the broken men or those who preyed on the weak as much as he could. Trapper studied people and saw few he wanted to remember.

As the sun set, he tied Midnight to the hitching post in front of the saloon. Be ready to ride had always been his motto. The town might be an important inland port, but Trapper feared trouble could be coming toward him just beyond the bend. A fast horse and lightning action had kept him alive many times.

A wreath of evergreen branches hanging in the bar window looked out of place. Three weeks away from Christmas, he thought, and the saloon boiled with unrest. In a few hours the place would be packed with men, angry and drunk. Like most, Trapper didn't care about the holiday. It was just another night.

He took a seat at a corner table near the kitchen. When he signed up for the War Between the States, he soon learned that one meal a day was a luxury. He always saved that one meal until sundown.

The thin cook, looking more kid than woman, brought him a plate of the nightly special. Trapper didn't look up.

"You want anything else?" The shy girl barely raised her head, and the worn hat she wore hid both her hair and her eyes.

"No, I'm good." He never talked to the women in the saloon more than needed, not even the kitchen help. He knew that as soon as this one filled out, she'd double, maybe triple her pay by climbing the stairs a few times a night. One night he'd see her in a fancy, low-cut dress, and not the rags she wore now. She'd be billed as a virgin for a few months, then the new girl for a while, and finally her rate would drop a bit and she'd simply be one of the doves. Her fancy dress would become ragged and her eyes dull from whiskey.

When the kitchen girl came back for his empty plate, he tipped her. She whispered a thank-you and moved away as a few men joined Trapper, ready to play cards.

Here among down-on-their-luck cowboys, outlaws, and river rats, the game was far more than poker. Trapper had to be able to read men. Sore losers, cheats, men looking for a fight, and even a few looking for a way to die.

But until he found work, it was his only way of making money. He could have just lived off the land, but he liked his bath in a bathhouse and he liked his one meal on a plate.

Trapper played his cards close. He never bragged when he won or complained when he lost. Tonight the game was casual, slow moving. It seemed the men at the table were simply drinking and playing to pass the time.

Trapper was about to call it a night when a barrel-chested teamster sat down at the table. He played with coins for a while, then offered his next hauling job as his ante.

"It's a three-week haul and pays five hundred dollars. Best part is I don't have to come back to Jefferson with the wagon. It's a one-way trip that pays ten times the normal rate. That should be worth money."

The drunks at the table laughed. "Yeah, all you have to do is stay alive between here and Dallas. Outlaws, raiders, storms, and who knows what. I heard this morning that one guy is already thinking about ambushing your wagon thanks to all your bragging. Must be something special if they pay so much."

Another man added in a mumble, "You shouldn't have been crowing so loud, mister. You just may have signed your own death certificate. There are men in this town willing to do anything for money."

The teamster smiled at the men. "But if you win this pot, and make it to Dallas, you'll have more than you made last year in your pocket. All you have to do is transport one wagon full of something priceless."

The big man patted his chest. "I may have got a bit drunk and said too much, but when I win this pot and take all your money, I'll be able to hire help. If one of you wins the pot, the trip will no longer be my problem."

Every man was in on the hand. A year's salary for a few dollars bet would be worth the chance.

Trapper didn't even smile; he simply played his cards.

Ten minutes later all were out but the teamster and Trapper. The pot was worth more than any since Trapper had been in Texas. If he won, he'd have money and a free ride to Dallas.

The teamster called. Trapper showed his hand. A pair of jacks.

The teamster smiled and laid down a pair of eights. "Looks like you win, stranger."

Trapper raised an eyebrow. The man looked too happy to have just lost.

The teamster leaned closer and whispered, "One thing I need to tell you. The cargo is five little girls. Spoiled and pampered rich kids. You'll need a lady's maid, a few men to ride shotgun, and probably a cannon to get them to Dallas. Every outlaw within a hundred miles has probably heard of the girls coming home and plans to ransom them after they leave you for the buzzards."

The teamster shook his head. "I might still have tried the trip except for one thing. The little girls' daddy has sworn to kill me if his daughters arrive with even a scratch. I figured out tonight that I'd be double dead if I took this job."

Trapper looked in the man's eyes and saw true fear. "Why don't the parents come to meet them?"

"Word is there's a big range war north of Dallas. If he leaves, he stands to lose all the land he's fought for. Some say he tried writing to the school to keep them over the holiday, but the girls were already on their way."

The teamster shrugged. "You'll spend all your money hiring guards and still not have enough." He stood. "Well, I'm heading home fifty dollars richer thanks to the advance they gave me. I'll keep the money left after I've bought the wagon and supplies. You can collect the rest if you make it to Dallas. If . . ." He walked away whistling.

Trapper didn't argue. It was too late. He'd won the pot. "Where do I find them?" he yelled at the teamster's back.

The man turned around. "They'll be arriving before noon tomorrow by paddleboat. The nurse with them will turn them over to you and return as soon as the boat is reloaded. A wagon will be waiting for you by the dock. It ain't big, but it's got a cover. I stocked it with enough food and water to last the trip."

"Aren't you going to be there to see us off?"

"No. I'm staying home with my wife. She's been complaining about having to go along since I signed on. She might be happy enough to be nice to me."

Trapper nodded. He'd faced worse odds before, like every night in the war, when he'd crossed enemy lines. Five hundred would give him a real start. So he'd take the job no matter what danger came with it.

Besides, how much trouble could five little girls be? They'd probably look at it as an adventure.

Chapter 2

Emery Adams watched the card game from the door of the kitchen. She usually tried to be invisible once she stepped into the saloon, but she liked serving supper to the tall man called Trapper. Once he'd glanced up at her, and she'd seen kind eyes in a hard face that rarely smiled.

He couldn't be much older than she was, twenty-four maybe, but he looked so confident. Sandy brown hair a bit too long, as most Westerners wore it, and blue eyes as blue as a summer sky.

He wasn't like the other men. He never tried to talk to her or kidded her about being so homely that men wouldn't take her upstairs even if the ride was free.

A few men would try to see if she was developing, but her mother wrapped her breasts every morning before Em slipped on the dress made of rough wool. It hung to her ankles and was hot in the kitchen, but it was the only way her mother would risk her working in the saloon.

If anyone knew she was twenty, she wouldn't be invisible. So she dressed the part of a girl not grown and shuffled her feet as she stared at the floor.

Eight years ago, when she'd just turned twelve, her father pulled her out of her bed before dawn and said it was time she earned her keep. Two of her sisters had married the year before and the third had run off.

Em was the only one of his worthless daughters left, and her father planned to take advantage of her shy ways. He knew she wouldn't fight him; he'd beat that out her when she was little. She'd do as she was told. Em, the baby, would never run away. She wouldn't have the energy after she learned to work. He'd make sure of that.

Em had to play the role or her father swore he'd turn her out to starve. She was small, but beneath her baggy clothes her body was definitely a woman's. Her mother cut her honey-brown hair blunt to her shoulders with bangs that hung in her eyes. As time passed, she braided it so her mother wouldn't cut it again.

At first she just washed dishes at the saloon where her father tended bar. She hauled supplies for the tiny kitchen, kept the fire going, and helped the old cook. When the cook died two years later, Em did both jobs.

Her father made sure she never saw her pay.

Though she had three sisters, her father swore Em would never leave him. Her hair was usually dull brown from the cook stove's smoke. As it grew longer, she stuffed it in an old hat she'd found left in the bar. Her skin was dull from never seeing the sun, and her body thin. Em's arms were scarred from burns. It had taken her a year to grow strong enough to lift the heavy pots without occasionally bumping her skin.

Her father reminded her now and then that she was worthless. She'd questioned him once about her pay, and he'd bruised the entire left side of her face with one blow. Em stayed, never owning a new dress or even a ribbon for her hair. Six nights a week she cooked, then cleaned at the saloon after midnight.

On the seventh day the saloon was closed. While her parents went to church, Em went in early to clean the upstairs. Half of the rooms were for the doves and their hourly guests. The other half were rented out to travelers. Once a week the sheets were changed and the rooms swept out, no matter how many times the rooms were rented.

The barmaids were nice and often left a quarter on their beds. A traveler once left a dollar. Em kept whatever money was left in the rented rooms hidden away in a rusty tin in the kitchen. It was mostly only change, but someday she might need it.

Long after Trapper's poker game was over and the saloon closed, she cleaned. In the silence she wished she could go on his journey. Even a dangerous adventure would be better than this. She'd grow old here, her days all the same.

When she finished cleaning, she heated one more pot of water and carried it upstairs to a back storage closet. At one time it had been a tiny room, but now the bed was broken, the windows boarded over to prevent a draft.

An old hip tub sat in one corner. Once a week, in the stillness before dawn, Em took a bath and pretended to be a lady. The drab, scratchy dress came off, as did the wrappings to make her look flat-chested. By candlelight she dreamed of more to her life than cooking and cleaning. If she just had a chance, she'd be brave, she told herself as she used the bits of lavender soap the girls tossed out.

In the silence, with warm water surrounding her, she relaxed and fell asleep. The tiny room's door was locked. No one would look for her.

When a noise downstairs jerked her awake, sunlight was coming through the cracks in the boards.

Em jumped out of the tub so fast she splashed water on her wool dress. Panic gripped her. She'd freeze walking the mile home in wet clothes.

She wrapped herself in a towel one of the barmaids had given her when she left, headed back to New Orleans on one of the paddleboats.

The barmaid had whispered, "Get out of this place, honey. It will rot your soul."

Em knew her parents wouldn't worry about her being late today. She often slept in the corner of the kitchen on the bench where deliveries were dumped. Her father never wanted to wait on her to finish her cleaning, and it never occurred to her that he might come back for her. She'd stayed in the kitchen a few times on Sunday so she could catch up.

As long as she did her work, he didn't care where she slept.

Em paced the tiny room. Over the years it had become a storage room for broken things no one had time to fix and lost luggage no one ever came back to claim.

A dusty black bag in the corner caught her eye. It was worn. The leather had been patched on one side. It had been in the corner for years.

She remembered the day she'd turned twelve and her father said she had to work. He'd almost dragged her into the back of the saloon. He'd showed her around the place and told her she'd have no more birthdays. She couldn't remember how long after that she'd found the forgotten little room. It became her one secret place where she could think and dream.

Now, feeling much like a thief, she loosened the straps on the old bag. Maybe she'd find a shawl or coat she could wear home. Em promised herself she'd return it tomorrow.

One by one she pulled the things from the bag. A black dress, undergarments, a shawl someone had crocheted with great care, and a pair of ladies' boots with heels too high to be practical.

It seemed to be everything she needed. She'd dress like a lady in the fancy clothes if only for a day. She'd walk through town with her head up. She'd be a woman and no longer pretend to be a girl.

In the bottom of the bag she noticed a thin black ribbon. When she tugged, a false bottom pulled open. Below lay three black boxes. They were made the same size as the bag, so unless someone looked closely, no one would see them.

Em pulled them out as if finding a treasure. The first was a small sewing box, packed full. The second was loaded with creams, a little brush, and a comb set to keep her hair in place. The third box held a Bible with money hidden one bill at a time between the pages. It wasn't much, but it might be enough to buy a ticket on the paddleboat or passage on the stage to the next town.

A gold ring lay in the corner of the third box.

Em slipped on the ring. It was a perfect fit. It was small, thin, the cheapest kind sold at the mercantile, but she'd never worn a ring before, so she felt beautiful wearing it.

Carefully, she began to put on the underthings. They smelled of dust, but they were clean. To her surprise, each fit. She'd seen camisoles in the stores, but she'd never felt one lightly touch her skin. The bodice pushed up her breasts and slimmed her waist.

With each piece she felt like she was shedding her old skin and putting on another. The shoes were a bit too big. The jacket a little too small.

When she stood and looked in the cracked mirror, Em didn't recognize herself. She pulled her damp, clean hair back with the combs and a woman stood before her. A lady in black with a widow's pin over her heart.

A plan shot through her thoughts. This was her chance. If she didn't take it, she'd wish every day for the rest of her life that she had.

Em rolled up the damp wool dress along with the towel and put them inside the leather bag. Then she circled the shawl over her shoulders, held her head high, and walked through the silent saloon. She quickly crossed to the kitchen and got the rusty tin that held her coins and rushed to the saloon's front door.

As a man entered, he held the door for her and said a polite, "Mornin', ma'am." He didn't realize his daughter was stepping out of his life.

"Goodbye, Father," she whispered when the door closed.

With shaking bravery she walked toward the dock where people were already gathering to welcome the paddleboat's arrival.

Chapter 3

Trapper spent the morning preparing for his new job as if it was an assignment during the war. He studied maps, learned a bit about his employer, the girls' father, Colonel Gunter Chapman. He'd been an officer in the Mexican–American War back in the 1840s. He was ruthless and came home with injuries. But that hadn't stopped him from moving farther west from the protection of even the forts and starting a huge ranch.

Trapper had seen that kind of man many times in the war. A king on his land.

Trapper bought clothes for winter, a new hat and a warm coat from his winnings last night. He'd worn most of his clothes too long for them to be presentable. Now, when he got to Dallas, he'd be dressed more like a cowboy, a Westerner. And, if the raiders killed him along the way, he'd have a fine funeral outfit.

Walking toward the dock, he planned. He'd meet the little ladies, tell them the rules for the trip, and get underway. He decided he needed only three rules. One: Be ready to travel at sunup. Two: Stop at midday for thirty minutes to rest, take care of private needs, and drink water. Three: At sundown make camp. He'd cook a meal of whatever he shot along the way or use the supplies.

When Trapper had checked the wagon, he noticed the teamster hadn't packed but two blankets, so he bought the girls each one. After all, they were little girls, and they'd need comfort.

He also added apples and canned peaches to his load.

Trapper was feeling hopeful about the journey. He'd bought two extra rifles and several boxes of bullets. He'd get these girls home safe and collect his five hundred dollars. Then he'd drive away in his new wagon with Midnight tied to the back.

A man who has a wagon, a horse, and enough money in his pocket to buy land was rich indeed. For the first time since the war he allowed himself to dream. He thought about something besides surviving one more day.

As he waited, he saw a small widow lady sitting on a bench near the dock. Trapper remembered the teamster had told him to hire a woman to travel with him, but surely he could handle five little girls.

There were so many women in black right after the war, it seemed like every woman dressed the same. Strange, he thought; the men wore blue and gray, but all the widows wore black. Mourning had no side, no color.

The paddleboat pulled up to yells and waves from the waiting crowd. As cargo began to roll off the side, passengers walked off the front in a thin line. It wasn't long before he saw a tall woman in a light blue cape marching with five little girls behind her. She had to be the nurse traveling with his cargo. They all wore a uniform of sunny blue and white. They reminded him of a mother goose and her goslings. He guessed he was about to become the father goose.

Trapper had no doubt these were his charges. The first girl was tall, only a head shorter than the nurse. Her blond hair was tied back, as if she was trying to look older. The next two were shorter, with auburn hair. The younger and thinner of the pair wore an old wool cap and seemed to be crying. The fourth girl was probably about five and was round as a goose egg. The last one, and the smallest, seemed to be having trouble staying in line. She weaved back and forth as she kept jumping up and down as if she could see everything if she was two inches higher.

Trapper straightened and removed his wide-brimmed hat. There were several families meeting travelers, but he was the only man standing alone in front of a small covered wagon. Eventually, the nurse would find him.

The tall woman weaved her way around groups of people and the girls followed in a row. Well, all but the last one followed. The littlest one seemed to be having trouble keeping up.

Finally, the lady noticed him and headed his way. She stopped three feet from him and the girls lined up behind her. Except number five, who bumped into four and almost knocked two and three out of line.

"Are you the driver for Colonel Chapman's girls?" The woman's voice was cold and held no hint of a Southern accent.

"I am." Trapper bowed slightly, not sure what to say or do. He decided to keep the poker game quiet. "I'm Trapper Hawkins, ma'am."

"I understood there would be a nurse traveling with you to take care of the girls' needs."

He thought of saying he could handle them, but for the first time he wasn't sure. Number five had lost her shoe and was starting to cry. The tall one, number one in the line, was glaring at him and the chubby one, number four, was laying her head on one shoulder, then the other, as if trying to see if he might look better from another angle.

"Mr. Hawkins, I'm sure you got the instructions. I assure you I will not be releasing my charges to you until you fulfill your part of the bargain. A woman to tend to their needs is essential."

He thought of giving up. Letting the oh-so-proper lady take them back. They'd be safer on the boat, if the rumors were true. "If I don't have a lady with me, you planning to turn around?"

"No. I'm going to file charges on you for breach of contract. Then I'll notify the girls' father and wait here until a proper escort can be arranged. Colonel Chapman will not be happy if his exact orders are not followed."

Trapper didn't even know if there was a crime called breach of contract in Texas. They had too many murders, robbers, and cattle thieves to mess with a breach of anything.

The woman pushed out her chest and made her stand. "If the colonel doesn't have his daughters home by Christmas, there will be hell to pay."

Trapper had no idea what she was talking about. He was starting to look forward to the outlaws on the trail.

"I'm loaded and ready, ma'am. I'll get them to Dallas."

She opened her mouth to fill him in on all the facts

when number five started limp-walking on one shoe and fell over her bag. Her foot went through the handle, so now she limped with one leg and dragged the bag with the other.

He just watched her. This last kid had the coordination of a day-old calf.

To no one's surprise, the tiny girl started crying.

The chubby one, number four in line, started to help the littlest one up, but the nurse cleared her throat so loudly several people turned in her direction.

Number four looked like she might cry too, but she let go of number five.

The nurse said to him in her lecture voice, "We don't baby our girls. Not even the littlest one. Understood? These girls are Texas princesses. Born in this wild state. They'll grow up to be strong women, not crybabies."

Trapper thought of pushing the nurse off the dock and seeing how strong she was, but he figured she'd file charges for that too.

Before anyone could move, a lady in black knelt down and lifted number five off the dock, freed her foot from the bag, and cradled the crying girl in her arms. "Come sit on the back of the wagon, child, and I'll put your shoe back on. It's far too cold a day to go without it."

The nurse glared at the woman for a moment, then seemed to relax. "I see the traveling companion for the girls has finally arrived. She'll be too soft on the girls and we'll have our work cut out for us when they come back to school in February. However, it is good to see you picked a proper lady."

As the widow tied the little girl's shoe, the nurse stepped away to direct the luggage to be loaded into the wagon.

Trapper leaned toward the widow. "Lady, if you have the time, would you act like you're traveling with me? Just till we get out of sight of that woman. I got to get these girls to Dallas and I'm not sure that nurse will let me do my job without a proper lady traveling with us."

"I was going to Dallas also." The widow's voice was low, almost a whisper. "The stage doesn't seem to be running this week. If you'll let me ride along with you, I'll play the part all the way."

Trapper was shocked. "You would?"

She nodded. "I'd be safer with you and five girls than traveling alone. If you prove to be a not-so-honorable man, I have a weapon and will shoot you."

He smiled. Her voice had a bit of the South in it and she could shoot. She had to be a born Texan. They understood each other. If he broke his word, she'd shoot him, no breach of contract needed.

"I'm Mrs. Adams."

Trapper removed his hat. "I'm Trapper Hawkins. You're doing me a great favor, ma'am."

The nurse came back as men finished loading the wagon. "I'd like to introduce my little ladies before I leave them with you."

She started with the oldest. "Catherine Claire, thirteen. Anna Jane, eleven. Elizabeth Rose, ten. Helen Wren five." The nurse pointed to the smallest, still in the widow's arms. "Sophia May is four. Colonel Chapman had three wives. All died in childbirth and none gave him a son. Poor man."

Trapper studied them as the nurse gave instructions to Mrs. Adams and marched back to the boat. The tallest daughter, with her blond hair, would probably be from the first wife. Two and Three from a redheaded wife. And

Four and Five from the third wife. He'd guess that wife had brown hair and big brown eyes.

Trapper turned to his charges. "Look, little ladies, I doubt I'll straighten those names out in three weeks, so how about I call you in order by number?" He pointed to the tall blonde, first in line. "One." Then the two auburn-haired girls. "Two and Three." He smiled at the next and couldn't help but laugh as she giggled, waiting for her number. "Four," he said, touching her nose. The tiny one waited for her new name. "You're Five. It's a game we'll play." He glanced at the widow. "A secret game. Like code names."

When he noticed the widow asked no questions, he added, "Only we have to call her Mrs. Adams. She deserves our respect. She lost her man in the war."

All the girls nodded except Five. She was spinning around again like an unbalanced top.

Chapter 4

After a stop at the outhouse behind the church, Trapper headed out smiling. He could almost feel the five hundred dollars in his hand. For once he was planning a future and not running away from a past.

This might work, thanks to the widow. She'd watch over the girls and help with the cooking. She didn't even want to be paid. Just a ride to Dallas. How lucky could he get? She was pretty too, but sad and pale. With no husband she probably thought she had the weight of the world on those little shoulders.

An hour out of town Number One crawled up on the bench with him. She looked as proper as if she was sitting in church. "Mr. Trapper."

"Just Trapper," he corrected.

"Mr. Trapper," she insisted. "I was wondering if I could man the reins."

"You know how to handle a wagon?" He swore her pointed little nose went up two inches. "A four-horse rig."

"I'm Colonel Chapman's daughter, sir. I assure you, I was driving a wagon by the time I was six, riding at four."

Trapper was impressed. He handed her the reins. The road was pointed straight west and dry. How much trouble could she get into?

Ten minutes later he decided she was better than he was at handling the team. "Any time you want to drive just let me know, One."

She smiled. "I'm thirteen years old, sir. I'm almost grown. We will get along fine if you remember that fact."

"Almost," he whispered as he watched the countryside passing. He'd been an "almost" when he'd joined the army. Now, at twenty-four, he felt like an old man. He'd seen enough fighting and dying to last him ten lifetimes.

He smiled. Widow Adams would take care of the girls and One could drive when he circled back to make sure they weren't being followed. This trip was going to be easy.

He heard the girls in the back singing songs. Farms spotted the land, and now and then a farmer waved from the winter fields. This was going to be the easiest money he'd ever make.

An hour later Trapper wasn't so sure. Number Four poked her head out of the canvas cover. "I have to stop to take care of private things, Mr. Tapper."

"Trapper," he corrected.

"I need to take care of private things, Mr. Tapper!"

She wasn't listening to him and he wasn't understanding her.

When Trapper raised his eyebrows, Mrs. Adams whispered, "Chamber pot."

"I didn't bring one." He started wondering if he needed to drive back to get one. He'd never been around women. He'd talked to girls in grade school when his dad let him go, and he'd managed to have a few conversations with ladies over the years, but he'd never asked about how they handled private things. In fact he'd never seen the nude body of a woman except in pictures over a few bars. Even if he'd wanted to court a girl after the war, none would have been interested in him.

To his surprise, all the girls looked confused including the little widow.

Number Five helped him out as her little hand patted him on the shoulder. "Please stop and help up us down, Mr. Tapper. We know what to do." The mispronouncing of his name was spreading.

"All of you?"

"Yes," Five answered. "If one goes, we all do. I think it's a rule written down somewhere."

Mrs. Adams took over. "We'll all have to make a circle, Mr. Trapper. It's a lady's way."

"Oh," he said, pulling up the horses though he didn't understand at all.

The girls nodded as he helped each one out of the wagon.

They walked over near a stand of trees and formed a circle, with Number Four in the center. Then they did the strangest thing. They turned their backs to her, held out their skirts, and waited.

One by one, each took her turn in the center, then

laughed as they all ran back to the wagon. He climbed down and helped each one up, counting as he loaded.

He noticed when he looked back into the wagon that they'd made their luggage into tiny chairs and tables and the blankets he'd bought were now cushions. Their bonnets were tied to the top of the cover, but Number Three still wore her wool cap, as if it might snow at any moment.

As he lifted Number Five, she leaned close to him and patted his cheek. Trapper couldn't help but smile.

When he looked around for the last girl, he couldn't see her. Number Four, the chubby one, was missing.

Great! He wasn't five miles out of town and he'd already lost one.

He looked around and saw her picking up rocks. "Four!" he yelled.

She paid no attention to him.

He walked toward her. "Four, it's time to go."

She looked up at him, and he saw panic in her eyes.

Trapper knelt to one knee, not wanting to frighten her. "Remember, honey, we're playing a game. You're Four." He told himself to be stern, but he couldn't. She had pretty, brown eyes and curls that bounced.

"I forgot. You want to see my rocks?" she whispered.

"Sure."

Four showed him two rocks. "I love rocks. My teacher said they hold the history of the earth in them."

"They are fine rocks," he said as he offered his hand. "How about we head back to the wagon and you show the others?" Her fingers felt so tiny in his big hand. As he walked, he added, "Do you think you can remember your name is Four for the trip, and that we all have to try to stay together?"

She smiled. "I'll try, Mr. Tapper."

Trapper didn't correct her. He never wanted to see panic in her chestnut eyes again.

After he lifted her in and climbed up on the seat, Trapper found Mrs. Adams sitting beside him. The widow might think he needed company, or maybe she felt she'd be needed as an interpreter.

They rode for a while, listening to the girls talk. Finally, as the afternoon dragged on, the conversations about school stopped.

Mrs. Adams touched his shoulder as she looked back. "They're sleeping," she whispered.

He nodded, still having no idea how to talk to the widow.

"They're sweet little things, aren't they?" she finally broke the silence.

"They are," he managed to say, then asked, "You got family in Dallas?"

"No. I just have to start over and I thought Dallas would be as good a place as any." She straightened. "I think that the war made widows and orphans of us all."

They rode along without talking after that. He didn't want to tell her all he'd lost and he guessed she felt the same. Now and then he did glance at her hands. Her fingers were tightly laced on her lap. Nothing about her seemed relaxed. The band of gold on her left hand reminded him of what she had lost. A husband. The safety of a home, maybe. Any chance of having children.

At sunset they camped by a little stream. The day was

warm for December. The girls took off their jackets and ran around, playing a game of tag. Trapper dropped a few fishing poles in the water, hoping to get lucky. Number Two, the shyest one of the girls, said she'd watch them.

By the time Mrs. Adams and Trapper set up camp and got a fire going, Two had caught three fish. The widow cooked a simple supper of fish and potatoes with biscuits.

"Tomorrow we'll be heading into open country." Trapper talked while they ate. "You all have to stay close to the wagon." He looked at Four.

All the girls nodded.

When he came back from taking care of the team and Midnight, he found all the girls asleep in the wagon. Mrs. Adams was wrapping biscuits to save for breakfast.

"Thanks for coming," he said.

"You are welcome. I enjoyed today more than I've enjoyed any day in a long time. It was good to see the farms."

"Me too." He thought it might just be the best day he'd had in years. "I know it's probably not proper for me to ask, but I'd like to know your first name."

She turned away for a moment, and he thought she might not answer. "My mother named me after her family, Emery, but people call me Em."

"What do you like to be called?"

"Emery." She smiled. "No one has ever called me by my full name."

"You think I could, Emery?"

She smiled. "I'd like that."

"How old were you when you married?"

She looked away again. "Can we not talk about the past?"

Trapper watched her carefully, wondering what hardships she'd faced. "Of course." She stood, and so did he. He offered his hand to help her into the wagon. "Good night, Emery."

To his surprise, when she stepped up equal to his height, she leaned and kissed his cheek. "Thank you. You don't know it, but you saved my life today."

Then she disappeared into the crowded wagon.

Chapter 5

Emery sat on the bench watching the days pass and the brown winter land drift by. The wagon of little girls was moving farther away from any civilization. Each mile she calmed knowing there was less chance her father would find her. He'd beat her sister the first time she'd run away. She couldn't walk for days, but as soon as she was strong enough she ran again.

Emery hoped she made it to that better life this time.

Farms and small groups of family homes often gathered in a circle. Trapper said they were often called forts because the group felt safer together. But she spotted homes or barns less and less as the road became more of a trail. Even the weather seemed wild away from all civilization and the wind howled at night like a wild animal.

A comfortable loneliness settled over her. She enjoyed the girls, but they weren't hers. She'd left her family and was surprised how much at peace she was about her choice. Part of her lived inside her memories when all she wanted to do was forget them. To do that, she'd have to make a new life.

Trapper was always polite. He never asked too many questions and when she didn't answer one, he didn't seem to mind.

They talked from time to time, but neither had much to say. He told her he'd been a gambler. When he asked if she'd ever been in a saloon, she knew he truly didn't know she'd been the ragged girl who'd served him dinner many times.

Trapper had no problem finding game, rabbits, wild turkey, and fish. Near the end of the day he'd ride ahead to set up camp. He'd have a fire going and the meat roasting before they arrived.

Number Three, the princess with the old hat for her crown, asked if she could ride Midnight. Trapper said she could if she'd stay close.

Em wasn't surprised when Three knew how to ride.

Emery decided she'd always sit next to Number One when Trapper left to find the next camp. The oldest of the colonel's daughters drove while Emery rested a rifle over her lap. Any sign of trouble and she'd promised to fire a shot. Two, an eleven-year-old and painfully shy, and her sister Three had orders to watch out the back of the wagon. Though they were only a year apart and had the same auburn hair, Two seemed much older. Number Three never took off the hat that looked like she'd found it on the boat. She usually did the talking for them.

All the girls had switched into what they called their Saturday dresses. They were plain but well-made, and much easier to climb around in.

Em had never had a Saturday dress. All of her clothes were hand-me-downs. By the time she was twelve she could sew as well as her mother, but the dresses she made were for her big sisters. Her mother told Em it would be foolish to make anything for herself.

Beneath the cover of the wagon, the girls played games and sang on the journey, but when they camped they wanted to help. Everyone gathered firewood, fearing that Trapper might get cold outside. Number One liked to help him with the horses and Two always helped Emery with the meal.

Chubby Four and tiny Five took on the job of washing the dishes and packing everything away. Five wanted to help fish, but after she fell in the stream twice, Emery appointed her the official lookout.

Every morning Trapper looked like he was silently counting as he helped each one into the wagon. Four was always the last one in, with her pocket full of rocks.

When he lifted her in, Four would always pat his cheek and say, "Thanks, Tapper."

Trapper would secure the back of the wagon, then walk around and help Emery up. She thought of telling him she could climb into a wagon without any assistance, but she liked the gentle way he lifted her. She loved it when his smile reached his blue eyes.

As the days passed, he rode Midnight, circling the wagon and riding ahead from time to time. He'd always come back to her side of the wagon and check on the "little ladies."

When the wind changed at the start of the second week, the nights grew colder. She worried about Trapper sleeping outside on the ground, but he insisted the cold didn't bother him.

Emery liked to stay out by the fire long after the girls were asleep. Trapper talked about the weather and the plans for the next day. Thanks to him hunting and fishing, they had plenty of supplies. A wagon they'd past a few days back had told them of a trading post two days ahead. Emery agreed they'd stop there.

"I'd better turn in." She stood still, wrapped in her blanket.

As he always did, he walked her to the back of the wagon. When his hands went around her waist to lift her up, he whispered, "You know, that first night when I helped you up in the wagon, you kissed me."

"I remember." She could feel her cheeks warming. She'd been so grateful he'd agreed to take her.

"I was wondering if you'd thought about doing that again. It was a great way to end the day."

She looked down, surprised he'd asked. "I thought it was a nice ending to the day also," she answered. "If you have no objection, I'd like to do it again."

He was smiling when she looked up. "I wouldn't mind at all. I'd be much obliged."

She took his hand as she moved up one step to his height and leaned over and kissed his cheek once more. His face was hairy from the beard forming.

"Thank you, ma'am."

"You are welcome, Trapper. You're a good man."

He smiled. "No one's ever said that to me."

"Maybe no one took the time to know you." He'd never mentioned any family or friends. Maybe he was a man who wanted to live alone. Yet her light kiss seemed to mean a great deal to him.

When she moved inside, she thought how nice it was to know a man well enough to kiss him on the cheek.

Rain started before dawn the next morning. Trapper tied Midnight to the back and took the reins. He told Emery and the girls to stay inside. By noon the ruts that had replaced the road looked like tiny rivers, and the wagon rocked several times, almost tipping them over.

Emery covered her hair and leaned out when Trapper called.

"There is a bend up ahead." He pointed, as if she could see it. "It's got a rock formation behind a stand of trees. In a flash of lightning I saw a few wagons camped there. I think we need to pull over and wait this storm out."

She nodded, hating how he was exposed to the cold and the rain.

"Tell the girls to hold tight, and make sure all is tied down. Once we're off the trail, it's going to get rocky."

Emery pulled back in and began getting ready. She crisscrossed rope between the bows holding up the cover. Then the girls could hold onto the ropes. Anything tumbling would hopefully be caught in the web.

Trapper must have pulled off the trail and into open land. The wagon leaned first one way, then another, but they all held tightly. The girls were wrapped in their blankets to cushion them against any bumps.

"One!" Trapper yelled over the storm.

The oldest girl jumped up and climbed out to the bench.

Trapper handed her the reins. "I need to guide the lead horses. Hold tight to the reins and don't let them bolt." The last thing he yelled before jumping down was, "If the wagon falls over, jump and roll in the mud."

Emery couldn't just wait for the accident to happen. She had to help. In as calm a voice as she could muster, she said, "Now, girls, bundle up and hold on. I'm stepping out to help Trapper."

Their eyes watched her as she stripped off her jacket and skirt. Next came her petticoats and shoes. Without hesitation, she climbed out of the back of the wagon and headed toward the team of horses.

The wind almost knocked her down. She balanced against the wagon and moved forward. By the time she got to the lead horses, Trapper was already there, trying to control the huge animals.

She grabbed the bridle of one lead horse. Trapper had the other.

For a moment he didn't see her through the curtain of rain. "What are you doing here?" he yelled. "Get back in the wagon, Emery!"

"No!" she shouted. When she pulled the horse back in line, they began to make progress. She felt like they were walking into an ocean. The rain was so hard she could barely breathe.

One step at a time they moved toward a thick stand of trees. It took what seemed like an hour to go the few hundred yards, but when they stepped behind the shelter of the rock outcrop, the wind slowed suddenly to a breeze as the rain dribbled.

Thirty feet more and they were in the shelter of the trees. Trapper pointed to a break in the tree line just big enough to pull in the horses and the wagon.

The wind and the noise of the pounding rain died, but the gloomy day remained. Now they were moving through a cloud sitting on the ground.

Emery held the reins, talking low to the exhausted team as Trapper began to unhitch the wagon. Four little heads peeked out of the wagon behind Number One, who still stood her post. She might be just thirteen, but she'd done her job better than most men could.

Trapper yelled for them to get back inside; then he helped One down from the bench. "You did great, Number One. I'm very proud of you."

She smiled. "I told you I could drive." She went to work, helping to settle the horses, and moved them twenty feet away to an opening beneath the overhang. It looked calm there in the shadows, and the grass was still green.

Emery started toward the wagon, carefully picking her steps in stocking feet. As she watched her path, she suddenly realized her bloomers were plastered to her legs.

She rounded the front of the wagon to the step up to the bench and noticed the thin material of her camisole was wet and lying like a second skin over her breasts. The pink of her nipples was showing proudly through the silk.

Before she could take the step into the wagon, she looked up and saw Trapper standing a few feet away. He seemed frozen as he stared.

There was nowhere she could run. If she stepped up, he'd see more of her, and if she turned to run to the back of the wagon, he'd see her backside.

She straightened and lifted her chin. "Turn around, Mr. Trapper."

For a moment he didn't move. She didn't think he was breathing. He was simply standing there. His eyes were wide open and looking at her.

"Turn around," she demanded.

"Why?" he whispered. "You're so beautiful."

The man had gone mad. You'd think she was the first woman he'd ever seen in her undergarments.

She glared at him, and he finally turned away, still smiling.

Emery climbed up as fast as she could and disappeared inside. Once in the wagon, she dried off with one of the blankets and removed her damp underwear. Then she dressed in her blouse, jacket, and skirt, feeling strange with nothing between her skin and her clothes.

None of the girls seemed to notice. Two and Three had curled up sleeping after their frightening ride, and Four and Five were leaning out the back opening, trying to catch raindrops on their tongues.

Emery combed out her long hair and braided it, then carefully twisted it into a bun at the base of her neck. Finally, she felt respectable again. It was raining and gloomy when Trapper had seen her. Maybe he hadn't noticed how her camisole clung to her.

Maybe if she forgot that one moment he'd forget it too. She'd never mention it, and if he did, she'd say the shadows were playing tricks with what he thought he saw.

Voices sounded outside. Emery made out Number One's light laugh and Trapper's greeting. She slipped into her shoes and moved to the back of the wagon to stand behind Four and Five. She might be in shadows, but she could see the outline of a tall, very thin boy, maybe a year or two older than One. The middle-aged couple behind the boy was smiling and appeared to be tickled to find someone else near.

"Come on down, ladies, and meet our neighbors in the storm." Trapper raised his arms and tiny Five jumped into his hug. Four followed. Both the girls stood close to him, and he put his hands on their shoulders.

Mrs. Miller shook both their hands, but Em noticed they still clung to Trapper's legs.

"Like us, it looks like the Millers are trapped here until the storm's over. Number One, meet their son, Timothy. He noticed our horses and came to see if he could help." Trapper looked down at the little darlings hiding behind his legs, but his words were directed to the Millers. "We're playing a game right now. I've numbered the girls off by age. These two are the youngest, Four and Five. We're all explorers looking for Dallas."

The couple, standing a few feet away, laughed. They explained that they also had children, so they understood games.

Trapper looked up at Emery as she neared the edge. He lifted his arms. When she hesitated, he circled her waist and swung her down. He was polite making the introductions, but the light in his blue eyes told her he was thinking of how she'd looked before.

She thought of yelling at him again, but she doubted he'd noticed the first lecture she'd tried to give him. His eyes had been so focused his ears hadn't seemed to be working. Plus, if she showed her anger, strangers would notice, maybe even ask questions or try to smooth over the disagreement.

This was between her and Trapper. What he saw. What she'd shown.

She slipped her hand around his arm and tried to act

like a lady and not a crazy woman running around in her underwear. She didn't risk saying a word, but Trapper kept the conversation going as he patted her fingers on his arm.

The Millers were farmers driving two wagons west to land they'd bought sight unseen near Dallas. They had two boys in their teens and two girls about the ages of Four and Five. Four was shy, but Five seemed excited to meet someone her age. Beneath the overhang, the Millers had built a fire and invited Trapper and his girls to a potato soup supper.

The girls grabbed their blankets and rushed to find a place near the campfire. Emery walked a few feet, then remembered she could add biscuits to the meal. As she hurried back to the wagon, she heard Trapper say, "Go along and get them out of the rain. We'll be right behind you."

He caught up with her just before she reached the wagon. Without a word, he lifted her into the back.

When she had the basket of biscuits in hand, she stood at the opening. "I can get down myself."

"I know you can, but I like lifting you down, Emery."

His hands gently circled her waist once more and slowly lowered her to the ground. "You're so light, one might think you were a kid, but I know different."

His words reached her like a thought he hadn't realized he'd said out loud.

"What happened in the storm never happened, Trapper. Whatever you think you saw was simply shadows."

He was so close she could feel the warmth of him. "I can't unsee what I saw, Emery, even if I wanted to. Which I don't."

"Stop acting like you've never seen a woman in her underwear."

"It's no act. I never have. Not like that, with so little covering your skin you might have been bare. I saw the tips of your . . ."

"Forget that. If you were a gentleman, you'd forget."

"I'm not sure if I died I could forget. The sight of you will probably follow me into heaven. I mean no disrespect, but you're a hundred times prettier than a painting I saw in a saloon in New Orleans."

Emery fought down a laugh. "The way you talk. You'd think you've never seen a nude woman in your life."

"I'm telling the truth. I haven't," he whispered. "Not a live woman. Only paintings."

She turned and faced him then. "Never?"

"Never."

She laughed. "Well, I've never seen a nude man, but I doubt I'd just stand there and stare if I saw you."

"If you want, I'll strip, and that will make us even."

"No. I'm fine. Keep your clothes on. We have a dinner to go to right now. I'll ask later if I need a viewing." They both laughed loving this new teasing. Laughter made her less shy and somehow what had happened made her more comfortable when they could joke.

He offered his hand. "Shall we go, Mrs. Adams?"

"Yes, Mr. Hawkins."

As they walked, he asked, "Why did you take off your clothes in the cold rain?"

"This black dress is the only one I have. I didn't want to get it muddy."

He didn't ask another question.

She finally added, "I didn't realize how I'd look once the silk got wet."

He held a tree branch out of her way. The night was dark, making all the world only shadows. "May I just say that you are beautiful with or without your clothes?"

"No. Forget what you saw."

"Not a chance."

Chapter 6

By the time Trapper and Emery got to the Millers' campfire, the half-frozen kids had thawed out and were laughing and talking as if they'd known one another for years.

There was enough supper for everyone and the biscuits were all gone by the time the basket made the second circle around the fire.

Trapper sat next to Emery on a bench. The night was still stormy, with the roll of thunder far away and an occasional flash of lightning brightening the sky.

For some reason tonight he wanted to protect her. Not just because he'd seen her body, but because the lady only had one dress. She'd taken off her black dress so she could help him. She must have been freezing out there.

What woman doesn't pack a change of clothes?

A very poor one, he decided, or one running with no time to pack. If that was the case, what was she running from?

She was a beautiful mystery. He'd never forget how she looked standing in the rain. She was a rare work of art now hidden away in mourning black.

He braced his arm behind her so she could lean back. Now and then their legs brushed. Nothing anyone would notice, but something both were very much aware of doing. For the first time, he'd found a woman who was as alone as he was.

During the war there was no time to court and when it was over no woman would have looked at him twice.

While trying to keep up with the conversation, Trapper attempted to understand what had happened between them in the storm. First, he'd seen her naked, or almost. He told himself that she shouldn't be too upset. She was the one who took off her clothes.

When he was honest and told her she was beautiful, she got mad. Then she told him she'd never seen a naked man. How was that possible? She was a widow. Surely she'd noticed her husband walking by now and then.

Maybe he was shy and they only did it in the dark. But then the husband would have missed seeing her body so nicely rounded in all the right places.

To top off Trapper's confusion, she seemed to think this whole thing was his fault. All he'd done was stand in the rain and look.

She'd told him to forget about what he saw, but that would take a shotgun blast to the head.

He decided he'd try forgetting one part of her at a time. Those round breasts, just right for his hands to hold. Her hips, so nicely curved. Her waist so tiny. He'd lifted her and never guessed how small it was. And, her legs with the thin material hiding nothing.

This wasn't working, he decided. Maybe he should start with her toes. They were muddy. They'd be easy to forget. In fact, he didn't even remember them now. Maybe this was working.

No. He hadn't even looked down to her toes. There were too many other body parts.

Trapper tried to act normal, but that was impossible. Every time he looked in her direction, he pictured her nude. He thought of how the silk had bunched up between her breasts and how it indented at her belly button.

Maybe if she'd take off her clothes again, he'd think about her with clothes on, but he doubted she'd go along with the idea.

As it got darker, Number Five crawled up in his lap. She patted his chest and said, "Night, Tapper," then went to sleep.

Trapper saw Number One and the oldest Miller boy walk over near the trees and stand so close to each other they were almost touching. He told himself he'd go stand between them if they got any closer.

How was it he felt so old one minute and so young the next? When he'd been the Miller boy's age, he'd been riding through enemy territory with a midnight sky as his only companion. He hadn't even tried to keep up with what day it was. He figured he had too few days left to worry about it.

As they walked back to their wagon, Trapper wished he could have some time alone with Emery, but that wasn't happening. She climbed up in the wagon and helped the girls settle down to sleep. It had been a long day and they were all tired.

Trapper found enough dry wood to build a fire. With the low-hanging fog, no one would notice the smoke so he felt safe tonight, but he couldn't sleep. The vision of Emery standing in the rain was now carved on the back wall of his brain.

At dawn he was grumpy, but the girls didn't notice. The sun was out and the storm seemed forgotten. Emery wanted to spend the morning washing clothes in the creek and cooking up a few meals. "The girls need a bath," she said. "We can't go into town looking this way."

Trapper thought they looked fine. All the girls except Emery looked like they'd been rolling in the mud, but that wasn't unusual to see in little farming towns. He decided to saddle Midnight and ride ahead to make sure there were no problems around the bend. By noon he backtracked to make sure they were not being followed.

All was clear.

When he returned, Emery had fish cooking along with a pot of beans. The Millers came to supper and added cobbler to the meal. They talked of living near Dallas.

Trapper saw the widow yawning a few times and wondered if she'd had as much trouble sleeping as he had. She was in the wagon by the time he waved goodbye to the Millers, so he had no chance of a good-night kiss on the cheek.

At dawn the next morning, the girls helped him pull

the wagon out of the trees and they were once again headed west. The Millers said they'd wait another day, but Trapper feared he'd lost too much time already. His goal was to get the girls home by Christmas, but he feared if more bad weather hit, he might not make it.

Once they were rolling, the girls were singing in the wagon and Emery was sitting beside him, so he thought he'd try to talk to her. "The girls look good with their hair in braids."

She smiled. "All but Eliza."

"Eliza. Who is Eliza?" Trapper asked.

The little widow smiled. "Trapper, you do know they have names."

"Of course, but I had it worked out with numbers. Once I hear or see something it sticks in my head."

"I'm aware."

When he glanced at her Trapper wasn't surprised to see her blushing.

He had a feeling one thing was on both their minds.

She tried to get back to their conversation. "Eliza is Number Three. The one who always wears a cap." She leaned close and whispered, "You want to know why?"

"Sure." He breathed in the scent of Emery. She smelled so good and he still smelled of trail dust and mud.

"She cut off her hair because she didn't want to go home. I tried to trim it, but I'm afraid she'll look more like a boy than a girl for a while if she takes off the hat."

"Why didn't she want to go home?"

"She says no one sees her there."

Trapper had no idea what Emery meant. Not being seen had kept him alive during the war. He felt like he'd gone half his life *trying* to be invisible.

When they stopped to make their circle, Trapper pulled farther off the trail than usual. Traffic was picking up. He'd seen two wagons coming from the trading post and a man on horseback rode past about an hour ago.

As the girls wore off a bit of energy and the horses rested, he rode to where he could see the road. Number Two wanted to follow along. She lifted her hand, so he pulled her up behind him.

She had done it before, but he'd barely noticed. One of the girls was usually walking close to him or sitting with him when he watched the road or collected wood. It occurred to him that maybe they were watching him or acting as his bodyguard. Who knows, maybe they were his tiny little angels.

When he knelt behind tall grass, Number Two did the same thing.

He hadn't waited long when four men, riding fast, came down the road. They weren't farmers. They didn't carry supplies on their saddles. Trapper touched his lips silently, telling Two not to make a sound.

Trapper had spent years learning to read people. These men were looking for trouble. Maybe running from someone, or riding toward something they wanted bad enough to exhaust their horses to get.

Who knows, maybe the men were even looking for him. Or worse, the girls. That knowledge felt like ice sliding down his back.

When the riders were out of sight, he swung Number Two onto Midnight and put his hat on her head. The big hat shadowed her face. "I'll stay here and watch to make sure they don't come back." He put his hand over hers.

"You tell Mrs. Adams where I am, then tie Midnight's reins loosely to the saddle. She'll come back to me."

Two looked frightened.

"Don't worry, I won't let anything happen to you, baby."

"Two," she said straightening. "We like our code names and none of us are babies, not even Five." Then she was off smiling. She was on a mission.

Ten minutes later Number One showed up atop Midnight. She was carrying two rifles.

"Mrs. Adams said you might need these and me."

He took the weapons. "Can you shoot?"

One made a face. "I'm the colonel's daughter. I can shoot."

Trapper had no doubt.

"So can Two and Three. The little two will learn in another year."

They sat down behind a fallen log and watched the road. After ten minutes of silence One said, "Mrs. Adams wanted me to tell you that we're all going back to the wagon if you want to wash in the stream when we get back."

Trapper scratched his dirty hair. "You think I need to?"

"Yes. You do. We took a vote and it was unanimous."

They waited until sunset and then they rode back to camp. Wherever the four men who'd passed were, they wouldn't be riding back tonight. Maybe they were headed toward Jefferson. On horseback they'd make double the time he was making with a wagon. The road was more of a winding trail now, too uneven to chance at night.

His little nest of ladies was safe tonight.

When he got back, supper was almost ready.

Trapper handed One the rifles and told her and Two to keep watch while he walked down a slope to where the horses were grazing. The sun was setting, with just enough light to see the towel and soap a foot from the stream. His saddlebags were there also.

If he was going into town, even though it was probably little more than a trading post and a few huts, he'd clean up. Trapper stripped and dove in. The water was cold, so he didn't waste any time. In ten minutes he was out of the water, dry, and putting on a clean set of clothes.

When he sat down by the fire for supper, each one of the girls walked past him and patted him on the shoulder. Number Four even kissed his cheek.

As they ate, he explained that tonight would be the first night he'd have a watch. After midnight he'd wake One and Two to stand guard while he slept a few hours. Emery said she'd take another two hours. Before dawn he'd take back over.

He felt they were safe tonight. They were too far from the trail for anyone to see their small fire. If a raid came, it would be after dawn.

To his surprise the girls asked questions. For them this might still seem like a game, but they wanted to know the rules.

If danger was coming their way, they needed to know what to do. Where to shoot to stop a man, but not kill him. How to hit a man twice their size and make him drop. How to read an attacker's movements. All that he'd learned in the army about staying alive poured out. They would have to be his troops if trouble came.

"If you can't convince them you're meaner and bigger, all you have to do is act crazy. Anyone with sense is afraid of crazy. Remember, anything can be a weapon."

Number Five crawled up in his lap and went to sleep, but the others listened and asked questions. They were little girls, too young to have to know all he said. But someday maybe they'd remember how to fight, and what he was teaching them might save their lives.

Chapter 7

The moon was only a sliver in the midnight sky when One and Two took over the watch. Trapper planned to stay awake, but he dozed, knowing they'd wake him if so much as a twig snapped.

Two hours later Emery took over the watch.

Trapper tried to go back to sleep, but he couldn't with her so near. They'd been little more than polite strangers for two days. He couldn't make himself wish he hadn't seen her almost bare, but he did wish they could go back to being close. He liked looking forward to her light kiss on his cheek, and the way she leaned close to whisper something. He liked watching her and seeing her smile when she caught him doing just that.

After a while he sat up and looked at her across a dying fire. "You going to talk to me ever again?"

"I talked to you today." She didn't look at him.

"Pass the bread. Tell Number Five to wash her hands. Do you want the last of the coffee?"

When she didn't comment, he added, "All that isn't talking, Emery."

She didn't argue. She wasn't even looking at him.

He tried again in a low voice. "I can't figure out what I did wrong. I didn't cause the rain or the storm. I didn't take off your clothes or tell you to come out to help. I couldn't act like I didn't see something so beautiful."

She was silent for a while, then she answered. "You are right. It wasn't your fault. I didn't think. It's all my fault."

"So you're not mad at me?"

"I'm not mad at you. I'm sorry, but you have to understand, it's hard to talk to someone who has seen me like that. I'm embarrassed."

"You have nothing to be mad or embarrassed about. You were just trying to help." He stood and moved to her side of the fire. He sat a foot away from her. "So we're friends again?"

She nodded.

"And you'll kiss me on the cheek when we say good night."

Emery leaned over and kissed his cheek. "I was never mad at you. I was mad at myself."

Trapper smiled. "Next time you're upset with yourself, would you mind telling me so I can get out of the way while you're beating yourself up?"

She laughed.

"And now that we're talking again, I need to remind you you're two kisses behind."

She leaned near and kissed his cheek, lingering a moment longer this time.

"That's one," he whispered.

He met her halfway when she leaned near again, and this time his lips met hers.

He knew she felt the spark between them as much as he did. Trapper raised his hand and lightly brushed the back of her hair as he held her in place. Her kiss was soft and he didn't want it to end.

Slowly, he learned the feel of her lips. When he ran his tongue over her bottom lip to taste, she shivered.

He put his arm around her and pulled her gently into his lap; he wanted her closer. When he opened her mouth slightly to deepen the kiss, he feared she'd pull away, but she didn't. She put her hands on his shoulders and drifted into the pleasure with him.

His hand rested at her waist as she moved her fingers into his hair. "I like touching you," she whispered against his ear.

He wasn't sure he could form words. He just held her and kissed his way across her face.

A thump came from the wagon, and Number Five climbed out. "I have to go take care of private things," the four-year-old mumbled as she tried to climb down.

Emery was gone from his arms in a moment and caught the little girl in flight.

"I'll take her to the other side of the wagon."

Trapper felt the loss of Emery in his arms. "I'm getting a chamber pot at the trading post."

He heard Emery's laughter from somewhere in the darkness.

When Number Five came back, she walked past the step up to the wagon and went straight to Trapper. Without a word, she curled up in his lap and went to sleep.

Emery stood in front of him. “It appears I’ve lost my spot.”

“Any time I’m open, you’re welcome to come on in. I loved holding you. For a few minutes I had heaven in my arms.”

She winked. “I felt like that too.”

Before she could say more, Number Four poked her head out of the wagon.

Emery lifted down the chubby angel, and without a word they went behind the wagon.

When she returned, Emery climbed up and tucked Four in, then reached out to take a sleeping Five. “Tomorrow,” she whispered.

“Tomorrow,” he answered, thinking a kind of happiness he’d never known had just slammed into his heart.

Trapper stayed wide awake. He knew trouble was coming. He could feel it in his bones. It was one of the reasons he’d stayed awake during the war. Only this time he wouldn’t be able to run. He had five little girls to worry about, and one little widow. They couldn’t disappear up a tree or roll in mud to become part of the land.

This time he might have to stand and fight.

And he would. He’d do whatever he had to do to keep them safe, even if it meant his life.

Chapter 8

They reached the trading post at about noon. The settlement was bigger than Emery had thought it would be. The stage line had opened a route a few months ago, but it wasn't dependable.

Em shuddered at the thought that if Trapper hadn't taken her with him, her father would have found her. He'd beat her, but not so hard that she couldn't go back to work.

She had enough money in the Bible to buy a ticket on the paddleboat, but it would have been hours before it was loaded. Years ago he'd beat her oldest sister for talking to a boy. Her sister had run away as soon as she recovered with that same boy. They were already married by the time her father found them.

Emery forced a smile. No thinking of the past. From now on she'd only look forward. This was a new world, wild and beautiful, she thought as she looked around. Even if Trapper moved on after they reached Dallas, he'd taught her there were men worth knowing.

Across from the trading post, someone had built a small bar furnished with barrels and boards stacked atop. There were a few tables for the stage customers to grab a meal under the overhang of the roof. Em could almost see the beginnings of a town that looked like a good wind would blow it away.

Trapper tied the team in front of the store and began helping each girl down. Number Five had lost a shoe again, but she didn't want to wait. She promised she'd just hop around the store.

Emery was as excited as the girls. She wanted to buy them all ribbons for their hair. She needed a proper gown to sleep in, and if the material wasn't too expensive, enough cloth for a proper dress. She pulled out three dollars from the Bible hidden away in her leather bag.

If the weather held, Trapper had told her, they had eight, maybe nine days of travel left. When he'd asked her if she needed any more supplies, Emery had given him a list of baking goods.

The little girls had pulled out little change purses. They weren't any bigger than her fist, but each had flowers embroidered on them. "We have money left over from our monthly allowances," Number One announced. "Is it all right if we buy candy, Mrs. Adams?"

Em loved that they asked her. "If you only buy what will fit in your bag."

When they walked in, all the girls stopped to stare. The rough, wooden building of logs with bark left on was filled with wonders. Hats made out of animal hides, bolts of material stacked high, rugs, guns, and knives beside pots and pans. Books, candy, and wood carvings of birds. Anything you could think of to buy was on display.

As near as Emery could tell, no one was in the store except an old man sleeping at his desk with a half-empty whiskey bottle beside him.

"Morning." Trapper woke the old guy. "Mind if me and my family look around."

"Nope. You're the first folks I've seen today." His words were straight, but his eyes didn't seem to be focusing on anything but his nose. "Wake me up when you're ready to check out." His head hit the desk so hard it rattled the whiskey bottle.

Trapper wandered off with his list in hand, and Emery moved to the material. She was deep in thought, trying to picture a dress made from each bolt, when Number Three and Four moved close to her.

"Mrs. Adams," Number Three whispered. Her hat hid her eyes from view. "May I buy a pair of Levi's and a flannel shirt? I got the money."

"Why, Eliza?" Emery asked. "Wouldn't you rather buy something pretty?"

She shook her head. "It'd make it easier to ride. I like riding just like Two does but it's not easy in a dress. When we met the Millers, the mom thought I was a boy in a dress when my hat got knocked off. I can't do anything about my hair, but I thought if I put on pants and a shirt, I wouldn't have to wear the hat all the time. I don't care if folks think I'm a boy."

Four pushed closer. "If she does, I want to get them too."

Emery thought of the terrible sack of a dress her mother had made her wear so no one would see her as a woman. In truth, Levi's and a shirt made much more sense on this journey.

"I don't mind at all."

Thirty minutes later Emery met Trapper at the counter with her material, ribbons, and a simple white nightgown. She feared she was spending money she'd need to get by in Dallas.

Trapper had collected all the supplies and a chamber pot.

He'd also bought Number One a pair of leather gloves for when she drove the team and Emery a sensible pair of boots. Ladylike, but practical.

He wanted to make sure Number Five now had a new bonnet; she'd lost hers on the second day out. Number Four had a leather bag to keep her rocks in.

Two would have her own fishing pole and Three would have a book to read because she'd told them she loved books.

"You're a pushover." Emery laughed, brushing his arm.

"I've never had anyone to buy anything for. It was fun."

When Trapper reached to shake the old man awake, Emery stopped him with a touch. She glanced around and saw there was no one around, then stood on her toes and kissed him on the mouth.

Trapper's blue eyes darkened when she pulled back.

"Why'd you do that?"

"I didn't want to wait all day to kiss you." She stared in his eyes. They both knew there was no time for more. No place they could be alone. But she saw what she'd hoped to see in his face. He felt the same way she did.

"One day, Emery."

"One day, Trapper."

The unspoken promise passed between them.

The old man lifted his head and looked at them as if he'd never seen them before. Trapper moved a respectable distance away from her.

"Where are the kids?" He looked around.

"They are changing. I told Two she could wear pants if she wanted to."

About that time she heard the tap of boots moving their way. As they moved out from behind the bolts of material, Emery smiled as five little princesses dressed in Levi's and flannel shirts stood before her. Each had on boots almost to their knees and wide hats like Trapper wore. Their shirts were dusty red and sagebrush green and their smiles were pure sunshine.

Except for a few braids hanging down, she could have sworn she was looking at boys. Number One swung a rain slicker over her shoulder and Two, Three, and Four did the same. Five tried but her jacket flew behind her.

Trapper cleared his throat. "Whose idea was this?"

Emery looked at the girls "It was Eliza, I mean Three, and mine. If someone is looking for a wagon filled with little girls, they won't find them."

"I needed a vest too," Number One commented.

Four giggled and added, "She's starting to bud."

Trapper looked like he had no idea what they were talking about.

Number One moved forward as she changed the subject. "I saw a corral full of horses when we came in. If we can buy a few, Two, Three, and I can take turns riding beside the wagon. We'd have a wider view of the surroundings."

All looked at Trapper. If he didn't like the idea, they'd all be heading back to change clothes.

"It is a brilliant idea," he said, smiling, "but I don't know if I can afford all this."

One ended his worries. "We've got enough to pay for the clothes and the horses."

"They'll cost you ten dollars a head," the drunk behind the counter finally joined in.

One turned directly to him. "That's outrageous, but I'll pay your price providing I pick the horses."

The drunk raised an eyebrow but finally nodded. "You do that, little girl."

As they headed out, Emery heard Trapper ask One how come they had so much money in those tiny purses.

She said simply, "The colonel doesn't want his daughters to ever go without what they need."

Trapper looked over at Four and Five, carrying two cornhusk dolls each. "I see some of the needs are questionable."

"No, sir." One smiled. "They needed them."

Trapper scratched his head. "You know, One, someday you are going to run the world."

"No, sir. I'm going to run the Rolling C Ranch."

Trapper looked at Emery and whispered, "I have no doubt she will."

Chapter 9

Trapper walked out of the trading post fully aware that the girls were imitating every move he made. They took long steps. Stuck their thumbs in their waistbands. Lifted their hats forward to shade their eyes.

He leaned close to Emery. "I have my army." He grinned. "They may be small, but I wouldn't trade them for gunslingers."

When they got to the wagon, each one insisted on swinging their now-free legs into the wagon. Five tried twice and almost made it the second time before she fell back into Trapper's waiting arms.

He tossed her inside, then touched two fingers to his hat in a salute. Number Five smiled and did the same. "Thanks, Tapper."

When Number Three climbed in, her short, auburn

hair was now free of the ugly wool cap. "I started something, didn't I?"

"Yeah," he answered.

"What do you think the colonel will say about this? Your father's bound to notice."

"I doubt it. He doesn't spend much time with us. Now and then he looks like he's counting us, as if to make sure we're all there or maybe he forgets how many daughters he has."

"He remembers the number and each of you. He's probably just making sure you're all there." Trapper had no doubt he'd counted to five a thousand times already.

He moved the wagon near the corral, and everyone seemed to have an opinion about which horses they should buy. Most looked worthless. Five wanted only white ones and Four wanted all the ones that looked like they were wearing socks.

One, Two, and Three climbed over the fence, laughing at how easy it was to do in Levi's. They walked among the horses and chose three.

Trapper joined them and checked each horse's teeth, legs, and eyes. He ran his hand from mane to tail and back again.

Each girl did the same.

"Pick your own mount, ladies. You'll be the one taking care of them."

Once they'd picked, Trapper took the time to show Four and Five how to saddle her horse. None of the mares were as big or would be as fast as his Midnight, but Trapper figured they'd do.

While the girls rode their horses around the corral, Trapper noticed the old drunk from the trading post was finally out in the sun.

"You picked my three best horses. Damn it."

"I didn't, they did," Trapper answered.

"I didn't sell you the saddles. You just going to take them? They are worth as much as the horses."

"I'll give you a twenty for the three."

"Twenty-five."

"Twenty. The girls can ride bareback to the next trading post if you don't take the price."

"Damn. You're as tough to trade with as your daughter, mister."

Trapper didn't correct the old goat.

A few minutes later he told One to drive the wagon, and he rode ahead with Two and Three traveling beside him.

They were not as skilled as Number One at riding, but both could handle their mounts. As the miles passed, he told them how to watch for trouble. How to move leaving the fewest footprints on the land. He said they had to feel trouble in their gut before their brains.

As the day aged, he traded places with One and let her ride with her sisters. The only rule was to stay in sight of the wagon, and the three ladies pushed that limit to the edge.

Before sundown they camped.

Emery and the two little ones made biscuits that looked like rabbits as Trapper made sure the older three took proper care of their horses. When he came back to camp, he whispered to Emery that he'd seen Number Three smile twice that day.

The old wool hat was retired to become the cornhusk dolls' bed.

After supper all the little ladies turned in. Trapper said

he'd wake up One at midnight so he could sleep for a few hours.

She nodded. He swore she'd matured these last two weeks. No bedtime stories or songs tonight; the girls were all tired.

Trapper kept the fire low even though the wind was kicking up from the north. He figured if the four riders were looking for them, they would have already been traveling back. Once they passed the trading post, it wouldn't take long for them to catch up.

Maybe not tonight, but Trapper guessed he'd be seeing them sometime tomorrow. Of course, it was just as likely that the men were simply riding fast toward Jefferson, but Trapper felt they were coming. Gut, not brains.

The next morning he was on edge. The wind was strong, with a bit of snow blowing like sand. All the girls stayed in the back of the wagon except Number One. She and Emery took turns riding shotgun.

By midafternoon the snow increased but still blew sideways from the north. The heavy clouds seemed to boil above them, promising a storm. Trapper ordered everyone inside the wagon as he drove, fighting to see the trail on a ground turning white.

Finally, before dark, he found a ravine about a quarter mile from the trail. It wasn't much deeper than the wagon was tall, but it would break most of the wind.

Though not perfect, he took the stop knowing that the horses needed rest. His three riders jumped out of the wagon and helped him with the horses. They walked them to the deepest part of the wide ditch. It was too rocky for the wagon, but here the animals were out of the wind, and they found a spot to form a corral.

When they got back, all the girls helped to push the wagon into a pocket in the ravine, taller and longer than the wagon. Trapper chopped down a few branches and small trees to block the one side of wagon that was exposed. The barrier might not keep out all the wind, but it would help.

Emery had a supper of apples and biscuits with leftover bacon sitting out on a tiny table made of bags. They all knew there would be no campfire tonight. They'd eat in the wagon.

Halfway through the meal, Number Five stood up and said that Tapper was staying inside with them tonight. It was too cold to sleep out, even if he did have a P-gun and didn't need the chamber pot."

"What's a P-gun?" he asked.

Emery whispered, "I believe it's spelled p-e-e gun."

He was the only one who blushed. The others all laughed.

"I never knew little girls thought of such things."

"We've seen them on babies," Three announced. "You take off their clothes and the pee gun shoots up like a fountain."

Two added, "Don't boys think things about girls?"

"We are not having this conversation." If he got any redder, he'd be stepping out in the blowing snow. He sat on the bench by the back opening that was now draped with the girls' dresses. Looking down at all of them settling in, he felt like an eagle watching over his nest of chicks.

Emery moved over to sit beside him. He wrapped his blanket and his arm around her. She spread her blanket over their knees.

He pulled her close and kissed her forehead, then looked at the sleeping girls. "I'm going to miss them," he whispered.

"Me too," she answered.

As the last light faded and the inside of the wagon was black as a mine, she touched his chin and turned his face toward her. This time she kissed him slowly and tenderly for a long while.

He didn't feel the cold or worry about the darkness. He was floating in heaven. He encircled her waist and pulled Em on his knee so he could feel her heart beating against his. As they kissed, he untied the shawl and pushed it back so he could feel the soft cotton of her nightgown.

She shifted so his blanket covered them from the shoulders down.

He spread his hand over her ribs and felt her breath quicken. When the kiss deepened, he knew she loved his touch as much as he loved the feel of what he'd once seen on a rainy night.

His hand moved up until his fingers passed over her breast and he caught a tiny cry of joy before it could escape.

He moved close to her ear and whispered, "You all right with this?"

She nodded, then turned to whisper back, "I'm loving it. I've never felt anything like this."

He wanted to tell her how soft she was, how perfect, but words would be dangerous. If one of the girls woke, what they were doing would be a lot harder to explain than the pee gun.

He moved to the buttons of her gown and slowly worked one at a time. Then he slid his hand beneath the cotton and felt her skin on skin. His hand was rough on the softest thing he'd ever felt. Her nipple peeked and he laughed in surprise.

They'd had no time to say the words of how they felt about each other. No mention of love or forever but he hoped she felt it in his touch.

Maybe neither believed in forever. But at this one moment in time, he wished he did. He had nothing to give her. She'd lost one man. What if she wasn't willing to lose another?

What if this one touch was all they'd ever have? It wasn't enough. He had a feeling that a lifetime wouldn't be enough.

He kissed her one more time and brushed her breast once more as he tried to memorize the feel. Holding her so close he felt like they were one person with two hearts.

Then, he relaxed. She rested her head on his chest and slowed her breathing.

He held her against him all night. It might be the only night they had. Tomorrow he might have to fight. He swore he'd die before he'd let anyone take Emery or the girls from him.

Chapter 10

The silence woke him at first light. The raging wind that had whistled down the ravine had finally settled. The storm was over.

He stood and gently lowered Emery to the bench. Covering her with his blanket, he kissed her head tenderly. He'd danced with a few women when drunk, and talked to a few when necessary, but holding Emery in his arms was a paradise he'd never expected.

Trapper had no way to put it into words.

Moments like this in his life were tiny stars in a million miles of darkness. They made all the hard times bearable. One night like this would carry him through seasons of loneliness. Strange, he thought, how he hadn't known how hollow he was until Emery filled his heart.

As he buttoned his coat, he stared at the girls sleeping. Texas princesses born on this land. Number Five, Sophia

May, she'd reminded him yesterday of her real name, had wiggled out of her blanket, but One, Catherine Claire, was holding her close and sharing her blanket with her little sister.

Number Four, Helen Wren, had hidden so many rocks beneath the back of the front seat he wouldn't have been surprised if they weighed more than him. He couldn't bring himself to tell her she had to toss out even one.

Four might be the next to the youngest, but she could read him. When he had to stop for the third time in one morning for the girls to "take care of private things," or Trapper was forced into one of their games, Four always came near and patted him on the cheek, like that one thing would calm him.

Strange thing. It usually did.

When he studied Two and Three, he couldn't believe he'd thought they looked just alike when he met them. They were as different as night and day. Number Two, Anna, was shy and organized, with a love of horses he'd rarely seen. Number Three, with her short hair and shorter temper, was emotional, unpredictable, and could talk him into anything.

As Trapper climbed out of the wagon and crunched his way down the ravine to the horses on a thin layer of frozen snow, he thought about what kind of men his girls would marry. He wished he could stay around to run off most suitors. If he were the colonel, he'd only let one in a hundred through the front door.

Trapper frowned. The colonel might want to think about nailing Number Three's windows closed. Short hair or not, she'd be a beauty and probably would grow up to be wild as a jackrabbit.

He thought he heard the horses moving restlessly farther down the ravine and was glad he'd corralled them so far away from the wagon. They might have kept the girls awake during the storm. Then Two would think she'd have to go check on them, and of course he'd have to go with her.

He'd better go check on them early, before he had two or three of the girls following him.

He'd like them to sleep a bit longer, for this morning there was no campfire to warm up around.

As he walked toward the makeshift corral, he realized something was wrong. Maybe some animal was trying to get to them. He'd heard that in cold winters mountain lions would come down this far looking for food.

He heard something strange on the wind. The tiny giggle of a spur. The sound of leather rattling and the shuffling of human feet.

Trouble! That gut feeling he always got. Every nerve in Trapper's body went on full alert.

He raised his rifle to the ready and moved into a heavy fog that had settled low to the ground.

Just as he turned a bend, something slammed into the back of his head, knocking Trapper to the ground. Someone or something hit the dirt a few feet to his left. Trapper turned left, but the fog blocked a clean shot.

Trapper took one step left as two more men, dressed in western clothes, dropped from above on his right. One man's knee hit hard into Trapper's middle, while another's fist got in two hard blows before Trapper could get in just one.

He was a trained fighter, but so were they. After delivering several blows, two of the men caught his arms, and the third man, with the stance of a boxer, delivered a fist to his chin that knocked back his head.

Trapper's world went black and he could no longer respond, but the boxer continued hitting as his partners kept Trapper from collapsing.

He hurt in so many places he could barely feel the new blows coming. He was seventeen again, thinking his midnight rides through the lines were exciting. Bullets flew past his ears, but he rode on believing he was somehow saving lives.

Suddenly, in his mind, he couldn't draw in enough air to breathe and his horse slowed. Now he was running. Not riding for a cause he didn't understand. Not trying to save lives. Just running.

In his nightmare he was reaching out, trying to touch someone. Running to Emery. He called her name, but the sound never met his ears and night closed in around him. The ground finally rose up to slam against him and all was silent.

When Trapper finally fought his way awake, the sun was high. The first thing he heard was snow dripping as it melted. All was silent around him.

Both his eyes were swollen, but he could see out of the left one. The three men who'd attacked him were huddled around a tiny fire drinking coffee. The boxer who'd delivered more blows than Trapper could count was beefy and bear-shaped. The other two looked more like gunfighters, with their gun belts worn low and strapped to their legs.

Trapper didn't have to ask what they wanted; he knew. He'd been watching for them to arrive, waiting for them since he left Jefferson.

Last night he'd talked to Emery and the oldest three girls. They'd agreed that Trapper would step out early and scout around until he was sure they were safe to travel.

Then he'd come back and they'd head out. From this time on they'd be traveling off the trail. Only now it was too late. The bad guys had found them.

The plan was still sound. The wagon was hidden. If Emery could keep the girls in the wagon, they'd be safe for a while. Only, Four might slip out looking for rocks or Two might decide to test her skills in tracking him. One of them could refuse to use the chamber pot and want to make their circle in the open. Number One might decide it was time for her to take over the world.

Trapper knew one fact: With Colonel Chapman's daughters, he needed to expect the unexpected.

His head was starting to hurt more from worrying than he did from his black eyes or split lip, or bruises and cuts.

A short little man who looked like the reincarnation of Napoleon appeared and strutted over to Trapper. The newcomer rocked back on his heels as if he was teasing. "You must be Trapper Hawkins. I must say, you are far more trouble to track than that fat teamster. We lost your trail the third day out. Since then we've been riding back and forth, trying to guess where you were. It was pure luck we found your horses last night."

Trapper didn't speak or move. It wasn't hard for him to look half dead; he pretty much was.

The little man turned and yelled at his men, "I told you to capture him, not beat him senseless. If he dies, one or two of you will be buried in the same grave."

The beefy guy grumbled and finally said, "I don't see that it makes any difference. You told us we was gonna kill him anyway."

"And that little widow with him," another added. "But I'd like to spend some time with her first."

All three started arguing over Emery.

Trapper sat calmly on the ground with his hands tied behind him and blood dripping from several cuts on his face. His one thought was which one of these outlaws he'd kill first.

The little Napoleon pushed them aside and stood in front of Trapper.

"Sorry about my men. They can't seem to follow orders," he said, as if there was nothing unusual about Trapper being tied up.

Trapper stilled. "Those are my horses. Take them and be gone and I won't shoot you."

The thin cowboy hiccupped a laugh and asked, "How you gonna shoot us? Your hands are tied and you don't have a gun." He tapped the barrel of his rifle against the back of Trapper's head.

The leader shrugged, as if not interested in anything the thin cowboy said. "I didn't spend two weeks tracking you just to take the horses. You insult me by even thinking I'm a horse thief. That's not what I came for."

Trapper saw no gun on the man. He might give the orders, but he wasn't a fighter.

"I heard you fought for the South, Trapper. Thought I'd make you an offer. One chance, you might say, from one soldier to another."

"You're here for the girls." Trapper made a statement. He wasn't asking a question.

"Yes, we are. We're not going to hurt them. They're worth too much alive. We just plan to keep them until their papa gives us enough money. Then we'll give them back, take the money, and head for California."

"I'm not turning them over." Trapper steadied himself. He sensed another man was standing back in the fog even though he could not see him. Once the shooting started, Trapper had to get two, maybe three, before they killed him. The man hidden in the fog was a wild card in this deadly game they played.

The three who'd beat him up were not ready for a gunfight. They'd done their job of beating him. The man in the fog might be the assigned killer.

Trapper put his palms together and twisted hard on the wet rope. It gave just enough to slip one hand out.

The short man was too busy making his point to notice. "Now think about it, Reb. You can get on your black devil of a horse and ride away, or you can die right here. Either way is fine with me." He smiled. "Either way we take the girls."

Trapper figured if he could bide his time a little longer, the sun would burn away some of the fog and his chances would be better. "What's in this for me? I'd already be dead if you didn't want something else from me. So, tell me what you want."

The outlaw leader laughed. "You're right. The old man at the trading post told us you were well-armed and you bought more. I only see one rifle on you, which means the others are in the wagon."

"They are." Trapper saw no reason to deny what they already knew.

The short man shrugged. "I'll give you a hundred dollars, your horse, and your life if you'll go tell the girls to come out unarmed. That includes that little woman you've got traveling with you."

Trapper shook his head and caught a glimpse of his rifle leaning against the ravine wall. If he rolled, he could grab it and get two, maybe three shots off before the men around him could raise their guns. But, the shadow in the fog standing twenty feet back might be ready. If so, Trapper would only get one man before he was shot.

The odds weren't with him this time, but he had no choice. He had to fight.

Chapter 11

Emery opened her eyes. Trapper wasn't holding her. Looking around, she realized he was gone. All was quiet. He was simply scouting around, checking on the horses, nothing more.

Maybe he'd gone to gather firewood for a meal before they started out.

She closed her eyes for a moment and remembered how he'd touched her. Very few words were spoken. He'd told her how he felt about her with his light strokes.

There was no time for words now, or maybe ever. He was a drifter who might not want to settle. But, last night, she'd felt cherished and his touch would stay with her no matter what happened next.

As quickly as she could, she changed into her clothes.

They all needed to be dressed by the time he got back. One by one she woke the girls. Before they were finished dressing, she heard a horse stomping, as if the devil was chasing him.

No breakfast. They'd be moving out soon, she guessed.

One and Two shoved on their boots. "That's Midnight," One whispered.

They were gone before Emery could stop them.

She ordered the three other girls to stay put and ran to the opening where One and Two had disappeared.

Branches caught her skirts for a minute, and she wished she'd been smart enough to buy Levi's like the others had.

Both girls were trying to calm Midnight.

"His right front leg is cut," Two said as she cried. "He won't let us close."

Emery didn't know much about horses, but she'd watched Trapper. He always talked to the horse before he touched the animal.

"Easy, Midnight. Easy. I'm not going to hurt you. Easy."

Midnight watched her, his eyes still fired with panic.

Emery kept talking. "I wish you could tell us where Trapper is. Did he go looking for you? Trapper will be worried about you."

The horse seemed to calm a bit as her soothing voice continued. "We want to help you, Midnight."

Finally, he stilled.

Number One touched the rope around his neck. "I've never seen Trapper put a lead rope on Midnight."

"Someone else must have." Emery felt fear cut off her

breathing. "We need to hide, girls. Get back in the wagon. If someone besides Trapper is out there, we don't want them to see us."

Catherine Chapman straightened to her full height. "No, Mrs. Adams. We have to split up. Eliza and you stay in the wagon with Helen and Sophia. If anyone you don't know comes near the wagon, start firing. Even if you don't hit anyone, they'll stay back."

Emery nodded. The girl was right.

"Anna and I will go look for Trapper. If he's hurt, we'll get him back here."

Emery agreed with the plan except for one detail. "Eliza will go with you. I'll make sure no one comes near the little girls. You may need her."

Eliza climbed out of the wagon, her arms full of rifles.

A tear ran down Emery's cheek. Three little girls, thirteen, eleven, and ten. Barely half grown, but they were now warriors.

And, they were all better shots than she was.

One took the lead and all three disappeared in the fog.

Emery asked the little ones to bring her bag and sewing box. Four and Five brought them, then stood close beside her, as if it was their time to be on guard.

While she ripped her ugly wool dress and bandaged Midnight's leg, they both asked questions.

Emery kept her voice low and calm. "One, Two, and Three have gone to get Trapper. We will stay here and on guard. If trouble comes, I want you both to get low in the wagon and stay silent. No matter what, don't say a word. Just hide."

Five straightened. “My father says Chapmans are fighters, not hiders.”

When she finished tying the bandage, she pulled the rope off Midnight and whispered, “Go find Trapper.”

As if the horse understood, he turned into the fog and vanished.

Chapter 12

Trapper sat with his hands still behind him, waiting for just the right moment. The shadowy figure in the fog was moving. Disappearing, almost becoming solid again.

The little man ordered the beefy boxer and one of the cowboys to saddle up. Trapper was pleased to see that the thin cowboy had a broken nose. The other cowboy close to Trapper was still cussing under his breath, like it was a twitch he couldn't stop. He circled around him and pointed his rifle at Trapper's face.

"Last chance. You go in and bring the girls out to us and we'll let you ride away." Little Napoleon moved in close, his tone low.

"They're nothing to you. Five little rich girls who won't ever amount to anything. Even if you got them back to their father, he probably wouldn't take the time to thank you." Napoleon shrugged. "And that little widow is nothing to no one or she wouldn't be traveling alone. If she vanishes, no one would miss her."

The little man put his hands in his pockets and rocked on his heels. "You're a good fighter, Trapper. If one of my men hadn't slammed you in the head, you would have taken all three of them down, even Big Hank. I wouldn't mind having a man like you in my gang."

"I'm finished fighting," Trapper lied. He kept his voice low and noticed the stranger in the fog moving closer.

With Big Hank and one of the cowboys gone to get their horses, there was a chance Trapper could shoot two of the three before they got off a shot.

But he didn't dare act until the rifle moved more than an inch from his head. The cussing outlaw kept tapping the barrel against his chin, as if teasing him.

Trapper growled as he looked away from the dumbest one of the group. In the blink of a moment, he saw blond hair move just above the top of the ravine. One.

Trapper forced his almost-closed eyes open and studied the edge of the small rise. Two's long, auburn hair flashed and disappeared. Two. Then he saw Three, ten feet away from her sister.

Trapper turned back to the head outlaw. "What if I did join up with you?"

Little Napoleon looked excited at the possibility.

To Trapper's surprise, the short man glanced at the man in the fog. The day was warming, and the stranger wouldn't be hidden for long.

"If I rode with you, would I get a cut of the ransom money?"

The short man hesitated, and Trapper knew that the true leader was in the fog, not standing before him. "Who's the shadow in the fog?" Trapper demanded.

"You never mind him."

"Oh, come on, Shorty, who is he? He's standing right behind you."

"Don't call me Shorty."

"Why not? I'm calling this one Drippy. Tell him to stop bleeding on me." Trapper pointed with his head to the man with the rifle pointed between Trapper's eyes.

Trapper raised his voice. "If I joined, I'd have three rules. One: Get rid of the shadow, Two: Drippy is yours, and Three: Take Shorty down. *Now!*"

Three guns blasted as one, ringing through the ravine like a cannonball.

Trapper rolled to his rifle and stood. Shorty was screaming that his kneecap was shot off. Drippy had been shot in his gun arm and was struggling to lift his weapon with his left hand.

Trapper kicked away Drippy's gun as the girls slid down the ravine, their rifles ready to fire by the time they hit the dirt.

When he saw Number One standing over the shadowed stranger, he limped toward her.

"You all right, One?"

She shook her head. "No. I know him. I think I killed him."

Trapper put his arm around her trembling shoulders. "Who is he?"

"He's the foreman at our ranch. I've known him all my life and he was trying to kidnap us."

Trapper knelt and pushed the blood away from the foreman's forehead. "He's not dead. You just grazed him. He'll live long enough to hang."

"Two," Trapper yelled. "Grab the rope off their saddles. We'll tie them up and doctor them later. I got to get to the wagon."

"One, come with me. Two and Three, keep an eye on these three. I'll be back as soon as I know the others are safe."

As soon as they were tied, Trapper grabbed one of the outlaws' horses.

Just before they rode out, he heard Three telling the prisoners that if they moved or cussed, she'd shoot their toes off one at a time.

Trapper smiled as he rode toward the wagon. He hadn't heard any shots coming from the wagon's direction. That might be a good sign.

The first thing he saw was Midnight, standing near where they'd hidden the wagon.

Big Hank was pulling off branches and dodging rocks.

"Stop that, lady!" Hank screamed in pain as one the size of a sharp egg hit his eye.

More rocks rained down. Some bounced off his big frame, but now and then one hit him and left a cut.

Trapper raised his rifle. "Step back, Hank, and raise your hands."

The beefy man did as he was told while rocks continued to pound on him.

Trapper handed his rifle to Number One. "Shoot him if he moves."

"Yes, sir," she answered.

"Emery, are you and the girls all right?"

"We are," Number Five answered. "Can we keep throwing rocks, Tapper?"

"Sure." He climbed into the wagon and hugged both girls, then let them go back to throwing rocks.

Trapper moved to Emery. He pulled her close, and they just held on tight to each other. Neither said a word. When he pulled away enough to kiss her, Trapper heard the girls giggling.

"There's one more man," Trapper whispered, not wanting to frighten the girls.

"We know," Emery said in a normal voice. She pointed to the back of the wagon. "He must have crawled under the wagon. When he started coming into the wagon, I was busy with that giant out there."

"The girls hit him with the chamber pot. It was full. I'm afraid the man doesn't smell so good."

Chapter 13

The next few days were hard. Trapper hurt all over. Hank had broken two of his ribs, but Trapper was able to drive the wagon by the second day. Five and Four stayed on either side of him on the front bench, wiping blood from his cuts and constantly talking about how bad he looked. The three older girls and Emery rode, surrounding the wagon as if guards.

They passed through the edge of Dallas but didn't stop. Number One was setting the pace and directing them over open country to her home.

Emery had insisted on doctoring the outlaws. Then Trapper tied them in the wagon and put the luggage on their horses.

When Number One said they were on Chapman land, Trapper thought they were home. He had no idea it would take two more days.

As the ragged, exhausted group neared the huge ranch house, armed riders rode out to meet them.

"What is the meaning of this? Are you drifters unaware you're on Colonel Chapman's land?" the leader of the not-so-friendly greeters demanded.

Before Trapper could answer, One moved her horse forward. The young girl not fully grown sat tall in the saddle. "Are you men aware I am Catherine Claire Chapman?"

All the men looked at her in shock.

"We were ambushed on the trail and almost killed. We have the outlaws tied in the back of the wagon. I want you to make sure they are locked up until my father decides what to do with them."

Catherine rode over to the wagon and lifted little Sophia May from the bench, then looked at the man closest to her. "Give Mr. Trapper Hawkins your horse and drive the prisoners in. We'll race to the house just like all Chapmans do."

All the men followed orders. One older rider, with a mustache that went from ear to ear, offered his arms to Number Four. "Come along, Miss Helen Wren, I'll ride you in."

"All right, Sam," Number Four said politely, "but while I'm here I plan to learn to ride all by myself. Will you teach me?"

"Of course. Just like I did your three big sisters."

Trapper slowly climbed onto the mount he was offered, then asked the cowboy to lift up the widow to ride with him. "My horse is almost lame, can someone see to him?"

Again the older man answered, "We'll see to it. Mr. Hawkins, right?"

Trapper nodded. "So you knew we were coming?"

"We did, sir. The nurse wired us. She said you'd make it by Christmas."

"Did we?" Trapper had lost track of the days.

"You did, sir."

Emery looked frightened when one of the men lifted her up in front of Trapper, but she obviously wanted to hold on to Trapper. All the little ladies seemed to think he might pass out at any minute.

Number One raised her hand and pointed toward home. "We ride to home."

They all took off, laughing and yelling. The cowboys at the wagon raised their rifles and fired in salute. The Chapman princesses were home.

By the time they reached the steps, everyone on the ranch was watching.

Trapper had no problem recognizing the colonel. White beard, white hair, and standing strong and tall. For a moment he frowned, as if he didn't know who was invading his ranch.

Number One lowered the four-year-old to the ground and she ran toward her father. She was halfway up the steps before anyone recognized the youngest daughter.

The colonel hugged her so hard, Trapper thought he might crush her. Within a minute all his daughters were around him, talking and hugging and laughing. He took each girl's face in his big hands and stared at them, then smiled. No matter how bad they looked or how they were dressed, his girls were back.

Trapper stood watching. He'd done it. He'd gotten them home by Christmas.

As the chaos began to settle, Trapper wasn't surprised to see the colonel's eyes focused on him.

"Mr. Trapper. I'd like to have a word with you. Now!"

Trapper remembered what the teamster had said about the colonel threatening to kill him if the girls arrived with one scratch. The girls were all sunburned and bruised, with scrapes and blisters.

He tried to stand up straight as he moved forward, but Number Three cut him off when she ran in front of him, almost tripping him.

"Now, Papa," she began, with her fists on her hips.

The colonel pointed his finger. "What happened to your hair, Elizabeth?"

"Never mind that. Right now Trapper needs a doctor and some rest. He is hurt and hasn't slept in days because, even injured, he's always watching over us." She crossed her arms. "And I go by Eliza or Three. You'll not lecture Trapper. I will not stand for it."

Anger reddened the colonel's face. "You telling me what to do, daughter?"

All five girls stood before him with their arms crossed and their boots set wide apart as if ready for a fight.

Anger looked like it might explode out of the colonel. Obviously, no one ever told him what to do. No man. No woman, and certainly no daughters.

The girls didn't back down.

To everyone's surprise, the littlest one stepped closer to her papa. "We're not taking a bath until you take care of our Tapper. He's still dripping."

"Who is Tapper?" The colonel lowered to her level and his tone softened slightly.

All the girls started explaining that Five never got the name right. And Trapper had told her she could call him by any name she liked.

"Who is Five?" The colonel tried to yell above them.

Then they all began with how they met on the dock.

Finally, the colonel yelled, "Stop." When all was silent, he said in a normal voice he rarely used, "Sam, go get the doctor."

"Yes, sir." Sam smiled, obviously happy to be leaving.

"Martha." The colonel yelled again.

A woman with an apron on, stepped from the crowd watching. "Yes, Colonel."

"Tell the kitchen to cook up a meal and keep buckets of hot water headed upstairs." He stared at his girls. "My daughters will be taking baths and dressing properly for dinner in one hour. I'll be busy taking care of our guests."

The girls all smiled and walked past their father. Each kissed him, and as they started up the stairs, Chapman grinned as if he just hadn't lost the first argument in his life.

When he turned back, he seemed to notice Emery for the first time. "Madam, I assume you are the girls' traveling companion."

"Yes. I met them in Jefferson."

"I'd be honored if you'd stay with us through Christmas. Martha will send a bath to your room, and I'm sure we'll find clothes that will fit you. I see you are a widow."

"Yes."

Trapper's hand was resting on the small of her back, and he could feel her shaking.

"Thank you for seeing my daughters here safely. I hope we have time to talk over dinner. It isn't often we have such a lovely lady among us."

Martha took Emery away. Trapper couldn't help but

notice she hadn't even said goodbye to him. But then, the little widow hadn't said anything to anyone but the colonel, and that was "*yes*."

Sam moved up behind Trapper. "I'll see you to your room, sir. The doc will be here as soon as he sobers a bit. He always comes for Christmas, but he prefers to stay in the bunkhouse."

"We have two guest rooms through here." Sam started down the same long hallway where Emery had disappeared.

Trapper followed, suddenly feeling the lack of sleep catching up with him.

"The old man was sure polite to the widow," Trapper said to Sam.

Sam nodded. "He's always nice to his wives and future wives."

Trapper decided he'd better stay awake a bit longer.

Chapter 14

Emery loved soaking in the big tub. They'd made the trip in less than three weeks, but it seemed like a lifetime. Someday she'd write down all that had happened and save it for her grandchildren to read. And there would be grandchildren, because after knowing the girls, she wanted a dozen kids, all girls.

Martha brought her a warm dress made of the softest fabric she'd ever felt. Without a word, the housekeeper took all her dirty clothes to be washed.

Emery's hair was clean and still wet. She combed it out and let it fall in curls down her back. When she stepped into the dining room an hour later, all the men stood.

Her gaze was drawn to Trapper. His wounds were all doctored and bandaged. His clothes looked new. His smile was the same as it always was when he looked at her.

Before she could take a seat at the table, the girls stepped in. They looked every bit the little ladies they were. Emery and Trapper remained silent as the girls entertained their father with stories of the trail.

She noticed none mentioned the trouble they'd faced in the snowy ravine. Maybe they didn't think it was proper conversation over dinner.

The girls invited Emery to join them for dessert in the kitchen so the men could talk. This apparently was a ritual in the house. Martha and the kitchen help had raised the girls and they wanted their time to talk.

Emery excused herself after two pieces of pie and retired to her beautiful room. She slipped into a nightgown far fancier than the one she'd bought at the trading post and brushed her hair until it shined.

Then, she stepped into the hallway and tried the door across from hers. Martha had mentioned it was Trapper's room. She wanted to check on him. He'd looked tired at dinner.

The room was dark except for the low light from the fireplace. She tiptoed to the bed and saw he was sound asleep. The man she thought was the bravest she'd ever known had finally let down his guard and slept.

Without giving it much thought, she crawled into bed with him, rested her head on the one spot on his chest that wasn't covered in bandages, and closed her eyes.

They'd never talked of the future. He'd never mentioned marriage. Neither had ever said they loved the other. But there was nowhere in the world she wanted to be but by his side.

Deep in the night, he moved and found her next to

him. Without saying a word, he pulled her close and kissed her.

When he finally pulled free, he whispered, "Am I dreaming?"

"No, I'm here."

He sounded half asleep when he asked, "Will you have kids with me?"

"No," she answered. "We're not married."

"Then will you marry me?"

"No. You don't know me."

"Sure, I do." He moved his hand over the soft cotton of her gown. "I know the way you kiss and the way you feel and how gentle and shy you are."

She had to tell him the truth. The whole truth. "I'm not a widow."

His body tensed, and she knew he was totally awake now. "Are you saying that your husband is alive? Did he leave you? Did you leave him?"

"No, he never was. I found the dress and the ring."

Trapper scrubbed his face. "You are not married. You were not in mourning?"

"Right."

"Can we go back to sleep, Emery? I don't want to think about this until morning."

"Why?"

"Because I've been keeping my distance from you for this whole trip because I thought you were a widow wearing mourning black. I couldn't tell you how I felt."

She laughed. "Start talking, cowboy. If we're going to make babies, I need to hear the words."

He pulled her close and told her what he'd wanted to tell her. If she'd give him a chance he'd love her every day and every night for the rest of his life.

The next morning everyone was up early for a Christmas breakfast.

Everyone had gifts under the tree and the girls' laughter filled the great room.

After breakfast the colonel finally got the chance to talk with Trapper. He made Trapper tell him everything that had happened.

Trapper swore the man's chest swelled with pride when Trapper described how the girls saved him.

When Trapper left the room, all five girls were standing outside the study.

He watched them walk into their father's study with determination in their eyes. Five closed the door.

He went in search of Emery. Whatever the girls were saying to the colonel, it had nothing to do with him.

Chapter 15

Trapper found Emery sewing with the women, and she seemed in no hurry to leave, so he wandered onto the porch and relaxed.

He had a great deal to think about but within five minutes he was asleep.

The colonel's booming voice woke him up.

"Mr. Hawkins, I believe we have business to finish. I owe you five hundred dollars, sir."

Trapper straightened in his chair. He hadn't given the money much thought. Getting the girls safely to the ranch had been his goal from the minute he'd seen them.

The colonel offered him a whiskey in his study, then sat across from him. "On another matter, I've just finished talking to my daughters, and they've informed me that you need to marry the widow right away."

"Why?" Trapper hoped the girls hadn't mentioned the pee gun again. A father might not think the conversation proper.

"They told me you like to hug her."

"I do." Trapper could not lie.

The colonel raised an eyebrow. "Does she return your affection?"

"She does," he answered remembering that she'd crawled in his bed last night. "But, she's a proper lady." Trapper felt he had to add.

"Then you've no objections to the idea of marriage?"

"None," Trapper looked down. "I don't have anything to offer her. It wouldn't be fair to her."

"You'll be a rich man with five hundred dollars in your pocket and I'm offering you a job. I'm in need of a smart man to be in charge of security. Nothing like this is ever going to happen again to my daughters. They said you risked your life to save them."

"Your daughters can take care of themselves."

"They will be able to do just that with your help, so what about taking the job?"

Trapper studied the man. "Did your daughters talk you into hiring me?"

"Of course not. No woman could ever run my life." He smiled. "I did love my wives. All three of them. I acted like I wanted boys, but truth be told, I wouldn't take ten sons for any one of the girls."

Trapper kept grinning. "They put some pressure on you?"

"Of course. Anna tried reasoning with me. Catherine told me she wanted you for her foreman when she takes over running this place. But it was Sophia who settled the debate. She said she wouldn't wear shoes ever, ever again if I didn't try my best to keep her Tapper around. From what I see, she's already halfway barefoot as it is."

Trapper leaned closer. "I'll make you a deal, Colonel. If Emery says yes to marrying me, I'll take you up on the job."

"Good. I'll have the former foreman's cabin cleaned out. It's about the right size for newlyweds."

"What's happened to the outlaws I brought in?"

The colonel shrugged. "I had a man ride into Dallas to get a Texas Ranger. He'll take them in as soon as their wounds heal, and I'll send a dozen men to ride along to make sure they make it to a trial."

"You mind if I'm one of the men going along?"

"It'll be your first assignment."

The colonel stood, happy with the deal, but Trapper feared the hardest part was yet to come. He had to ask the little widow to marry him first. Since she was already thinking she'd like to have kids with him, he thought he knew what the answer would be.

It was evening before he caught her alone in a big room the housekeeper called the great room. The fireplace was tall enough for a man to stand in, and tonight candles lined the windows. Garland climbed the staircase. The center table was covered with sweets for the neighbors and the employees and their families. It didn't take long for Trapper to realize the ranch was a small town.

When Emery entered, dressed in a dark-green dress with white lace, she took his breath away. He took her hand and pulled her into the empty study.

"You're beautiful." He kissed her hand. "Almost as beautiful as you were that night in the rain."

"Thank you."

She seemed so shy now, as if they hadn't spent three weeks together. As if he hadn't touched her. As if she hadn't slept in his arms.

"I don't know the words, Emery."

"What words?" Her shy whisper brushed his heart.

"The ones to tell you how much you mean to me. I feel like I've been walking around holding my breath all my life and suddenly I can breathe. I've been half dead for years and you make me want to live forever."

When she didn't answer, he looked away. "I don't have anything to offer. I own a horse and a wagon." He took a long breath and let it all out. "I do have enough money to buy a little place or the colonel offered me a job. But without you I don't think I could settle down."

All at once he couldn't find the words. He'd lived from day to day, never dreaming for so long he was afraid to wish for more.

She smiled. "What do you really want?"

"I want you to be with me forever. I want to have a bunch of kids. I want to sleep next to you until I die."

"You have me," she said so low he wasn't sure he heard her. "You've had me since the day we left Jefferson and you couldn't be stern with Four. You had me when you let Three be her own person and you let One become a leader. You watched over us all."

"I know who you are, Trapper Hawkins. I saw the truth the first time I saw your blue eyes. You're a good man. You have everything I want even without the money or the land or even the job. I want you."

"Any chance you'd marry me?"

She smiled. "You can bet on it."

As he kissed her, Trapper swore he heard five little girls laughing just outside the window.

"Look, One," a four-year-old whispered, "Tapper got what he wanted for Christmas."

Read on for a preview of Jodi Thomas's next novel . . .

DINNER ON PRIMROSE HILL

A Honey Creek Novel

Available November 2021 wherever books are sold

Prologue

March 8
Friday

Professor Virginia Clark stared out the third-floor window of her office on a campus so small it seemed more like a set for a Hallmark movie than a college.

Tomorrow would be the start of spring break and at forty-three years old she no longer cared. In her college days she'd loved the break. A time to travel, have fun, and maybe go wild, but now it was only a time to clean her office and catch up on paperwork.

If she could turn back time, she'd live one more wild spring break.

But she had a survey to conduct and a paper to write and an office to organize. No fun in that.

Mischief crawled up her spine. Maybe, even at forty-three, she might enjoy the break of another kind.

After all, you're not dead until you're dead.

Chapter 1

Friday

Benjamin

Dr. Benjamin Monroe folded his notes and placed them in the worn leather briefcase he'd carried since graduate school. His lecture room at Clifton College was empty now. Peaceful. He always liked the stillness after class. He'd done his job, and he took pride in that.

As he often did, he turned to the long narrow windows behind his podium and looked out over his hometown. From the third floor he could see east all the way to the river and north to where the land rose in rolling hills. There was a balance here that calmed his soul. A wide valley that nestled three small towns, but his town, Clifton Bend, was the best because the college rested in its center.

Benjamin hadn't missed a class in twelve years. At forty-two he always came on time and well prepared. Routine ruled his life. He liked working with his dad on their farm every weekend and loved biking through the valley on sunny afternoons. The exercise kept him lean and tanned, just as his work kept him sharp.

What he didn't like was spring break. It interrupted his routine. A worthless holiday, but he'd help his father on their little farm and manage to keep busy.

"Doctor Monroe?" A nervous, high-pitched voice bombarded his thoughts. "May I speak to you about something? It's important."

A creature with auburn hair, glasses too big for her face, and huge blue eyes leaned around the door. Professor Virginia Clark.

He plowed his long fingers through his straight, mud-colored hair. If teachers were allowed a nemesis, Miss Clark, the biology instructor, would be his. As far as he was concerned all they had in common was age.

Benjamin thought of saying, "No, you can't speak to me," but that would be unprofessional.

To her credit, Miss Virginia Clark was bubbly on a down day. Her voice was too high, her manner of dress was in no way appropriate, and her legs were too short. On a good day she was exuberant and misleadingly thought they were not only colleagues but friends.

He'd always hated bubbly people; they made him nervous. But she taught two doors down in the biology lab and officed next to him. Some days he swore he could hear her laughing or running around her tiny workplace like a squirrel in a box.

Right now, she was charging toward his podium like

Grant taking Richmond. Too late to say no or run, so he just watched.

Another observation: professors should never bounce.

Miss Clark bounced. She was a bit on the chubby side; a head shorter than him, and the white lab coat did not conceal her curves. Her corkscrew hair seemed to be dancing to hard rock and her breasts . . . well, never mind them. Unprofessional, he thought as he watched her coming down the steps row by row, breasts moving to their own beat.

"I need your help, Doctor Monroe." She stopped one foot too close to him.

He fought down the urge to step back.

"Of course, Miss Clark, I'm at your service," he offered. Maybe she needed a ride or she was locked out of her office, again. He could make time to be kind. After all, they were colleagues. "I'd be happy to help any way I can."

"Good. I was afraid you'd say no. It's a great opportunity and we can split the work and the money."

Benjamin raised an eyebrow. "What work?"

"My research paper entry for the *Westwin Research Journal* has been approved as one of five finalists. The winner's findings will be published in the journal as well as winning the ten-thousand-dollar prize." She smiled. "Just think, we'll be famous. Last year's subject was how aging relates to location. The winner was interviewed on the *Today* show."

She was bouncing again. This time with excitement. "I might finally get to go to New York City. I've always dreamed of seeing plays and walking through Central Park. They say you can hear the heartbeat of the whole world in the streets of New York."

Benjamin fell into her pipe dream for a second. "If I had money to blow, I'd go to Paris and see Marie Curie's office and lab. I've read every book about her dedication, her work, her life. Imagine walking the streets she walked."

He didn't mention that he'd also find his mother, if she were still alive. She'd left him when he was four years old, saying she must paint in Paris for a few months but never coming back. He only had one question for her. Was the life she'd given him up for worth it?

Miss Clark frowned at him as if measuring his sanity, then shrugged. "Paris, really, Benjamin, sometimes you surprise me."

When he frowned at the use of his first name, she rolled her eyes back, obviously reading his thoughts.

"Doctor Monroe," she corrected. "We could split the research and the writing. I've already obtained the president's approval for a small survey. All we have to do is the work in the next month, and we've got spring break to kick off our start with a bang."

He nodded slowly, not willing to jump in, but willing to listen. "What is our topic of research?"

Blushing, she added, "Redefining sexual attractions in today's world."

Benjamin straightened slightly.

Miss Clark giggled. "We could call it, 'The Chemistry of Mating.'"

He swallowed hard as she turned and bounced out of the room.

Benjamin forgot to breathe. Calamity had blown in on a tornado with red hair.

The only good news: spring break wasn't going to be boring.

The Mistletoe Promise

SHARLA LOVELACE

To all the women back then who made eye contact and wore pants. You made this possible.

Chapter 1

1904 (present day)

Josephine

I would prefer to be dragged behind my horse. Through manure. And then run over by what was left of our meager cattle herd.

"Repeatedly," I added through my teeth as I told all this to the only woman who would understand. "This party is—" I shook my head, making the stupid curls I hated bounce around my shoulders. "The most mortifyingly horrendous thing I've ever stooped to do."

Lila, a slight, elderly woman with sharp eyes and a quick mind that had kept me in line since I was a baby, pinned back a rebellious lock of my hair that refused to be manipulated. I felt its pain.

"The *most* horrendous?" she asked, lifting a gray eyebrow as her gaze darted to mine. "I highly doubt that."

"Then you'd be wrong," I said.

"Josephine."

"Lila," I retorted.

"You will be fine," she said, walking away from me to carefully unwrap something from yellowed paper. I hadn't noticed it lying on my cedar chest when she came in.

"I will be the laughing stock of the community," I said. "Henry Bancroft's society-scoffing, failure of a rancher, failure of a *daughter*. Still scandalously unmarried—"

"Interesting that you listed that last," Lila muttered.

"—who *never* steps a foot on Mason Ranch property," I continued, closing my eyes. "Ever. Now shows up begging with her tail between her legs."

"Honestly, Josie," Lila said, looking up from her unwrapping, her brow furrowed in disapproval. "I realize you're more comfortable on a horse than in a dress, but have some couth."

I stood there in my underthings in front of the wood-framed, full-length mirror that once belonged to my mother. Where Lila used to dress *her* for galas probably much like the one across the bridge tonight, because my mother's family came from some of the original money that settled in Houston, Texas. Marrying my father and taking on the cattle-ranching lifestyle on the outskirts may have changed some things, but she would have loved this party. From what I understood anyway.

She died the night I was born.

"All my couth disappeared, Lila," I said, gazing into my own dark eyes.

"Nonsense," she said.

"When the storm wiped out Galveston and cut us off," I said. "When the herd got sick, when buyers stopped buying, and the Masons took part of our land, and then Daddy—" I shut my eyes tight against the burn.

"Listen to me, young lady," Lila said, coming back up behind me, something draped over her arm. Her pale-blue eyes glittered with something between love and a desire to put me over her knee. "Your daddy was the most honorable man I've ever known. And he raised you to be the same. He knows that you've been pulling out all the stops and doing everything in your power to keep the Lucky B going since he passed. You are not a failure. He *knows* that you're struggling. But he also expects you to hold up your head and be the lady of this house now. It's been three years since he—"

"I've never been a lady, Lila."

"Bullshit."

My mouth fell open, and not even a shocked laugh could fall out. In my twenty-three years of life, I'd never heard Lila say anything stronger than "cockleburs," and that was when I nearly burned down the kitchen attempting to fry sausage.

"Lila!"

"Oh, don't act like you have virgin ears, baby girl," she said, waving a hand. "You *are* a lady. You come from the finest lady I ever had the privilege to—call my friend," she said, her eyes tearing up before she blinked them away. "And I did everything I could to nurture her spirit in you. You may not live it actively, Josie, but you have stronger stock in you than you think. And your parents would expect you to call upon that now. You've done everything else."

"Everything else," I said bitterly. "Except find a husband to save me?"

"To save this ranch," she said, her jaw twitching with the same pain I felt. She averted her eyes to check my hair for the fiftieth time, as if it held all the answers. "I know how you feel about going to the Mason Ranch, but at least the party is no longer held on Christmas Eve, so there's that. And there will be benefactors there, Josie. Possibly even that Mr. LaDeen, who has come calling twice."

"Benefactors," I said, swiping under my eyes. "Such a nice, benign word for available, rich men. And Mr. LaDeen is old enough to be my father. He never looks me in the eye either. He's . . ."

"Rich?"

"Creepy."

"Call him whatever you want, my girl," she said with a sigh. "But the cold, hard truth of the matter is that you need help. And fast. You like saying 'Masons' like there are hordes of them lying in wait, but you and I both know there's just one now. And you may not want to believe it, but Benjamin Mason didn't *take* the bridge and creek junction of Lucky B property. He bought it fair and square to help your father."

"He bought it to stick it to me," I snapped—a little too hard. I took a deep breath and tried to blink back the sudden burn.

"You need to let all that go," she said, walking up behind me and meeting my eyes in the mirror with a tired hardness. "Men make pretty vows when it serves their purposes, and a promise made under a silly plant is about as solid as oatmeal."

I refused to let my mind drift back to the worn-out memory.

"Didn't my father propose to my mother under the mistletoe?" I asked dryly. "I'm quite sure I've heard that story a time or twenty."

"Your father was a romantic git," she said. "And one of the few who always kept his word. Don't think for one moment that because you've carried around this anger the past five years that Benjamin Mason had any memory of it two weeks later."

"It wasn't about any stupid promise," I said. "It was all the lies preceding it." I shook my head, pushing away the old memories. It served no purpose going there now. "It was personal, Lila, him buying that particular section," I said. "I knew it, and so did he. If he'd really wanted to help us out, he could have just given Daddy the money free and clear."

"If you think *that* was ever a possibility, sweet girl," Lila said, scoffing, "then you didn't know your daddy at all." She held up what was on her arm. "Now—enough of this. Quit crying; you'll mess up your face. Time to put on the dress."

"I should go looking like I really do every day," I said, crossing my arms over my chest. "If I'm trolling for a husband, shouldn't they know what they're paying for?"

"Josie, if you go over there dressed in men's riding breeches and a top shirt, you'll get more attention than you ever want, and not the good kind." She hung the dress in front of me, layering a corset in front of it. "Put this on."

The dress was a deep burgundy velvet, and simpler than what Lila had pushed on me in the past. A simple cut with a scalloped neckline and a tailored waist. The full-length sleeves were sheer. It was actually beautiful.

"Where did this come from?" I asked. "I haven't seen it before."

"Just put it on."

"I'm not wearing the corset."

"Josie."

"It's torture," I said. "And they are going out of fashion anyway."

She closed her eyes. "So am I, but I'm still necessary, it seems."

"The dress?" I asked again.

Lila opened her eyes. "Was your mother's."

Staring at myself in my mother's gown was . . . eerie. Not that I had memories to pull from, but I'd seen photographs. Elizabeth Ashford Bancroft had been a stunning beauty, with wavy, chestnut hair and an easy smile. Her eyes were light in the images, a pale blue according to Lila and my father, whereas I had inherited his dark-chocolate ones. Outside of that, I could pass for her. With my dark tresses done up and curled instead of the quick, single braid I went with daily, and her incredible dress forming to my every *natural* curve—to *hell* with that damn corset—it was like seeing that handful of photographs come to life.

The tears brimming in Lila's old eyes said the same.

"I wish your father could see this," she said, blinking them free and swiping them away.

"I never saw this in her trunk," I said.

Lila waved a hand, tightening the laces in the back of the dress to make up for my audacity. "When we finally sorted her things, he asked me to keep this aside for you. He knew the Ashfords would go through the trunk and plunder her things, taking what they wanted, and *he* gave her this gown as a Christmas gift right after they married. He wanted it for you."

I ran my hands along the elegant fabric. A gift from my father. Twice.

"Why didn't he give it to me sooner?"

She shrugged. "Probably because he knew you'd never wear it."

This was true. Running a cattle ranch didn't call for fancy gowns and pretty coifs. I didn't make up my face or stay out of the Texas sun to insure the feminine, milky-white complexion that men loved. I spent my days either on my horse—full saddle, thank you—checking on the dwindled herd, working with the stable manager on supplies, riding the perimeter for issues, or at my father's desk poring over bills. Lately, that last one took up more time.

None of it worked well with skirts in the way. It never had. Even when we had more staff and I didn't have to do as much. Ranch life was too busy for frilliness.

It was too busy for *anything* else.

I was the son my father never had, and I desperately needed to help him with the ranch. I was also the daughter he adored and very much wanted to see accepted into nearby Houston society and married off—mostly to appease my grandparents. I couldn't pull off both and was actually okay with that.

It wasn't that I was averse to the idea of marriage and family, or even of men. I liked men. I accepted an occasional lunch date or a picnic out to my favorite pecan grove if the man could work it around my schedule and didn't mind taking a horseback ride, but most didn't understand that. Or me. Rarely did anyone come calling a second time.

I'd even go so far as to say I'd loved a man once, but that was a hard lesson learned.

It was also the reason for the dull ache behind my temples tonight, and the clamminess of my palms as I rode silently in the covered buggy we kept in the stable for special occasions. The damp chill was right on par for mid-December in Texas. No snow yet, but cold enough to seep into the bones after sunset and make me pull my coat tighter around me and adjust the blanket higher on my lap. It could have been thirty below, however, and my palms would still be sweaty as I headed to Benjamin Mason's home.

Lila was right about one thing: We needed help, quickly. This evening would make or break the Lucky B. With everything failing so abysmally, taxes had been in arrears for the last two years. We'd limped our way through calfing season. All that I knew, all that I kept trying fell flat. Now we had till year's end—literally less than two weeks away—to pay our debt in full.

I didn't have it.

And unless I successfully sold my soul to one of the wealthier men tonight, convincing them to take on a hobbled cattle ranch as a dowry and bail me out, the Lucky B would belong to the bank on New Year's Day.

My stomach roiled just thinking about it. My father would turn over in his grave.

Lila was right about something else as well. At least it wasn't Christmas Eve, my birthday. That would have been too much. Benjamin's uncle, Travis Mason, had always held this "community get-together"—that was what he'd called it—on the holiday itself back in his day. When Benjamin inherited the ranch and married, he'd carried on the tradition at first. Since his wife died giving birth to his daughter shortly afterward, however, he'd changed it to a few days prior. Probably in mourning over the love of his life. As if he knew what love was.

I shifted in my seat. Malcolm, the last stable manager left who I could afford to pay, insisted on driving for propriety's sake, and sat silently as we jostled and listened to the carriage horse's hooves. As with Lila, I let him have his way. Most of the time. They were only looking out for the woman they still saw as a girl. To be honest, I kind of felt like that girl again as we crossed the bridge that once connected our separate properties. Before Benjamin Mason made it his.

I'd made it a point not to come here except in passing, to inspect the fencing over the last five years, but once upon a time that young woman who'd thought she was all grown up then, met up with a certain ranch hand just on the other side on a fairly regular basis. To the little stone formations that were hidden from the eye on the other side, that made their way down to the water and a little cubby under the bridge. A beautiful, private spot.

That young woman had been a fool.

Chapter 2

1899 (five years earlier)

Josie

I slid down from my saddle, running a loving hand over Daisy's neck. She turned to nuzzle my cheek, and I chuckled. Anyone could say whatever they wanted—and they usually did—but horses were the best kinds of friends. Loyal to a fault, silly when they wanted to be, fiery when they needed to be, and they were the absolute best keeper of secrets.

Daisy knew all of mine.

Being the only girl my age among a world of cattle-men didn't provide much in female companionship, so when the mysterious new ranch hand arrived at the Lucky B, she heard all my thoughts.

Ben—I never asked for a last name, and he never offered one—was different from the others. Quiet and to himself. A little dark and sulky, maybe, but oh so beautiful. Light hair that wasn't quite blond but not brown either, peeked out in wavy locks from beneath his wide-brimmed dark hat. Hazel, gold-flecked eyes gazed at me boldly when I'd gotten close enough to see them the first time, sending my insides into a flutter I'd never experienced before.

And at eighteen, I'd had plenty of opportunity lately.

My grandparents on my mother's side were active in Houston's social circle, and hell-bent on pulling me from "that ranch life" that they felt was beneath me. It was beneath *them*, really. I couldn't wrap my head around the endless galas and dinners and teas and formal etiquette they loved so much. I'd find myself on the other end of some boring so-and-so's son's diatribe about what he was going to college to do, or what business his father or uncle or grandfather was in to . . . and staring out a window at the land in the distance. Fantasizing about being back on my land. Sitting under the pecan groves and feeling the grass under my fingers. Riding Daisy until my hair shook loose from my perpetual braid.

My father insisted I go. I knew it was to keep the peace with his in-laws. Maybe even assuage some guilt that my mother left them behind and then died having me . . . I didn't know exactly what his reasons were. But he told me to keep my mind open, and that I could do both. I could love the ranch and still be cultured in polite society. I could marry a suitable businessman and still be connected to my own family's legacy. The ranch was doing well, rising in status every year in the cattle auction circles. The Lucky B was making a significant name for itself, and I would be considered quite the catch.

I felt *quite the catch*, all right, every time I met a new suitor. Like I had a sign around my neck listing my assets for bidding.

Ben, however . . .

Ben wasn't interested in my assets. Or not *those*.

Ben would smile when I'd accidentally on purpose ride by where he was working, or resting, or taking a break. While the other hands I knew were warned not to look at me that way or speak to me in any manner other than as the boss's daughter, he would meet my gaze and the darkness would leave his face, and that smile—that smile made my whole day. Every day.

And once we started talking, we never stopped.

He knew about my mother, my life, my inevitable shoveling off to some business heir one day. I learned that he was four years older and from Colorado. A rebel of sorts, come to Texas to work for the great Travis Mason, our nearest neighbor and a horse rancher, and my father's oldest friend. Mr. Mason soon traded Ben for one of our hands, sending him to work for us. Ben hinted at disagreements being the reason, but that wasn't my business. He was trying to stay out of trouble, he said.

I told Ben that I secretly dreaded Christmas because it made my father sad. I knew he tried not to be, to give me the excitement of Christmas and my birthday, but I always saw it in his eyes.

I learned that Ben had recently broken off a serious relationship back home—with a tempestuous girl who he realized he barely liked anymore, much less loved. Leaving his whole world behind, he'd come here to start over. He said that he didn't have to worry about marrying anyone now because no one would want to deal with his past, and he learned with our first timid kiss that I very much wanted him. Past or no.

My father would hate it. My grandparents would revolt. It was unacceptable and improper from every possible angle for Ben and me to meet in secret the way we did. The way I was today, waiting in our spot under the bridge that connected the Lucky B to the Mason property.

I didn't care. Once he'd kissed me, it was all I could think about. Those lips on mine. His hands, rough and callused, on my face, threading into my hair, which I'd pull down loose just for him. The way he'd groan against my mouth when I'd press close, and then break away, holding me at arm's length but looking at me with those eyes like—oh, God, I knew it was wrong and improper in a hundred different ways, but I couldn't get enough. I was falling for the wrong man and couldn't stop it if I tried.

I was shaking with anticipation when I heard the gait of hooves overhead, and pushed my palm against my stomach to stem the flop it did when he appeared, jogging down the rocks that ran alongside the little bridge, ducking to avoid hitting his head as he joined me on the rocky ledge. It was beautiful here, watching the water bubble by, tucked away in our own little world. Even more beautiful, as he set his hat on a protruding stick and sprawled out on his side next to me, his head propped on his hand.

Something was different, though. There was trouble in his eyes. Trouble he didn't want me to see as he smiled and reached for me.

"You aren't cold?" he asked, noting my riding jacket on the rock underneath me.

"It's a beautiful and rare dry day. It doesn't get better than this in Texas," I said with a smile. "Haven't you learned that yet, Colorado boy?"

"Come here," he said, tugging gently on my hand.

"What's wrong?" I asked.

He shook his head. "Nothing that the next five minutes won't cure," he said, pulling my head down to his.

I couldn't agree more. Kissing Ben made the whole world go away. All the incessant letters from my grandmother, the stress on my father's face, the nagging from Lila to be a lady, when all I really wanted to worry about was whether the herd had food and medical attention, and what calves were due to be birthed. What fence needed tending.

And lately . . . how I could keep my tumbling, crazy heart at bay.

"Ben," I said breathily against his mouth, almost lying next to him but holding myself up by sheer will. "Tell me."

He shook his head slowly, narrowing his eyes as if studying me. Or gauging what to say. His fingers played with a lock of my hair.

"It's not important."

"Important enough to make you frown," I said, running a finger between his eyebrows and relaxing the muscle there. I kissed it, and he closed his eyes. "Talk to me."

"The Christmas party is coming up," he said.

Thrown by that, I backed up an inch. "Mr. Mason's party?" I asked. "The one he has every year?"

"Yes."

I lifted an eyebrow, waiting. "How do you even know about that? And why would that bother you?"

Travis Mason had hosted a Christmas Eve party at his

house every year for as long as I could remember. Adults only. He and my father would frequently plan it over cigars and whiskey. This year brought my first invitation, even though I'd technically qualified last year, turning eighteen that day. Although I generally avoided any event I wasn't forced to attend, this invitation was something I'd waited my whole life to garner. It was a thing. Probably a really boring thing, but the mystery made me want to see for myself.

"Have you ever been?" I asked when he didn't answer, something feeling off.

"No," he said, blinking away. "Of course not. I'm new here."

I brought his face back to mine. "Don't lie to me, Ben. We have enough secrets to keep up with."

That sentence looked to settle on him like a dark blanket as he met my gaze.

"I just have a little too much on my mind these days," he said, caressing my cheek. I knew he was diverting, but I didn't push. I wanted that smile back. "One being the thought of you paired off with some guy with manicured hands."

I laughed, and the smile I needed so badly lit up his face.

"There aren't too many of those around here," I said. "Not to worry. Maybe in the city, but around here it's mostly smelly cattlemen and ranchers." I balled my fists, not wanting him to see the state of my unladylike hands. "They put on suits and forget about the manure under their nails."

He took my left one in his hand, opening it and caressing my palm with his thumb. Tingles shot up my arm.

"I know you want to go," he said, his gaze fixed on my hand. "Especially on your birthday."

"My birthday means nothing to me, Ben," I said, feeling the familiar cloud that always shrouded it. "It's just a day when my father lost one girl and gained a faded version of her."

"Josie Bancroft," he said, his tone scolding. "Don't you dare say that. There is nothing faded about you. And your birthday should be special. It's the day you came into this world, and I for one am damn glad of it."

My heart swelled at his words. "But you don't want me to go."

"I just—" He shook his head. "I hear the other hands talk. They don't see you like I see you. They see this rebellious girl with her smart talk and riding breeches."

"And they would be correct," I said, watching that thumb of his work magic on my palm. "I've grown up with most of them. I've trained them well," I whispered playfully.

"That's only a very small piece of the amazing *woman* I see," he said, meeting my eyes, completely serious. "A woman who's making me crazier every day, and—" He stopped, as if weighing his words. "Other men will see you that way, too. Every party, every gala you have to go to—"

"Wearing silly, frilly dresses, flaunting on my father's arm like a prized calf at auction," I said. "It's not glamorous."

He chuckled. "I'd love to see you like that, all haughty with disgust while looking like a dream."

"A nightmare."

"I assure you," he said, letting go of my hand to trace my bottom lip with a finger, "that every man there will trip over themselves to get close to this nightmare."

"Ben, are you jealous?" I said, my heart skipping with delight.

"Ridiculously so," he said, making me laugh again. "Avoid doorways with hanging greenery. I can't stand the thought of anyone else kissing you under the mistletoe."

"I don't suddenly become dizzy with stupidity when standing under silly plants," I said, dramatically putting the back of my hand to my forehead. "Nor do I allow any man's lips to touch mine without permission."

"I wish I could be there with you," he said softly, gazing at my mouth and stealing all the breath from my lungs with his intensity. "Kissing you under that silly plant on your birthday in front of everyone and granting you any wish you'd like."

I stared at him in awe. "That would be my wish."

He brought my hand to his mouth, kissing my palm. Sensations shot all the way to my heart, down to my toes, and straight to a place he'd woken up lately with his ardent kisses. My breathing quickened.

"So soft," he whispered against my wrist, moving up. "Your skin is so soft." The bell sleeve of my blouse was loose, and he moved it up farther, dragging his lips up the inside of my forearm, making me gasp. "Like velvet." He stopped and placed that hand against his face, his gaze heavy with desire. "I love how you feel. How you touch me."

"I love you."

The words were out of my mouth before I realized I'd

said them, and I pressed my lips together as the flush came over my face. It was too forward. Everything with Ben was too forward, too much, too unexpected, too inappropriate. I knew that I had to go to the Mason party, whether he wanted me to or not, because of my father if nothing else. He'd know instantly that something was off if I didn't.

But I'd just declared my love to this man in front of me, knowing that my father would be on a matchmaking hunt. Ben was right. It was insane. And the way he looked at me as I said it made me dizzy with a need I didn't even know I had. It was like all decorum dissolved into smoke when we were this close.

He didn't look put off by my forwardness. Or amused. Or afraid.

A long breath escaped his chest, and his gaze was loaded with every emotion I could ever imagine.

"Oh, God, I love you, Josie," he whispered, as if to himself.

I was all reactive sensation as my hand wound into his hair and pulled his face to mine. Something in the back of my brain said to slow down, not to react to my thighs clamping together over the feel of his stubbled face against my tender skin, over the sound of those words, over the suddenly much deeper kiss we fell into, our tongues exploring desperately. Something said to resist as he pulled my body down to his and I felt all his hard lines and something else very hard pressing right against—oh, sweet Jesus, right against *there*. Something said that his hands on my body and his mouth tasting his way down my neck to the hollow of my throat and unbuttoning my top buttons was wrong.

But nothing felt wrong.

"Josie?" he groaned against my mouth.

"Yes," I breathed.

We were in love. Everything felt incredibly right as I gave myself to the man I loved, body and soul, our murmurs of love and my moans of pain and pleasure being carried off by the sounds of the ever-trickling water below.

Chapter 3

1904

Benjamin

Looking around the large sitting room I rarely inhabited, along with the adjoining parlor and dining room—equally unimpressive to me—now spilling over with a bunch of starched-up people I barely knew, my opinion hadn't changed over the last five years.

I tugged on my too-tight collar and glanced at my uncle's old grandfather clock, mocking me from the corner. He knew. That damn codger knew from whatever direction he was watching that there was little in this world that I despised more than this godforsaken party.

"Benjamin."

I closed my eyes.

Except for maybe that person.

I resisted the urge to roll my shoulders away from him or to duck out of sight the way I'd done when I was younger, but he and this place had sucked the life clean out of me. The only bright light in the whole place—in my whole world—was currently asleep upstairs with a homemade doll tucked under her arm. I wished I could go climb in with her. I felt double my twenty-seven years as I turned for the umpteenth time to see what Theodore needed.

"What?" I asked, knowing that it sounded clipped, and losing the will to care.

Theodore had run this house since long before I came, working for both my uncle and his parents before him. Even before my Uncle Travis made a name for himself in the horse ranching business, his father had run a profitable farm there, and I was pretty sure Theodore was just spawned out of the woodwork or birthed in a stable. I had no illusions of whom the real master of the Mason Ranch was behind the scenes, but right now, I'd just about reached my limit of his hard, emphatic *Ben-ja-mins* at every turn.

"It's seven on the hour," he said, as though that was of vital importance. "It's time to announce—"

"That the food is out," I said, giving a tight smile. "Yes, I know. You've mentioned it. Also, I've done this once or twice."

"Not like this."

Theodore gave me his standard disapproving look, the

same one he'd worn since the day my uncle passed and all this glory was shoved into my hands. He never thought I was worthy or able to take those reins, and he was right. I was fifteen shades of green back then, and only cared about the unthinkable manipulation that had just twisted my life.

I liked to think that I'd done it justice. That I'd taken on a ranch I didn't know how to run, a woman I was forced to marry, and the hatred of the one person that ever mattered with some amount of grace. Because in all the chaos, God dropped the sweetest little angel into my arms.

I was bucking the system tonight, however, and Theodore wasn't happy about it. Setting out the food on the long dining table I hated, with the small serving plates my late wife called dessert plates. I figured that guests could serve themselves and continue walking around and talking while they ate. I sure as hell did it all the time. I rarely sat down to eat anymore, except for breakfast with Abigail every morning.

But using dessert plates for regular food evidently *wasn't done* in social settings.

Well, it would be done now.

I couldn't abide another insufferable sit-down with these people, all pretending interest, when we rarely spoke the other 364 days. It was ludicrous, and if I had to have all these damn hypocrites in my house, whispering about my singleness and ability to raise a little girl by myself, then they could be grown up enough to walk, talk, and eat at the same time. If they didn't like it, they could leave. Hell, maybe I was on to something.

"The dessert alone is reason to sit down and savor it,"

he said, looking physically pained by the thought of not obliging it. “Imported chocolate cake, Benjamin. It’s divine. And not something one stands up to eat.”

“Why on earth would you import cake, Theodore?” I asked.

“Your sweet wife and uncle would—”

“—say nothing, because they can’t,” I finished for him. “They’re dead. Please go make sure our guests’ coats are secure.”

Striding away before Theodore could puff up again, I snatched the silver handbell from the sideboard.

“Friends,” I said loudly as I rang it, clearing my throat as the word stuck in my throat. “Ladies,” I said, nodding to a dapper older woman with a tall, intricate hat. “Gentlemen. Welcome to my home.”

There were murmurs and smiles and the rustle of dresses as people turned to face me from all around the room and the parlor doorway.

“I’m honored that you could all be here tonight,” I lied. “I know the weather looks like it could be stirring up something soon, so thank you for braving it. Some of you are new to the event, while others have been coming since my uncle kicked off this shindig in—” I narrowed my eyes toward an elderly man in a topcoat. “What was it, Mr. Alford? Eighteen seventy-five?”

“Before that,” the old man rasped with a grin. “After the war. Back before your father left Texas and the Mason brothers would do anything for a party.”

I joined the room in amused laughter, in spite of the sour taste the mention of my father left in my mouth. I felt nothing for the man who’d sold me out.

"Well, I'm sure you would know," I said, raising a glass of bourbon, to which the older man smiled among the chuckling with a shrug to his wife. "But seriously, to you all, we're a small community here, and this is one night every year that Uncle Travis loved. Having you all in his home to break bread and mingle for the holiday." The front door squeaked from the other room as the bustling sound of a late arrival reached my ears. I heard Theodore's tone pitch oddly as he asked for a coat or wrap, and I wondered if it was another of my investors from the city. He despised anyone who openly talked about money. "I realize we still have a few days left—"

"Four days," called a young woman I recognized from the feedstore, where she worked with her father. It was her first time here and she was grinning ear to ear. I almost hated to short her of the full experience, but she was young. She'd be fine standing.

"Four days," I said with a laugh, pointing at her and not missing the pink that flooded her cheeks. I hoped that Mrs. Shannon, my daughter's nanny, wasn't watching from a corner somewhere, or I'd never hear the end of that. "So, eat up and enjoy. Theodore will introduce our new dining style tonight," I added, grinning wider at the look of repulsion on his face. "We're going very modern. So, Merry Christm—"

My lips froze as my eyes fell on the newly arrived guest.

Dark hair hung in curled ringlets around her shoulders, grazing bare collarbones as a scalloped neckline and fitted bodice of a burgundy velvet gown hugged curves I could still feel under my fingers if I closed my eyes.

Dark-chocolate eyes met mine, her sun-kissed skin

flushed with the cold, perfect brows lifting as she raised her chin haughtily.

"I apologize for being late," she said in a stilted tone, adding with a pause, "Mr. Mason."

My jaw twitched at the formality, and all I could do was tumble back five years since she'd last graced this room, to another night when words had failed me as well. And had turned my world upside down.

Chapter 4

1899

Ben

I tied the tie. Combed my short waves into submission. Pulled on the jacket and rolled my shoulders to let it settle.

This was a bad idea.

For three months, I had stayed incognito at the Lucky B Ranch. Henry Bancroft and Uncle Travis were convinced that someone was stealing supplies from both ranches, and that it might be from the inside. When I first left Colorado to work for my uncle, it was to get away from my manipulative father and his incessant badgering for me to marry a wealthy girl and be set. For *him* to be set was what he really meant. My jaw couldn't take the clenching anymore. While my uncle was pretty much a stand-up guy as far as I knew, his brother would do anything to help himself.

I'd even proposed marriage to a girl I'd tried to love for a year, just to placate him, and finally couldn't stand for it. I had to go. I had to get away. Winifred was pretty and cultured and nice enough, and would probably make someone a very nice wife and give someone's family a very sizable dowry, but that wasn't for me. *She* wasn't for me. Winifred Harwell was spoiled and high-strung and too entitled for her own good.

So, to Texas I went, to my father's childhood home, to the horse ranch their parents and grandparents ran, that was now run by his brother. Uncle Travis had no children and no heir, so he took me in, showed me the ropes, and put me to work straightaway. It was exactly what I needed. Then things started disappearing at his best friend's cattle ranch that bordered his property, and so they devised a plan. I'd go to work for his friend, and keep my eyes and ears open. See if anything sounded off. No one paid much attention to new hands—they were the lowest rungs of any working ranch—and I was new in town, so I'd just blend in.

In return, I'd be paid double wages, and if I listened up and learned well, I'd glean some excellent skills on the workings of two different ranch operations. Because while it wasn't announced or even planned anytime soon, the two ranch moguls were talking about merging their assets. Horse and cattle ranching together in the same business could be hugely profitable for both of them in the upcoming year. The century was turning, and things were happening. Some people in the city had electric lamps lighting their homes, and a handful even owned the new electric automobiles. It was an exciting time.

And then a beguiling creature named Josephine rode up with extra water canteens one day where I was working at the Lucky B, and everything I considered normal in my life blew up. She was breathtaking in a way I'd never seen before, beautiful and confident. Riding full saddle like a man, with breeches and a top shirt and a long duster riding jacket and knee boots. A black cowboy hat sat atop dark hair that she wore in a long braid down her back, with loose tendrils around her face. No makeup colored her dark, expressive eyes or pink, full lips.

There was no pretense or concern with her looks or societal standards. No coyness or games. She was comfortable in her own skin, easy to smile, with an infectious laugh that the other men seemed accustomed to, but that damn near knocked me to my knees. There were no words for the effect Miss Josephine "Just Call Me Josie" Bancroft had on me.

And she was the boss's daughter.

I knew I was doomed.

When she started to come around more often and I knew it was for me, there was no turning back, and when I finally got the nerve to kiss her . . . God help me.

Nothing in this world was better than kissing Josie. Tasting her. Feeling her respond to me as her breathing quickened and she wanted more. It was all I could do to keep my hands to myself and not take what her body kept offering with every close press and embrace. I had no intention of taking advantage or doing anything her father could shoot me over, but then she said those words, and—

Damn it, the second she said them, I knew. I knew it

was more than just physical attraction with Josie Bancroft. I knew as the embarrassment took second place to the boldness in her eyes that all the conversations and banter and laughter and getting to know her had shoved me right over the edge. So the cursed words fell out of my mouth, too, and then it was on. Right there under the bridge on that slab of rock, in the most undignified way she could lose her virginity, she gave it to me, heart and soul.

I should have stopped it. I should have been the gentleman who saved her purity for her future husband, but it was out of both of our control. She was all fire, gasping with little moans at every new touch, and it lit me up inside like a volcano. Every taste of her skin as I exposed it was like a sweet dessert. Her body was perfect, soft and tight at the same time. Her muscles were toned from riding, making her movements glorious to watch. Beautiful pink nipples begged to be sucked, and I obliged, nearly losing my own control when she'd arched into me and fisted her fingers in my hair.

This inexperienced girl knew instinctively what she wanted, and wasn't afraid to ask for it. And I was done for.

The next three times—yes, three, over the last two weeks—had only gotten better. Just thinking of her face, now. Her smile, her beautiful body under my hands, her way of giving and receiving with complete abandon . . . unlike other women I'd bedded who remained stiff and compliant, like they were doing me some obligatory service. Like they all attended the same schooling for how to appropriately not enjoy sex. Even Winifred, who was going to be my *wife*, had just lay there sweetly, not daring to like it.

Josie, on the other hand . . . Josie loved to be touched, and to touch me. She was all liquid warmth and breathless moans, shaking violently when she came undone around me. Alive, and exquisite.

Any man would love that. But it was what followed, what came before and every in-between moment. The way she looked at me, touched my hand or my face or my arm, the way her whole face lit up when she'd see me. There was so much love there. So much raw emotion. We'd play a silly lovers' game about who loved who the most, and it was all in fun, but at night when I lay in bed alone, the realization would hit me. It was so much more than just fun. And as that hard reality would wrap around my chest with a mixture of elation and fear, I'd be hit with a dark wall. We'd have the deepest conversations about life and love and the world, talks that shattered all our defenses and boundaries. Except for one.

I was lying to her.

Doubly lying. Not only did she not know that I was Travis Mason's nephew, but being paid by him and her father to spy at the Lucky B. I hadn't found anything, or heard one negative comment from any of the other hands, but that wasn't the point.

I knew enough about her to know she had a deep sense of integrity. Granted, she didn't yet have any world experience to test it, but still. My instincts told me that she would walk away if I was honest with her. Possibly even lose respect for her father.

I couldn't stand the thought of losing her, but my own integrity was eating me alive.

And now, with my uncle and Theodore insisting that I be at this ridiculous thing—for what? To blow my cover? It made no sense. No hands would be there, but it was a huge risk. Theodore didn't know about the ruse; he just thought I was working elsewhere, but he was nosy and prone to eavesdropping.

I was sure Josie would still come, regardless of my pleas. It was her birthday, after all. Of course, she'd want to come to a party. To try to bring a special memory to a day she dreaded every year. I'd swallowed my pride and the bitter bile that rose in my throat when I'd played the jealousy card, like a lesser man would, but I couldn't think of any other way to get her to stay home. The real kick in the pants was knowing that it was that very streak of wild independence that made me so damn crazy about her.

She would show up, on her father's arm and look directly at me, and the whole room would know. She'd be surprised, and then confused, and then that thing we had would radiate off us and her father would punch me, and my uncle would kick me out, and chaos would ensue, and all the ridiculous Christmas decorations would be for nothing.

But what could I do? Hide in the kitchen?

No.

I met my own eyes in the mirror with acute clarity. *No more.*

"It's done," I murmured.

I would tell her tonight. All of it. As soon as she arrived. She might get mad, but I had to hope that her feelings for me would win and she'd give me a chance to explain. We had no future if I kept up this lie, and no chance of being together at all if we didn't come clean with her father.

He might kill me.

But I'd take that chance. Because—

"Shit," I muttered, realizing with a stab to the chest what came after that *because*. "You want to marry her."

"Ben-ja-min," Theodore intoned outside my door, making my jaw clench.

"What, The-o-dore?" I responded, pulling open the door to his perpetually unhappy expression.

His right eyebrow lifted. "Your uncle asked me to come tell you that guests are arriving and you should come down."

Go down into hell, or the moment of truth. I blew out a breath.

"Tell him I'm on my way."

"I'll rush right to it," Theodore said dryly. "And by the way, one of them is asking for you specifically."

My stomach flipped over. "The Bancrofts are here?"

It was now or never. I'd pull her into the library and tell her everything. And then hit one knee and—God, that was terrifying. I'd done it before, and it was cold and awkward with no love and a lot of giggling, but I hadn't been nervous. I hadn't been anything. I had no idea it could feel like this. Like my whole life depended on her words.

I had no ring, but that could come. Winifred kept hers, and that was a small price to pay for my freedom when I left. I couldn't wait to see Josie now, my nerves shot to hell for a whole different reason. It would be okay. I had to believe that. And then afterward, I'd bring her here, to this room, and make love to her properly, in my bed instead of on a rock, watching her rumple my sheets. Well, no, that would have to come later, too. When her father wasn't here.

"Benjamin!" Theodore said, startling me.

"What?"

"I asked you why on earth the Bancrofts would be asking for you?"

I blinked. "So, it isn't them?" I asked. "Who is it?"

"I believe it was a Miss Harwell," he said, turning and continuing on.

My feet took root in the wooden-planked floor, as his steps moved farther away.

No.

Winifred couldn't have come here. All the way to Texas. Alone. But he didn't mention my father being with her, and he would have known him, even after so many years gone. Suddenly propelled into panicked motion, I sprinted down the long hallway to the stairs.

I heard her high-pitched laughter even before I reached the bottom. Saw her perfectly coifed blond locks and fake smile and head tilt that many perceived as graceful and quaint. I knew how much time she spent practicing that movement with her own reflection, so it was lost on me.

"Winifred," I said, a little more harshly than I intended.

Her green eyes darted to me, her smile faltering a little, just for the span of a second before broadening into a dazzling greeting.

"Benjamin!" she exclaimed, rushing to me. "It's so good to see you!"

I grabbed her hand and held her fast before she could hug me, stopping her show of affection. What I felt on that hand made me glance down. The ring.

"What are you doing here?" I asked, forcing my voice to stay low. "And how did you—"

"My cousin escorted me to Houston," she said. "We arrived last week, actually, but I needed to rest and recover after such a long journey. I can't believe you did that alone."

"Why?" I asked. "*Why* did you make the trip, Winifred? And why is this"—I squeezed her finger discreetly, forcing my words through my teeth—"still on your finger?"

"Because you gave it to me," she said softly. "And I came because we need to—"

Another hearty laugh divided my brain and turned me on my heel, shooting darts of worry straight through my chest. Henry Bancroft clapped Uncle Travis on the shoulder as they laughed mightily about something. As old friends do. All I could see was the vision on his arm.

Josephine. My Josie. In a dress.

I'd never seen her in a dress, oddly enough, and it was more than just an article of clothing on her. It was deep blue and fitted, and covered nearly every inch of skin, save for a frilly collar that she'd left partially unbuttoned. Purposefully, knowing her. The skirt flared out from her waist in a series of layers I instinctively knew she'd despise, but sweet Jesus, just looking at her made me forget my own name.

"Benjamin," Winifred reminded me.

I walked straight past Mr. Bancroft, instead, to the stunning girl with the waterfall curls, and hoped my trousers weren't giving me away as I gazed down into her surprised eyes.

"Ben," she whispered.

Chapter 5

1899

Josie

So many thoughts bombarded at once, tumbling over one another. Contradictions clashing with what I knew as fact. The first being that Ben was here. My heart about leaped from my chest at the sight of him. The second was the automatic response to hide that feeling. Third—wait, why was he here? And looking like—good Lord, he was beautiful in a dark brown suit that made his eyes—but why would he be in a suit? How did he get an invitation?

I glanced up at my father to see if he noticed, but . . . I was quite sure *everyone* noticed.

Because Ben was standing directly in front of me. Holding out his hand. A very odd expression on his face.

"What—I mean—" I stammered, unsure what tack to take.

"Happy birthday, Josephine. May I speak with you for just a moment," he said, darting a glance toward my father before meeting my eyes again.

"Ben," I said, licking my lips. It was okay. Of course we'd know each other. I knew all of the ranch hands at the Lucky B, but none of them would be at this party. "What are you doing?"

"What's going on?" my father said, his tone low. When I looked up, he wasn't looking at me. He was staring at Ben. Something was strange.

"Josie," Ben said. "Please. Just five minutes."

My hand was off my father's arm in the next second, and onto Ben's. Without another thought. Well, with quite a few thoughts, actually, and with the weight of a million eyes boring into me, but I didn't care. I loved him so much. We'd been declaring our love since that first day under the bridge, when I'd given every part of myself to the only man I could ever imagine loving like this. I told him every time I saw him, and he'd pretend to be insulted and say *I love you more*. Then one day I'd gotten really brazen and told him to prove it. He had. That was quite pleasant.

"I'll be right back," I said to my father, daring to meet his gaze. "It's—fine."

I had no idea if it was fine.

"Benjamin," called a female voice nearby. Something in the back of my brain said it might be relevant, but I was swimming too deeply in the fog.

"Josephine."

My father's voice. And my proper name. Never a good sign from his lips. But it landed at my back as I followed Ben into the library. And we closed the door to the outside world.

Once again, it was just us, the way we knew how to be, but—nothing about this situation felt like us. Above my head, hanging from a hook on the nearest bookshelf, hung a branch of fresh mistletoe. It was the third one I'd seen since I walked through the front doors of Mr. Mason's home. Someone here was a romantic.

"What's going on, Ben?" I asked, echoing my father's question. "This is a bit much to steal a kiss, don't you think? What on earth are you doing here?"

Ben glanced fleetingly above our heads, and then closed his eyes, his hands warm on my upper arms. I felt goose bumps travel from the back of my neck down to the soles of my feet. Something big was happening. Something—possibly not good.

"I love you, Josie Bancroft," he said. "I swear on my life, I will love you until the day I die."

That was ominous. And the way he held me now, the way he looked at me—those goose bumps intensified.

"I love you, too, Ben," I said, winking at him. "I love you more." My hands rested on his suit coat, bringing down my gaze to the fine leather I was touching. Nothing like the work clothes he wore every day. But then, I didn't normally don fancy dresses either, so . . . But maybe it was about my birthday? It felt so off-balance. "Why are you here? How—"

His lips were on mine, stopping my words. Soft. Bold.

Incredibly needy, as his hands moved to hold my face as he kissed me as though he were memorizing the feel and taste of me.

This wasn't about a birthday surprise. Or Christmas anything. Something was wrong. Or big. Or both.

I pulled back and looked into his eyes, narrowing mine.

"Tell me," I said. "Whatever it is. Tell me, right now."

Ben took in a long breath and released it slowly, while never breaking my gaze. My last thought as he opened his mouth to speak, was that nothing would ever be the same again.

"Travis Mason is my uncle," he said.

Blinking, I pulled back an inch.

"What?"

"His brother, Lawrence, is my father," he said. "and the long and the short of it is that I came here to work and—"

"Wait," I said, pushing back against the leather suit that suddenly felt foreign under my touch. "You told me—how did you end up at our—"

"The theft at the Lucky B," he said. "The food. The supplies."

"That's you?" I cried, pushing harder against his hold.

"No!" he said, shutting his eyes briefly. "Damn it, this isn't going right," he muttered. "Please just listen."

My mind was going in every direction but in listening mode, but I tilted my head to let him continue.

"I was new in town, so they—"

"They, who?"

He sighed, frustration working on his patience. "My

uncle. Your father. *They* sent me to your ranch to see if I could learn anything. Keep my eyes and ears open."

I felt my jaw drop.

"You are at the Lucky B to spy on us?"

"Not you," he said. "The other hands. They think it's someone working there."

"You lied to me," I breathed.

Ben—or whoever he was—stared at me.

"I just told you, my uncle and—"

"I don't care what you did for them," I said, the burn building behind my eyes. "I care that you didn't tell me."

"It was a secret," he said. "Strictly forbidden."

"So was I, but you broke *that* rule with no problem," I said. "You could have confided in me."

"Josie."

"We talk about everything," I said, tears spilling over my lashes that I angrily swiped away. "Everything. Our pasts, our dreams. I gave you—" I sucked in a breath as a heat wave washed over me. "I gave you all that I have. All of me."

"And I love you for that," he said, crossing the space I'd put between us. "I wanted to tell you so many times, but I'm telling you now, love—"

"Only because you're caught," I said, backing toward the door as realization dawned. "That's why you didn't want me here. It wasn't about other men's attention on me. It was about *my* seeing *you* here."

"No," he said. His eyes said otherwise.

How could I have been so stupid?

"I trusted you," I said, my breath hitching.

"Josie, please," he said, his jaw tight. "It wasn't like that."

"No? How was it?"

"It was doing a job and ending up falling in love with the boss's daughter," he said roughly, blowing out a breath. "Yes, I maybe should've told you, but I won't apologize for feeling the way I do." He took my face in his hands again, his large thumbs wiping away tears. "Damn it, Josie. I mean it when I say I'll love you forever."

He dropped to a knee.

"What—what are you doing?" I cried, covering my mouth with my hand. "Get up."

This couldn't be happening. He couldn't possibly be—no—not after everything he'd just told me. Not after knowing that I've been lied to and played for a pathetic fool for months. This man who I gave my heart and virginity to, who I'd loved beyond reason—it was as if a knife kept turning in my chest with every second that passed.

"God is my witness," he said, looking up at me with something so passionate and palpable that the naïve girl of ten minutes earlier would have believed it. He looked like he loved me to his very soul. "I want nothing more than to spend the rest of my life with you, Josie. I know this is smack in the middle of chaos, but I need you to believe me and trust me that *this*—right here," he gestured between us, "is real. You're the other half of me. I don't know what we'll do or how we'll do it. We can stay here on either ranch, or go anywhere you want to go. Any town. Any state. I don't care, as long as you're by my side."

It was dizzying. Was he actually saying these things in the same breath as the other horrendous sentences?

"Marry me, Josie," he said, his voice almost a whisper as his eyes pleaded with me, so full of everything I thought I knew about him. His hands gripped my hips softly, and he bowed his head against my stomach. "Please be my wife."

Hot tears flowed freely down my face as my every breath trembled and hitched. I gazed down at his beautiful head, my shaking hands touching his hair tentatively. I needed the grounding sensation to balance the horrible twisting ache in my heart.

His fingers tightened on me at my touch, and I felt him exhale a rough breath.

Nothing made sense. Nothing would ever make sense again, but—

"Benjamin Mason!"

I jumped at the shrill female voice and whirled. I'd never heard the door open, or the whispers of the crowd peering in around her. The blond, petite, impeccably put together woman standing in the doorway, her cat-green eyes fixed on Ben. Who was still on his knee.

Then she raised that gaze to me.

I knew instantly who she was. Or some version of it anyway.

Benjamin Mason.

She knew his last name.

Ben rose to his full height, stepping in front of me protectively. That told me the rest.

"Winifred," he said, shoving the word through his teeth. "This is a private conversation."

"Conversation?" she said on a biting laugh. "Hardly an appropriate one, considering."

"Considering?" I managed.

Her gaze slid to me as though I were a bug on the floor.

"*Considering,*" she seethed, lowering her voice so that the many ears behind her wouldn't hear, "my fiancé is behind a closed door, on his knee, with the likes of you."

"How dare you," Ben said, stepping toward her. "You know—"

"Fiancé."

The word fell from my mouth as it shot through my brain and around the room like a shooting star, bouncing off every surface. The horror that had given way for two seconds as I came up for air was back, shoving me under.

He was—*engaged*?

"No," Ben said, turning to me. "That's a lie."

"Is it?" Winifred said, holding up her left hand. A beautiful square diamond sparkled from her ring finger.

"I allowed you to keep that when I broke things off, Winifred," he said, anger rolling over him now. "And you're using it against me now?"

"I'm not using anything, Benjamin," she said, holding up her chin defiantly. "Just because you throw a fit and leave, that doesn't break our bond."

"We have no *bond*."

"Oh," she said, lowering her hand to her belly, resting it against the fancy layered fabric of her dress. "But we do."

God himself could have crashed the very roof down on top of us, and it wouldn't have had the crushing blow that that one simple movement delivered.

My feet wouldn't move. It felt as though they'd taken root in the floor, punishing me forever by forcing me to watch this scene. To watch Ben's eyes follow her hand, to see the two of them look at each other, to lock the image in my mind of him making love to her the way he had to me. His desperate growling of my name as he spilled into me—being *her* name instead.

Making a baby. Making a family.

"That's not possible," he breathed.

"Really?" she said under her breath. "Are you unclear on the method?"

"That was months ago."

"*Three* months ago, to be exact," she whispered. "And you need to make this right. Quickly."

"Excuse me," I said, my feet suddenly finding wings. Blinded with mortified tears, I pushed past both of them, past the line of nosy gossips, in search of my father or the door, whichever came first.

"Josie," I heard him say from behind me, but I couldn't get away fast enough. From him, his voice, his pleading eyes, or his lying heart.

He'd deceived me, almost convinced me to forgive him, and then proposed to me while engaged to someone else. A *pregnant* someone else. His surprise didn't matter. His deception did.

A scream from another room halted my anxious steps, and I turned to see the crowd, ever curious for more, move en masse toward the sound. Another shriek, and another, followed by two women in tears, and Theodore, the houseman, looking pale and distraught.

My dilemma slid to the side as worry moved to the forefront. My father was nowhere to be found, and fear sped my steps back through the hordes of hideous busybodies.

"He was just—" one woman was saying through her tears.

"—so still," another one cried.

"—face was like a ghost."

"It's not working!"

I broke through the wall to gasp at the vision in front of me. Travis Mason, sprawled on the floor beside his favorite chair, a half empty tumbler of brandy on a table. My father, coat off, hair swinging free of his oiled-back style as he pumped his fists on Mr. Mason's chest.

His face was red with exertion, his eyes wet as he looked up and spotted me.

Instantly, I moved forward and dropped to my knees, feeling for a pulse like my father had taught me. *Ranch life requires you to know a little of everything, Josie.* I shook my head, looking down at the lifeless face of my father's best friend and pushing back the latest information I had on their little secret scheme.

It didn't matter. Business was business, and the state of my heart was inconsequential. Irrelevant. My father had bigger problems than an irate daughter, especially when he didn't know my role in the whole horrible thing.

He would never know.

There was no purpose to it.

There was movement to my right as the wall of people parted, letting through a wild-eyed Ben. Benjamin Mason. Travis's nephew. His jaw tightened as he dropped to his knees next to my father, and his eyes went red with the burn of telltale tears.

"Uncle," he choked out.

I pushed to my feet, unable to bear the mixture of anger and sadness warring within me, and backed straight into hands holding my arms. Turning, I stared straight into clear green eyes that held not one ounce of sympathy, Theodore, in contrast, hovering behind her like a confused bee, looked ready to collapse.

"Benjamin will be busy," Winifred said stonily. "You may leave now."

"Oh, my Jesus," Theodore said, a hand over his face. "Benjamin gets everything. He's the—he's in charge. This is awful."

Winifred raised a perfect brow, palming her abdomen at the same time, her gaze never leaving mine. "As I said."

Chapter 6

1904

Josie

I clasped my fingers together so tightly they ached, but it was better to stem the tremble that began the moment Benjamin Mason locked eyes with me.

It had been a full five years since we simply stood across from each other and took it in. Yes, I'd seen him here and there, from a distance, but we didn't talk, and one of us always turned away. I didn't leave the ranch much; we had staff for those things. Or we did. So, most of the time, any sighting I had was while I was out riding the perimeter or checking on the herd. And most of the time, that sighting was of him and his little girl, either riding his horse, or in his family's tiny private cemetery.

That, I understood. I'd done that with my own father all my life, visiting my mother via a gravestone. It was the times he was alone that reminded me who he was. *What* he was. A liar I'd almost trusted with everything. Most of those times, he wasn't visiting his uncle, because I knew where that grave was located. He was kneeling in front of his late wife.

That told me all I needed to know.

Winifred Mason, from the three excruciating minutes I'd shared air with her, had been an abominable, horrid, witch of a woman, and if he loved someone like that, then they'd deserved each other. That poor little girl—I knew what it was like to grow up without a mother, but I had to believe she might have dodged a bullet with that one.

And I was probably going to hell for that.

Now, looking into the face of a man I once thought I knew, I tried not to be affected by him. He was so much the same, and yet different. With no hat to cover his dark blond waves, they were combed neatly back in a gentleman's style. His face was shaved clean of the stubble I remembered, and his eyes—well, nothing could change that. Except that something had.

There was a sadness there. A hollowness.

I guessed losing his wife had taken a toll.

I held up my head and breathed in a steadying breath. No time for walking memory lane or analyzing the present. I had to somehow get through this interminable party, find a suitor, sell my soul, and maintain some semblance of dignity before I went home and hid in the stable to come undone in private, with my horse, Daisy, and a bottle of my father's whiskey.

That's what I'd done the last time. I'd run on foot from that house, running with no mind to the biting, wet cold on my skin and the bushes and rocks tearing at my gown. I got a tongue-lashing from my father later on the indecency and embarrassment of leaving in such a way, but I couldn't take anymore. Ben suddenly being a stranger, lying to me, then proposing, his fiancée showing up pregnant, his uncle dying in my father's arms, and Winifred's icy hatred . . .

All within the same half hour. It was too much.

I turned away from the flash of his eyes now as I called him by his surname. Let that burn a bit. I wouldn't leave here like a distraught girl this time, but if I had to be here suffering, he could go with a little stab.

No one appeared to notice the pause in his greeting as he continued, or else they were too polite to gawk at the tension between us. And that wasn't likely in this crowd. The rumors of that fateful night's melodrama had not escaped me. I had very much stayed to myself and the ranch in the past five years, purposely avoiding public gatherings and prolonged events like this one that loosened mouths and reminded people of old gossip.

Now, to be back here, in the same place where my life had so publicly disintegrated in front of everyone—it was all I could do not to shake my head at my own ridiculous predicament.

As he finished and the guests began to move and murmur among themselves about the new "modern dining," I drew an easier breath. I could do this. I could be social, and civil, and nice.

"Miss Bancroft."

Then again, this evening's torture might never end.

Falling into step beside me was Benjamin Mason himself. So much for avoiding the gossip. I swallowed hard and kept my fingers intertwined, determined to ignore the foreign yet familiar pull of his body so close to my side. I had no business remembering that.

"I'm sure you have other guests to bother, Mr. Mason," I managed, realizing that that crossed "nice" off my agenda.

"Possibly, but I've already achieved that," he said nonchalantly, facing forward as we walked slowly. "They've had their dose of me."

The rumble of his voice resonated to my very toes, sending goose bumps down my spine.

Stop that.

"How fortunate."

He blew out an impatient breath, but I was saved by the approach of our long-time accountant, Mr. Green. I never cared hugely for the man, finding him a bit smug most of my life, but I smiled in his direction as if he were my closest friend.

"Josie," he said, taking my hand in his and patting it. "Good to see you, my dear. May I help you with your plate?"

I blinked, taken aback. "My plate?"

Mr. Green chuckled, his bald head gleaming in the soft, flickering lantern light that glowed from every few feet. Benjamin had spared no expense for fuel.

"Our host has quite the progressive plan tonight," he said, glancing up at Benjamin. "Kind of a walk and carry."

"Progressive?" I said, not daring to look up to my left, where I could feel the gaze bearing down. "Is that what they're calling moving cattle through the chutes to graze now? I think we've been doing that for some time."

Mr. Green laughed heartily. "She has a point, Benjamin."

"I'm fairly sure I can handle the inconvenience," I said, taking the older man's arm. "But I'll be glad for the company."

With that, the presence to my left stepped away, and I cursed my disappointment. What the hell was wrong with me? Why did I have to fight the urge to turn in that direction and see where he went?

"I have another reason to want a few minutes of your time," Mr. Green said, his voice lowered as we continued our slow progression toward the dining room.

I took a deep breath and released it slowly, thankful for the distraction. "Oh?"

"I know you're aware of the year-end tax deadline," he said.

My gratefulness dissipated, replaced with the despair that had become much more commonplace. Yes. I was aware. As I let my gaze sweep the room and take inventory of the obvious businessmen talking in clusters, I felt so painfully aware.

"Yes. I'm working on some ideas," I said.

He darted a sideways glance my way. "Well, you'll need to work faster," he said, nodding toward those same clusters. "The bank has stated an extended holiday this year, closing next week between Christmas and New Year's. Meaning—"

"No," I breathed, knowing exactly what that meant. "They can't. The holiday is—"

"I know," he said, patting my hand again. "But they can choose to give their employees additional days off, and they are."

I felt my scalp begin to sweat. It was already mostly impossible. Now it was swimming in the land of bleak and hopeless.

"So, I have less than—" My chest ached as my heart clenched inside it. "I have only days left."

"Four," he said. "You have until Christmas Eve."

He clamped his hand down on mine as if that would calm me somehow. As if that would fix the horror that once more rained down on that horrible date.

My mother's death.

Ben's betrayal.

Now, I would lose everything my father created on that day as well.

My burning eyes moved over the room. I couldn't afford to be proud anymore. I had to save my home. The jobs of my last few employees.

"I don't like what you're having to do, Josie," he said as we approached the table and he handed me a plate. "It doesn't set well with me."

I scoffed. "Me either, but what choice do I have?"

"Have you considered asking your grandparents?" he asked. "They have the means."

"To save the thing that took their daughter from them and tainted me?" I responded with a sad chuckle. "They've been waiting for years for this to happen. Especially since Daddy died."

"Even for you?" he asked.

I met his gaze. "If they knew how shaky things were, they'd work even harder to get me there."

Mr. Green rubbed at his jaw as he averted his eyes and appeared to be fascinated with the food spread.

"There is one other option," he said.

"What?" I asked, stopping short and gripping the plate as he placed some kind of meat pastry on it. There was hope? "Tell me."

At this point, I'd do anything, and not having to hand over my life and inheritance to some stranger to bail me out sounded divine.

"Merge with the Mason Ranch," he said under his breath.

The slight flutter my heart had felt for half a second died a horrible death.

"That's not funny," I said.

"I wasn't trying to be."

"Or an option," I continued. "How dare you even—"

"Josie, just listen."

I set down the etched-glass plate with a loud clank, bringing faces already bewildered by the new dinner plan staring my way with curiosity.

"No."

"Josie—"

His voice was a distant, tinny sound as I pushed against the human cattle flow to exit the dining room.

"Excuse me," I said repeatedly as people did their best to let me through. Blindly, I sought the front doors, instinctively wanting out of this house. Wanting away from everything this place represented.

Everything negative from the past five years began . . . here.

Learning about the thefts and the missing food supplies. Mr. Mason's death, followed by the horrible storm that destroyed the island of Galveston the next year. It damaged our stables and cut off our supply connection for months on end. Finally, my father's subsequent decline in spirit and health, his death, and then the illness that wiped out two thirds of our herd and sent what was left of our buyers and breeders running for more reliable cattle sources.

All of it started right there, under that roof, in the beautiful, wooden beamed entryway of the Mason Ranch. And that didn't even include my own personal loss. Finding out that my Ben was Benjamin Mason, that he'd betrayed me with a pack of lies, was engaged to another, and expecting a child.

It was like the portal to hell, and all I wanted was out, but my feet halted at the doors. I shut my eyes tight against the burn that wanted to win, that wanted to make me give up and retreat to a dark corner. I didn't have that luxury now.

Taking a deep breath and turning slowly, I swiped under my eyes and watched the last remnants of the crowd wander through the dining room door, some of them still whispering among themselves as they glanced over their shoulders. I'd reminded them. Glorious.

Let them talk. I didn't care. I had bigger problems.

The library door stood ajar ahead, and a burst of painful laughter escaped my throat before I clapped a hand over my mouth. The irony was almost crazy. But before I knew what I was doing, I found myself inside, raising my eyes overhead. No mistletoe now.

I closed my eyes as I leaned against a shelf and breathed in the quiet. The last time I was in this room, my world turned upside down. I could still see him down on one knee, his head bowed, begging me to—

"Who are you?"

I sucked in a very ungraceful breath, knocking two books from their place as my right hand flailed sideways. They clattered to the ground, and my gaze landed on two little bare feet near where one of them lay open on the wood floor.

A little girl with silky blond hair, a long nightdress, and her father's golden-hazel eyes peered up at me from the corner as she sat cross-legged, a book on her lap.

"Oh my God, you startled me," I said, blowing out a slow breath.

"You aren't supposed to take God's name in vain," she said, holding one finger in her place on the page.

"Well, I'm pretty sure you aren't supposed to be sneaking up on people at a grown-up party either," I said.

"I didn't sneak," she said. "I was reading. You came in *here*."

I bit back a smile. "So I did. What's your name?"

"Abigail Winifred Mason," she rattled off automatically. "Winifred was my mommy's name. What's yours?"

Of course she would have a version of her mother's name to carry around with her. I understood that burden.

"Josephine Elizabeth Bancroft," I said. "And Elizabeth was my mother's name, too."

"Is she dead?"

This girl was direct.

"She is."

"Do you remember her?" she asked, her eyes clear.

I shook my head. "She died when I was born, just like yours did."

Abigail closed her book and leaned forward. "Kind of makes us half orphans, don't you think? Never knowing our mommies? Did you know mine?"

I swallowed at the barrage of questions. "I met her once."

"What was she like?" she breathed.

God, I knew this conversation. I'd had it at least once a week with my father for the first ten years of my life. Any speck of information, of knowledge, of anything that would make me feel closer to the woman I never knew.

"She was very pretty," I said, digging hard for that. "Just like you. Shouldn't you be in bed, Abigail?"

She shrugged. "I couldn't sleep."

"So you came down here to be nosy?" I asked, raising an eyebrow.

She shook her head. "We don't care about the people."

"We?"

"Me and Daddy," she said. "But Uncle Travis did, so Daddy plays pretend once a year to give him a belly laugh in heaven."

I chuckled in spite of myself. "And you? What's your excuse?"

"I like to read," she said. "Books are nicer than people."

"You are absolutely correct about that," I said, dabbing under my eyes to get myself in order.

"You aren't wearing a hat," she said. "Most grown-up ladies do."

"I don't like hats unless I'm riding," I said. "They make my head feel heavy."

"I don't think I'll like them either," she said. "My daddy doesn't like this room." My hands stopped in midmotion. "He says it's a sad room, but I love it. So I come in here to get some quiet sometimes."

A sad room.

I cleared my throat. "I understand that. I have a place like that, too, at my house."

"A library?" she asked.

"The stable," I said. "I like sitting with the horses."

"Me too," she said, her bright eyes lighting up. "Mrs. Shannon doesn't understand that."

"Who's Mrs. Shannon?"

"My nanny," she said. "She takes care of me. Does the mommy things."

I laughed. "I have one of those, too. Her name is Lila."

"But you're a grown-up."

I tilted my head. "I wasn't always."

Her eyes grew wide. "And she still takes care of you?"

I nodded. "More than she should have to."

"Why were you crying?" she asked.

Jesus, this girl.

"I wasn't."

"Daddy says that lying is bad," she said.

I snorted. "I'm not lying."

"I saw you."

"Abigail!" boomed a voice from behind me that simultaneously fired the anger in my blood and made me weak in the knees. "What have I told you about sneaking out of bed?"

I whirled, ready to defend her, but the ire in Benjamin's tone was in full contrast with the mockery in his eyes. Love emanated from him as he gazed upon Abigail, stealing my words.

"I told Josephine I didn't sneak," she said. "This is just the best room in the whole house."

His eyes darted to mine, and the playfulness faded slightly.

"Apologies," I said quickly, turning to move around him before this highly observant, well-spoken *toddler* picked up on the animosity. "I just stepped in here to get a moment of quiet, and—"

"Abigail is good at finding those places, too," he said softly, the low rumble of his voice giving my feet reason to slow. "Tell Jo—*Miss Bancroft* good night, Abigail," he amended. "And go back to bed."

"But—"

"You can take the book with you," he said. "I'll be up to tuck you in *again* in a minute."

Abigail sighed and rose to her feet, padding across the room with her book under her arm. "Good night, Josephine."

"Miss Bancroft," he corrected.

"Actually, you can call me Josie," I said, kneeling to face her and whispering conspiratorially, "We half orphans sometimes have to bend a rule or two."

Her serious little face broke into a grin. "G'night, Josie."

" 'Night, Abigail."

Then she was gone.

And the déjà vu suddenly swam with a vengeance. This room, filled with the smell of old books and older wood, was my permanent memory of the worst night of my life. Along with the company.

His hand was outstretched to help me up, but I rose without it, not needing or wanting anything from him. Not even common courtesy.

"She's quite something," I said, smoothing my skirt. "I know you're proud."

"She's my world," he responded, and something in his tone made me look up.

This close, I saw more than just sadness in his face. Tiny lines fanned from his eyes, and something like anger set his jaw. His full mouth looked hard.

Anger . . . at me?

That was absurd.

"I didn't seek her out, if that's what you think," I said. "I didn't know she was in here."

"Why are you here?"

I narrowed my eyes in confusion. "I told you, I was just looking for a quiet place."

"I'm not talking about the library, but yes, I find it ironic that you'd come here for solace," he said, his tone sarcastic, his eyes darkening. "Of all the choices in this house, you'd come in *here*."

My jaw dropped. "I don't know the other *choices* in this house, Mr. Mason, because I've never been farther than this in the five minutes I've spent here. *Either* time." I felt my blood heating and my mouth was sure to overflow soon. "If you'll excuse me, I have—"

"You have what?" he asked, closing the space between us. I could feel his body heat radiating off him and I curled my short nails into my palms to keep my hands from doing something stupid. "Why are you here?"

"I believe I was invited."

"You're always invited," he said smoothly. "And you've never come. Not once since—"

"Since *when*, Mr. Mason?" I said, lifting my chin defiantly as he leaned closer. "*Please* finish that sentence."

I watched his jaw muscles twitch in response.

"So, why now?"

It took all I had not to avert my eyes. To steel myself against his hard gaze and remain composed with his face just inches away.

"Maybe I came for the exquisite dinner," I said finally, acid dripping from my tone. "Why do you care?"

The question backed him up, as if he'd just realized how dangerously close he was and remembered that we didn't like each other. I tried to focus on that, too, fighting my body's automatic desire to pull him back.

"Do whatever you want," he said, rubbing a hand over his face. "I need to go check on my daughter." He glanced back at the open door behind him. "Do you want to go out first? I can wait a few minutes so the other guests won't talk."

"Please," I said sarcastically, walking past him. "It's a little late to worry about my reputation. If you'll excuse me, I have business to take care of."

Chapter 7

1904

Ben

After doing everything short of making Abigail take a blood oath to stay in her room, I finally left her with her book and a cup of water—and a pastry from the dessert table—and went back downstairs. I couldn't have her wandering around down there with strangers. Call me overprotective, but I didn't know most of the people in my house.

And she was all I had.

She was my miracle baby who survived a premature birth that Winifred had not. As horrible as the woman I was forced to marry could sometimes be, the memory of her huge, terrified eyes as she screamed through her contractions that something was wrong haunted me.

Of course something had been wrong; the baby was too early. The doctor had been summoned, and yes, there was concern, but Winifred was a professional at being melodramatic. Crying wolf was her forte for just about anything. And my mind was distracted with thoughts of betrayal. Being almost a month early—what if my wife had lied to me? What if it had all been a ruse to trick me?

Anger had blinded me to the pain in her eyes. The baby was positioned wrong, and when Winifred went stiff and then limp in the middle of pushing Abigail out, I thought she'd just fainted from the exertion. It wasn't until the doctor cut the cord and tried to rouse her to meet the tiny person needing her attention that we realized her heart had stopped.

No amount of lifesaving measures worked.

I'd finally stared down at Winifred's lifeless eyes as I held our child and realized it was all on me. This was the reason my life had turned inside out. Why I'd had to lose everything. It was because this moment was coming. I had to figure things out, and take care of our daughter. Keep her safe. Keep her happy. Be her father.

Abigail Winifred Mason wasn't full-term; she truly was early and needed to be transported to Houston for care for the first few weeks. It was terrifying, and out of my control, and humbling.

And the reason I went to Winifred's grave every week with Abigail, and sometimes without her, was to silently apologize for my doubt and for not being the husband she needed in her most frightening moment. To tell her about the child she never got to see. I might not have loved my wife, but she gave me an incredible gift that I never knew I wanted. I could swallow my resentment to give her at least that.

Abigail had had a rough start, but my little firecracker was tougher than her petite little frame showed. At just under four and a half years old, she never met a stranger, and had her mother's strong confidence, albeit rooted in grace and sweetness instead of greed. That's why I worried for her. She didn't care for crowds, but she'd talk to anyone, and trusted *everyone*.

And had already made a friend in Josie Bancroft.

Damn it.

I even doubted that Josie had wanted to be her friend. Hell, she'd probably tried to leave the library fifty times once she realized who was in there, but Abigail had that way.

My eyes drifted to where I knew Josie was talking to an older gentleman, a permanent smile affixed to her face as she tilted her head, pretending fascination in whatever he was saying. I knew it was pretending because she wouldn't smile like that, unmoving, not speaking her mind. Josie was animated when she spoke, her whole body coming alive in mesmerizing motion. Or she had been, five years ago.

She didn't even show repulsion when the man—who at second glance I realized was someone I once knew and was a lecherous cad even back then—unabashedly appreciated the view of her perfect cleavage to the point that I thought he might just dive in.

What was she doing? He was the second old asshole I'd watched her corner since she left me in the library. Again.

I'd mostly given Josie a wide berth since that fateful night. I understood her ire and sense of betrayal that I'd kept the truth from her, but what I never understood was her inability to forgive. I'd attempted twice to see her afterward, wanting to apologize, but her father had turned me away. I didn't know what she'd told him about us, but he was cooler with me after that night, cooler with everything, actually. As if losing his best friend in my uncle turned off his spark. He was gone, himself, a couple of years later, and then I stopped trying. I wasn't the only one who had amends to make, after all.

Yes, I was in the wrong, but I'd loved her enough to go to her. She never even tried to come to me. She'd walked away from me in that library and never looked back. What level of love was that?

When the current jackass touched her waist and leered suggestively, I couldn't take it anymore. I scooped a fresh tumbler of bourbon from a passing tray and headed their way.

"Martin, I've brought you a fresh drink," I said, stepping closely enough to force him back from her several inches. "How are you? It's been too long."

It hadn't been long enough as far as I was concerned. Back when I was working at the Lucky B, Martin LaDeen was a senior ranch hand. A senior with an ax to grind and a lot of mouth, but Mr. Bancroft trusted him. He'd been the only one in the stables who was aware of my role.

I knew my actions were rude, interrupting them, but Josie was here unaccompanied. That alone put a bull's-eye on her back for unwanted attention, and the way she looked in that dress didn't help. I didn't know what she was thinking, but I knew damn well what every red-blooded single *and* married man here was.

"Fine," he said, blinking in irritation before covering with a tight smile. "Thank you, I appreciate it."

"Enjoying the move out of the field?" I asked. "Banking, is it? Or—"

"Oil," he said, lifting an eyebrow. "It's a massive wave of the future, Mason. You should look hard at it yourself."

"Got it," I said, dismissing him. "Miss Bancroft, may I have a quick word?" I asked, not wasting a moment, especially when I saw the fire in her eyes. "Martin, be sure to try the chocolate cake. Theodore assures me it's divine."

The words weren't even all the way out of my mouth before I turned her and guided her off. Three steps and she stopped short. I hadn't expected anything less.

"What are you doing?" she hissed.

"I could ask you the same," I said under my breath. "Do you know—"

"What I know and what I do are none of your business," she said sharply, covering the vitriol with a polite smile as an older couple passed us. "I'm a grown woman with no attachment to you."

"Who's acting like a fool right now?" I said. That wasn't going to win me any rounds, but winning wasn't in the cards anyway. "You can't come in here alone and talk to men like that without it going in a direction you won't like."

She blinked at me and shook her head. "Of course. Because men are such spineless, stupid, crotch-ruled creatures that they can't possibly be held to a higher standard."

She moved to walk around me, maybe to chase after Martin, I didn't know. But my hand shot out of its own accord.

"Josie," I said, feeling her warmth against my arm as she walked into it, her breasts heavy and soft. I felt the gasp she bit back at the solid contact, and fire shot straight to my groin.

Dark eyes shot up to meet mine, her cheeks flushed.

"Please let me go," she whispered through her teeth.

"What are you doing?" I asked through mine, echoing her words.

Her breaths were shallow and fast, belying the calm of her face.

"Whatever I have to," she said.

What did that mean?

That question plagued me for the next interminable hour as I watched her chat with Harris Green, our mutual accountant, and then, in turn, make her way to discreetly introduce herself to two well-to-do men he'd pointed out.

There was something nefarious going on, that was without question now. Anyone with eyes and an inkling of suspicion could see that.

"Mr. Mason?" an older female voice belonging to the sheriff's wife was saying. "Do you think so?"

I blinked back to her, clueless as to what she'd asked me. "I'm sorry?"

"I asked you what you thought of the Lucky B's situation," she said, which continued to tell me nothing. "Do you think she'll let it go to the bank?"

"The—bank?" I echoed.

"Oh, I know I'm speaking out of turn," she said. "But

it's no secret the trouble they've been having the past few years, since that disease took her herd. Three of her hands are Charlie's deputies now. They needed jobs. I heard a rumor that—"

"Will you excuse me?" I said as pleasantly as I could. "I need to speak to someone before he leaves."

I made a beeline for my accountant.

"Benjamin!" Harris Green said jovially as I approached, probably looking anything but. He held up one of the little glass plates filled with slivers of meat. "Great idea! Love the modern twist." Lowering his voice, he added, "I was dreading Theodore's seating chart this year. Last year I was stuck next to that taxidermist who always smells odd."

"What's going on with Josie?" I asked.

He looked at me like I was speaking in tongues. "I don't understand."

"Yes, you do," I said. "You've been coaching her all evening. Sending her to various boneheaded fools she'd never give the time of day otherwise. And now I just heard that her ranch might be foreclosing?"

My head started banging out a rhythm against my skull, and guilt had a big role in that. Not so much the distant past anymore—that was done and couldn't be undone—but as Josie's neighbor, I should have known if they were in real trouble. I knew about the cattle disease, or at least that something had hit the herd hard. I'd heard through my men that the loss was pretty bad, and I'd worked out something the year before with her old man to help out after Galveston's supply ports were destroyed. He was pretty frail then, but still wouldn't accept a handout, so I'd purchased a tiny piece of their property. The only part that meant anything to me. I hadn't heard anything more after the cattle debacle, but then, I hadn't gone looking for myself either.

Green sighed and put down his plate, glancing around as if ears were lying in wait to listen in.

"You know that I can't talk about another client with you, Benjamin," he said.

"And you know how little I care about legalities," I responded. "Her father and my uncle were best friends, even almost business partners," I said. "We're neighbors." I wanted to say "friends," but I knew that was pushing it. "She's by herself now, and if she's in trouble, I want to know."

He looked at me wearily.

"She would rather be trampled by her own horse than have you know anything about anything," he said. "You realize that."

"Duly noted," I said. "Now tell me."

Chapter 8

1904

Josie

I hadn't been able to strip out of that dress fast enough.

Yes, it was beautiful and my mother's, and I felt dreamy in it, and all the things that women are supposed to feel upon dressing up, but that all wore thin in the first hour. Actually, I was pretty much done after the library.

So, after more mortifyingly insulting encounters with benefactors than I ever cared to stomach again, smiling and playing the meek and weak female in need of a big, strong man to save the day, I left. Threw propriety to the wind and begged a waiting carriage man to run me home in the then steady mist. Being that it was so close, and whoever he was waiting for would likely never know—and that I probably looked pathetic—he complied. So, I came home, stripped naked, and climbed into my bed, just like that. Rebellious and improper and everything the ridiculous pompous asses at that party would thumb their noses at.

I'd started out thinking I could talk it up as a business deal. Appeal to these men's financial prowess. But none of them were interested in anything a woman had to say that involved more than a few introductory words, an anecdote about my father, and silly laughter at whatever inane thing came out of their mouths. I would have had better luck writing it across my chest, where the majority of the fools' attention was spent anyway. Had I taught my breasts to speak, I could have sealed the deal.

Today was a new day, I told myself as I headed out to check on the herd and make note of some needed fence repairs Malcolm had told me about. He'd given me a list, but I needed to see them for myself. See if costs could be curtailed somehow. He wasn't physically well enough to do them, so with the lack of other hands now, I'd have to hire it done. I cringed at the thought. Fencing was vitally important, but . . . I was running out of funds. Depending on the severity, I might be able to do it myself. I had helped the guys fix a fence or two when I was young, back when I thought it was fun.

So, I dressed in my daily riding breeches and boots, my favorite lace-trimmed white blouse tucked in, with a duster jacket and my hair in a side braid. The rain was soft, but picking up, and it whipped at my face as Daisy trotted the perimeter of the Lucky B. No corset to hold me together. My hat down low. This was me. This was comfortable and practical, and if no one liked that, they could kiss things I was too polite to say. There were no ranch hands left to maintain appropriateness around, but the jacket was enough cover. I could almost ride completely naked and no one would know. The ranch might be limping right now, but it wasn't broken completely. Someone with an eye for business—or just the funds for business—could help me get it all back on track. I knew what to do, from the fences to the breeding to the auctions. I'd done it my whole life. I just needed the money.

I sagged in my saddle as that reality hit me for the fortieth time in the last eight hours.

That horrible party had been my last shot. I was now down not only a week I hadn't planned to lose, but also all the hope for potential marriage candidates. That had been nauseating enough, knowing that my family's legacy would be handed legally to a stranger simply by my marrying him. That it would no longer belong to me. Now, it seemed that even that indignity was beyond my reach.

Four—well, now, *three* days.

Foreclosing with the bank would be my only option.

Save one.

And that thought made me want to vomit.

Especially when I rounded my favorite grove of pecan trees, and saw that option perched atop King, the same big black stallion, dressed like I remembered him in his worn jacket and black hat, and looking every bit as heart-stopping.

I couldn't think about that, though, as my blood sped up for different reasons.

"What the hell?" I muttered, touching my heels to Daisy's soft sides.

She picked up her pace on command, but her ears

twitched and she whinnied as we approached, as if she remembered King and was happy to see an old friend.

Great.

He turned at the sound, a scowl already darkening his face.

"Excuse me?" I called out as Daisy's gait slowed. "What are you doing here?"

"How long has it been this bad?" he asked, gesturing with a sweep of one hand.

I didn't have to look. I knew it all too well. The meager herd, if it could even be called that these days. The stables, once so impressive due to constant maintenance, were in serious need of attention and repair since the Galveston storm, one of them listing slightly. The Southeast Texas sun and deep, salty humidity from the nearby Gulf of Mexico was additionally hard on the wood, and we hadn't been able to keep up. The fence—my chest tightened as my quick glance told me volumes—was worse than I'd hoped. Still, I might be able to pull it off alone.

I moved a stray lock of wet hair from where it stuck to my face.

"Better question—again—is what are you doing on my property, Mr. Mason?"

He and his horse turned to look at the fence in tandem, as if that explained it.

"That doesn't give you permission," I seethed. "I assumed you had better etiquette than the simple ranch hand you pretended to be, although no hand I've ever known would breach someone else's property line."

His jaw tightened. Good. Maybe he'd leave and I could get back to the business of breathing at full capacity.

"I'll apologize later," he growled. "What the hell happened over here? And how long has it been this way?"

"Galveston happened," I said, stiffening my spine. "No supplies for months on end. Then the disease that damn near wiped out my herd, which no breeder wants to touch and no buyer wants to get anywhere near, regardless of how many years pass. We're tainted. And what's that other thing?" I said, exaggerating a tap to my temple. "Oh yes, my father died. So what has you suddenly so interested?"

"Maybe just finding out that my nearest neighbor has been going under for some time and hasn't said a word to me," he said.

"Didn't realize that was required," I said. "And Mr. Green has a big mouth. Maybe I need to find a new accountant."

"Well, you might need to after you sell yourself off to the highest bidder," he said.

My jaw dropped, air escaping that I couldn't form into words. I took a deep breath.

"How dare you judge me," I breathed, the cold rain seeping through my clothes. "From your castle on high with a million lamps, a fire in every hearth, a massive table heaped with food you can afford to waste, staff at your beck and call."

"I'm not judging you."

"How far would you go to protect what's yours?" I asked. "To protect Abigail's legacy?"

"This isn't about my daughter."

"No, this is about my property," I said. "That you've come over here yelling at me about, so clearly there are no boundaries."

I slid off Daisy and walked to the nearest section of

rotten fencing, picking up the largest piece. I heard him blow out a frustrated breath, followed by the sound of leather and his boots hitting the ground.

"I don't need your help," I said, my back still to him as I weighed one side of a post in my hands.

"Then have your hands come fix this," he said. "Why have they let it slide like this?"

"Because I had to let them go," I retorted, dropping up the post and whirling around to face him. "They likely all came to work for you."

He stopped short, looking shocked. Maybe a little humbled. Ranch owners didn't usually know all the minute details. They had managers for that. *I* used to have managers for that.

"Who's working the herd every day?" he asked.

"Malcolm," I said. "And me."

"You?"

"Yes, me," I said, indignant as I shrugged out of the restrictive jacket and draped it over the fence. I turned to pick up the post again and look down the line. "I'm perfectly capable of it. And with it so small now, it's really nothing." I set the post back down and nodded. "I'll go into town later and get supplies. I can probably fix this tomorrow."

"You?" he said again.

I turned back around, fixing him with a look as I shielded my eyes from the rain. "We've established that."

"You're going to fix the fence." He said it as a statement.

I dropped my hand and crossed my arms, suddenly a little too aware of my state of dress, or lack of it. Especially wet. And white.

"I'm a rancher's daughter," I said. "I've done every job on this land at least once, and fixing broken things is a daily chore."

He wiped a hand over his face.

"You can't go on like this, Josie. You need help to run a ranch."

I snorted. "Really, now? Come up with that all by yourself?"

"So that's why you were interviewing for husbands last night?"

I shook my head. "Are you—do you *mean* to keep insulting me, or is it just your natural charm?"

"I'm sorry, but do you realize the dangerous position in which you put yourself last night? Not all men are gentlemen, Josie."

"Do you realize I don't have a choice?" I spat, stepping up to him just as the rain went a little more horizontal. It didn't matter anymore. There came a point when you couldn't get any wetter. "And I suppose you're calling yourself a gentleman?"

"I try to be," he said, rain dripping off his hat as his gaze burned down into mine. "Every day. I try to be some sort of standard my daughter can use to measure a good man by."

Words stuck in my throat at the sincerity that emanated from him with that sentence.

"Well, here's a tip: Don't be a cad."

His jaw ticked, and being close enough to see that wasn't a good idea. I backed up a step and turned back to survey the damage. *Think, Josie.* If Malcolm and I went into town together, we could probably get enough precut railings to take care of this. He was getting too old to do the physical work. I could do that; I just needed help manhandling the timbers.

"Get the horses out of this," he said behind me, already leading both under a nearby tree.

"Feel free to leave," I said. "You aren't needed—"

"I'll take care of it."

I whirled around. "No, you won't. I just need to get the materials, and I will do this myself. It's not your problem, *Mr. Mason*."

Anger flashed in his eyes, and that's what I wanted: to make him mad enough to leave. I couldn't keep up this back-and-forth bantering and seeing good in him. I didn't want to see good in him.

"Well, because it borders on my property and your three cows might wander over, it does become my problem," he bit back. "I'll have my men over here in an hour."

I curled my nails into my palms, relishing the burn.

"It's more than three," I muttered. "Did you miss the part about not being an insulting cad?"

"Yes, well, sometimes I fall short," he growled, loosely tying both horses to low branches. Walking back to me, he grabbed my arm and pulled me under the tree before I could register that my feet were moving. "You're soaked. Get out of the damn rain."

I yanked my arm free, glaring up at him. "Don't tell me what to do."

"You—" He blew out a breath and ran a hand over his face again. "God, you are so infuriating." He stepped closer and I backed up the same distance. "You should have said something. To *someone*. Anyone. Let people help you."

"I don't have *people*, Benjamin," I said, hating the hurt that worked its way into my voice at the admission. "I have Lila and Malcolm. That's it. I had my father, and—" I swallowed hard. "And I had you. Both of you are gone now."

I watched that land on him like a punch to the gut.

"I know what I did was horrid, Josie," he said, his voice low, his words slow and measured, as if I might fly off and away at the wrong one. "I can't say that any of my reactions that night five years ago were smart. I was floored."

I scoffed. "*You* were floored?"

"Yes," he said emphatically. "I was spinning out. Uncle Travis dying in front of me. Winifred appearing out of—nowhere. Pregnant." He shook his head, looking off past me somewhere in the distance. "I thought I'd left that chapter of my life far behind me. Like in another state."

"She had your ring on her finger, Benjamin," I said, reminding him. "That's not leaving things behind."

"A ring I let her keep to ease the breakup—I thought," he said. "She loved fancy things. I told you then that she wasn't for me." He stepped forward again, and I backed up, feeling the bark of the tree against my back. My breathing increased, and I cursed in my head. Not out of fear. Out of another response that I had no business having. "That never changed, Josie, not then and not later, but once she was carrying my child, I had no choice. Everything I wanted . . ." His eyes seared me, the gold flecks in them burning like little fires. "It had to wait," he finished softly.

I closed my eyes. "You're a good father, Benjamin."

"Please stop calling me those things," he said, the hoarseness in his voice and the proximity making my eyes flutter back open. My stomach flipped at the rawness in his. "I'm Ben to you."

I shook my head, or it felt like I did. Maybe I didn't move at all. I wasn't even sure I was breathing.

"That was another lifetime."

"Josie."

"And you know damn well that it wasn't just about Winifred," I said hurriedly, my voice pitched oddly. Anything to break the gravity, the draw, the heavy pull that was sucking us down into that place where we used to get lost together. He was right there. Almost touching me as the wind ripped around us. I was on a precipice, about to fall. "That was just the icing on a very sour cake."

"Because I didn't tell you—"

"Because you lied," I said. "There's no pretty way to color that. And nothing has been pretty since."

His brow furrowed. "Let me help you."

I laughed, and his eyes dropped to my mouth, making every one of my nerve endings stand at attention and all things south begin to tingle. *Stay focused.*

"So selling myself to you is better than all the others?"

His eyes narrowed. "Now who is insulting who?"

"And yet—"

"I didn't offer to *buy* you, Josie," he said, so close I could feel the breath from his words. His chest met mine, and my body instantly arced to meet him, betraying me with the need for a man's touch. It had been so long. "I'm saying let me *help* you."

"I don't need you," I whispered, lying. Blatantly, flagrantly lying.

"Oh, I know," he said, removing my hat and dropping it to the ground. "You've made that clear."

I was tumbling down into an all-consuming fire as his mouth got closer, his eyes unblinking as they demanded I not look away.

"So, then—"

"Maybe I need you," he said against my lips.

Chapter 9

1904

Ben

Her soft moan as I cradled her face and took her mouth just about sent me over the edge before it had even begun. I'd been hard as steel since the moment she came riding up in all her angry glory, her breasts bouncing unencumbered and barely covered by that joke of a jacket. The rain soaking her thin clothes to her body, her nipples hard and erect against the fabric, all while she dressed me down like a little general, ire flushing her wet skin.

Jesus, I'd tried to walk away from her, even make her angrier with crazy, ridiculous insults so she'd get on her horse and ride back in the direction in which she came, but she just kept plowing forward. Weakening my resolve. And once I got close enough to feel her heat and her energy, there was no going back. I had to touch her, to taste her, or I'd go mad.

My intention of something soft and searching to cross that boundary went flying away with the wind the second our lips met. Her sweet taste sent my mind reeling through the past and pushing all logic aside. I dove deep, needing more. Her fingers curled into my jacket, tugging me closer before moving up to knock off my hat and scrape through my hair as she pulled me deeper into her kiss.

I felt leaves and grass and God knows what else pelting us as the rain and wind whipped around the tree we were one with. I didn't care. I'd waited five long years to have Josie Bancroft in my arms again this way, and nothing had ever felt more right. I lifted her as she arched into me, and the wild woman I remembered responded, wrapping her legs around my waist, burying my hardness in her soft heat as I pinned her against the tree.

"Oh, God," she moaned, breaking the kiss as I grinded against her, growling against her mouth. Her hips bucked then, her legs tightening around me, and I was gone.

"Josie," I breathed against her skin, my mouth traveling down her neck, licking the rain from her skin like a man starved.

One hand cupped her ass, holding her tightly against me, as the other moved up to fill it with her breast. My thumb squeezed a hard nipple, and she cried out, pulling down my face. God, she still knew what she wanted, and I was dizzy with the need to give it to her. Taking that nipple into my mouth, I sucked her through her blouse, both hands kneading her perfect breasts as she gripped my head and moved against my hard length, her body shaking violently as her orgasm chased her.

Primal noises escaped her throat as she rode the waves down from the fastest and sexiest orgasm I'd ever seen. Especially fully clothed.

When her eyes drifted open and reality dawned, I knew I'd be visiting my own hand later on. The embarrassment and mortification were all over her face. Before I could say anything to soothe her, however, a crack of lightning split the sky and both horses reared, spurring us into action.

"Daisy!"

I set her down and grabbed my horse's lead as she grasped hers, and we bolted from the trees, slinging our bodies onto the animals' backs and heading for the horse stable near the main house, ducking our heads low against the bitter bite of the icy rain.

She was shivering when we made it inside, and I instantly grabbed a blanket from a stack by the door and wrapped it around her. Scoffing, Josie pulled it off herself and draped it over her horse, grabbing another one to rub her down with.

"There are plenty," she said, her voice shaking with cold as she quickly lit a lantern. "Dry him off."

"Dry yourself off," I said.

"We'll go to the house and get dry when we've taken care of them," she said, scrubbing at Daisy's coat. "We need to get out of these wet clothes."

I nearly dried on the spot.

"Yes, we do."

She stood up and gave me a look, her eyes looking huge in the flickering light.

"We can't—" She shook her head and went back to rubbing Daisy's legs like it was her sole mission in life, wavy, dark locks swinging loose from her braid. "That was a mistake. I got caught up in—I don't know what I was thinking."

"You were thinking that things felt incredibly perfect for the first time in years," I said, picking up a blanket and setting to work on King, the regal, nine-year-old stallion that had adopted me when I first got to the Mason Ranch.

Her hands slowed, pausing for a couple of beats before they jumped back to the task. A telltale sign that I'd struck a nerve. Or perhaps a vein of truth.

We worked like that in silence, listening to the rustle of the rough blankets and the howl of the wind around the old stable. Only when the animals were dried and draped with fresh blankets and had been given some oats did she speak again, not looking up.

"You destroyed me, Ben," she said softly.

It didn't escape me that she'd called me Ben, but the pain still evident in her tone cut me to the core.

"I know," I said. "You destroyed me, too."

She turned to look at me then, and I could tell she'd never considered that. I watched the thoughts play over her face.

"You assumed the worst of me and left. Forever."

A shaky breath left her chest. "I did," she breathed. "I'm sorry."

I nodded. "Me too."

Chapter 10

1904

Josie

We were sitting on the big stone hearth, stripped down to our underthings and wrapped in blankets, fire almost licking at our backs, as Lila fussed around Ben and me, and Malcolm came in with two steaming mugs of his spiced tea concoction.

Yes, I called him Ben. After what we'd just done out there . . . it seemed frighteningly fitting. My God, I couldn't believe I'd done such a thing. Out in the wide open, humping a man's crotch while he sucked my nipple until I came apart? Against a tree. In a rainstorm. Let's forget for two seconds that the man was Benjamin Mason, the man who'd shattered me into a million pieces five years ago.

Who does that?

Me evidently.

You destroyed me, too. You assumed the worst of me and left.

His words stabbed into me like a hot poker.

Lila's eyes kept meeting mine knowingly, and I couldn't quite read her thoughts. I'm sure I looked a mess, but we were out in a storm, after all. Maybe it wasn't my physical appearance. Maybe I just reeked of animalistic orgasm.

God, I wanted to jump into that fire.

I hadn't been able to stop myself. Every bit of logic that poked at me when it came to Benjamin Mason went zipping off into the raindrops and the driving wind when he got that close, and when he kissed me—I was done for.

Maybe I need you.

Yes. Truly done for. Nothing on this earth tasted as good as him on my tongue. His mouth. His skin. His smell. The feel of his hands on my body as he touched me. Rough and tender. Sweet and scorching. Two people so desperate to memorize every inch of the other that we couldn't get enough. Because yes, I was just as needy.

I couldn't look him in the eye now, and maybe that was what Lila was picking up on. What he'd said in the stable—about things feeling right for the first time in so long—it was exactly what I'd been thinking.

And what I couldn't afford.

But more than that, my heart hurt. What he'd also

said—that I'd hurt him, too—my God, I'd never even thought about that. That I'd never given him the benefit of the doubt, I'd just taken it all at the hideous face value in front of me and bolted. Left him to deal with all that landed on him, without even a friend to lean on. Granted, I thought Winifred was that friend at the time, in my haze of anger, but still.

My anger was gone now. Talking to him the last couple of days, meeting his daughter—it helped. Either I was just older and less dramatic, or possibly just more open to listening after all this time, but I understood him better now. I could finally see past my own pain and wrap my head around the choices he'd had to make.

The sacrifices.

But could I chance risking my heart again with him? And with my family's legacy? I didn't know. I didn't think so. I couldn't afford to trust in that. In anything. But at what cost? Losing it all?

I chanced a sideways glance at him, taking in his messy, slightly damp hair that my fingers had twisted in. At the lines next to his eyes and the rough calluses on his hands where they wrapped around his mug. He wasn't cut out to be the big boss. He was a worker at heart. Clearly more than just at heart.

"Good to see you again, Mr. Mason," Lila said, cutting her eyes my way with a subtle eyebrow raise. "It's been a bit."

"Yes, you too, Lila," he said softly, smiling at her, although it didn't quite reach his eyes. There was a sadness there that I'd noticed last night as well. I hadn't recognized it then, but today—today felt like I'd lived a week in this man's presence. Other than with Abigail, he didn't seem very happy. Not like when I'd met him. Back when both of us were . . .

I closed my eyes. That couldn't matter. This was business.

"Last time I saw you was at the funeral, I believe," she said, busying herself with nonexistent dirt on a table as my head snapped her way. "At the back of the crowd."

"Yes, ma'am," he said, his gaze dropping to the floor. "I—didn't want to intrude," he said. "But I had a lot of respect for Mr. Bancroft. He was a good man."

Ben was at my father's funeral? I never knew that. I'd noted his *marked* absence, adding it to his many sins at the time, and Lila had never corrected me. By all appearances, she was saving that little tidbit for some choice moment. Like possibly now.

"He and Uncle Travis were about to merge," Ben continued, lobbing another surprise swing my way. "They were joining forces."

"What?"

"The day my uncle died," he said. "They were making plans."

I shook my head. "I don't believe that."

"Well, you didn't believe they conspired to have me watch things at the Lucky B either," he said. "But I lived it and your father told me that himself. Can't prove it, but you'll just have to trust me." He leveled a sideways look at me that said so many things his mouth didn't. Things that were packed up with old memories that had very recently been shaken out. "Or not."

"What do you mean, joining forces?" I asked.

He looked back down into his mug. "They had a plan. Make the two places into a larger ranch, with the individual specialties benefiting both."

"Why?"

He shrugged. "I don't know. I didn't ask. But now that I'm in this position, and see the numbers on a regular basis, I get it. It makes sense. They were thinking way ahead of themselves, but I'm willing to bet it would have worked."

"It's crazy," I said under my breath. I had to be insane to even entertain the idea.

"Something to think about," he said.

"To think about?" I echoed, standing and wrapping my blanket tighter around my body. "Just yesterday, we hadn't spoken in five years, Ben. Now we're—"

I stopped and swallowed. Hard. He looked up at me with a mixture of the old and new in his expression. The fiery young man who had loved me so fiercely. Or had claimed to anyway. And the present-day ranch owner and father who just looked tired and sad. Who had kissed me into oblivion less than an hour earlier.

"What are we, Josie?" he asked softly.

Malcolm cleared his throat, and we both blinked quickly, remembering we had an audience.

I ran a hand over my face and moved to massage my neck. My hair was tied up on top of my head, and tendrils fell loose over my hand.

"I can't—I can't do that, Ben," I said.

I felt the collective disappointment in the room, and the weight pressed in.

"What else are you going to do?" he said. "Marry

Martin LaDeen and be Josephine LaDeen?" Lila snorted, and I cut a look in her direction. "He's in oil, Josie. He's going to put big oil rigs on your land and milk it for all its worth."

I frowned. "He never said such a thing."

"He doesn't have to," Ben said. "All he has to do is get the place in his name and he can do whatever he wants. Why bother you with those pesky little details now?"

I narrowed my eyes. "That's rude."

"That's real," he said. "Forget the cattle. They'll be sold, mark my words. He didn't like them when he worked here."

I was pacing and I stopped and turned back. "Worked here? What are you talking about?"

Ben's brows furrowed. "He—was a senior ranch hand when I first came on."

"What?" I stared at him, "No."

His expression grew more serious. "He didn't mention it?"

"No, and I would remember. I've known every man who worked here." I raised a brow. "I brought the water every day, remember?"

"Well, he never did anything," Ben said. "Never worked any of the outdoor jobs, and found things to sit, stand, or lean on while everyone else worked their asses off. Guys called him Heavy Lean Deen."

I gasped. "Oh my God, I remember that. Or—indirectly anyway. I remember hearing you all talk about him—"

"I do, too," Malcolm said. "I didn't remember his real name, but I remember the nickname."

“You do?” I asked.

Malcolm nodded. “One of only two men I’ve ever fired in my life.”

“You fired him from the Lucky B?” I said, widening my eyes. “When? Why?”

“Right after . . . Mr. Mason left,” Malcolm said, pointing awkwardly at Ben. “Caught him stealing tools. Sacking them away in his horse’s saddlebags. I had a feeling it wasn’t the first time.”

I thought of what Ben had told me about their theft suspicions, which, sadly, just helped to confirm all he’d said.

“So, he was the one,” Ben said. “He was the only one down there who knew who I was. How convenient. He works for an oil company out of Houston now.”

“God, the whole world is crooked,” I breathed, closing my eyes. “I can’t trust anything.”

I heard a sharp release of breath, and I opened my eyes to see Ben drop his blanket and grab his nearly dry shirt.

My throat went just as dry, and Lila turned around and busied herself as Ben made the inappropriate movement of being shirtless in mixed company. But that was the thing with him. It wasn’t inappropriate in his world; it was just life. He and I were much alike in that regard, not giving a damn about etiquette, albeit easier for him. Men could get away with that line of thinking, while I sat there not looking away, soaking up every inch of skin and wanting to lick every muscle. His back was even better, but I didn’t see much of it as he yanked on his shirt and whirled on me.

“I have to go check on Abigail,” he said tightly.

"O—okay," I stuttered, not quite understanding the crisp coldness coming from him. I stood. "I need to go check on the herd myself."

"I'll do that," Malcolm said, pushing to his feet. "The storm let up. Might even turn to some flurries, as cold as it's getting out there."

"No, Malcolm, I've got it—"

"Let him *go*, Josie," Ben said, his voice booming. I stopped, stone still, as did Malcolm and Lila.

Chapter 11

1904

Ben

I couldn't listen to another word about how she couldn't trust anyone. To hell with it all. I had enough to deal with in my life, with Abigail and the ranch and all the little details of both that kept me running. I didn't need Josie Bancroft's drama.

Not even when I could still taste her sweetness on my tongue.

I didn't mean to raise my voice, but damn it—the constant need to do everything herself made me want to shake her till her teeth rattled. Or until I could shut her up again with my mouth. Which if we were alone, I would do in a heartbeat.

"He's offering to help," I said, pointing at Malcolm.

"But—"

"But nothing," I growled. "Let *him* help you." Yes, let that inflection set in. "I'm going to make sure my daughter is all right, and then I'm coming back with some men to give him a hand—"

"Ben," she began, that chin going up in the air already.

"I don't give a damn what you need or don't need, Josie," I said, making her blink quickly. "I don't care that you don't want my help. I'm doing it." I pulled on my shoes roughly and looked around for anything else of mine that might be lying about. "Be out there if you need to, but I'll be there, too. You aren't alone anymore."

Josie looked away, her jaw tight. "I'm always alone."

"That's a load of bull, Miss Josie," Malcolm said, turning back. Her eyes went wide. "I'm sorry, and maybe it's not my place to say, but look around you right now, young lady. Are you alone in this room? Did you fetch that tea? Did you warm that blanket? Did you stoke that fire?" He shook his head, running veined hands through his silver hair before shoving his hat on top. "We might not be blood, but no one cares for you more than we do." He gestured toward me. "You've been praying for help. Get out of your own way and pay attention."

Malcolm nodded toward Lila as he turned and left the room, touching the brim of his hat.

"Miss Lila."

Both women stared after him, slack-jawed, Lila a little

flushed. I guessed they'd never seen that man be a stable boss. He ran a tight ship, once upon a time.

"Miss Lila, thank you so much for this," I said, taking the older woman's hand in mine and covering it with my other one. "If I don't see you, have a very Merry Christmas."

Her eyes warmed, looking a little wistful. "Thank you, Mr. Mason. I'll send some sugar cookies over for your daughter."

I smiled. "Just Ben. And she'd love that, thank you."

When I moved my gaze to Josie, Lila immediately slipped from the room. We were alone. I could have kissed her if I'd wanted, but I had to stop thinking like that. What had happened outside was a fluke and a mistake. There was too much water under this bridge. Right now, things needed to be said. Whether she wanted to hear them or not.

I love you.

I love you more.

Our old banter filled my head and I had to shake it free.

"Josie, I was hired to do a job five years ago, and then I fell for you and handled everything after that like a lovestruck boy. I did nothing right. And I'm sorry."

Her eyes looked distant as she gazed off at nothing. "I still can't believe my father hired a spy to watch his own people. That he did that without telling me. That *you* did the same."

"Things were happening that he felt in his gut but couldn't prove, and no one knew me," I said. "And I was sworn to secrecy."

"From me."

"From everyone," I said. "But I told you that night—"

"Only because you were stuck," she said, her gaze coming back to meet mine. "If I'd never come to that party . . ."

"My hand may have been forced, Josie," I said, stepping forward. "But what you don't know is that I'd already decided that night that I was done with it all."

I could feel the heat radiating from her as I moved closer to her, to see her breathing quicken, her tongue dart out to wet her lips as she worked equally hard to neutralize her expression. I gritted my teeth and focused back on her eyes instead of her mouth.

"Before I saw you, or Winifred, or anyone," I continued. "I was upstairs putting on my coat, practicing what to say to you, how to lay it all out there and ask you to marry me as soon as you arrived. That very night." Those huge, dark eyes widened, her eyelashes fluttering in a way I knew she'd hate but that sent a zing straight to my cock. "There was nothing contrived about that, Josie. Or my feelings for you. I didn't care where we'd go or what we'd do; all that mattered was that you were with me."

Her eyes filled with tears, and when one spilled over, I reached out to brush it from her cheek. The contact was like an electric jolt through my body, but I stayed where I was. All the next choices had to be hers.

"Everything might have blown up afterward, but that was as real as it could be," I said, forcing my hand back down to my side. "That's all there is to my story. There are no more secrets. You can tell yourself you're all you have, but Malcolm was right. You ran from me once and never looked back. If you do that again, it's your own choice. I can't make you trust me. You do what you have to do."

Before I could change my mind and sweep her into my arms, I walked away. Out of the room, out of the house, lifting my collar against the wet cold as I headed to the small horse stable for King.

Chapter 12

1904

Josie

I didn't go.

It killed me, and went against every fiber of my being not to be out there, dealing with my own cattle, my own business, but Malcolm's words kept echoing in my head. All that afternoon and into the night, as I lay in bed until the sun peeked in on the next dreaded day.

Malcolm's, not Ben's.

Malcolm telling me to get out of my own way.

I couldn't think about Ben basically telling me it was all up to me. Or that he'd brought up the marriage proposal from five years ago with as much fervor and passion as he had the night he'd made it, fire burning in his eyes. Or that after just one day of him back in my world, I couldn't stop thinking about kissing him. About how good he'd felt pressed against me, his hands on my body. My hands on his.

How that one singular moment when our mouths met was the happiest and most complete I'd felt in years. Like I'd found my home.

I sat up in bed quickly on that thought. My *home*?

My home was right here. I shut my eyes tight against the burn. "At least for today," I whispered to the walls.

There was a soft knock at my door, and Lila peeked her head in.

"'Happy Birthday,'" she sang in a whisper, smiling. Pushing the door open, she walked in with a bed tray.

"Lila," I said, standing. "You didn't—"

"Hush, and sit back down," she said, clucking her tongue. "It won't kill you to get a little special treatment today. Sit down and enjoy it."

The tray was set beautifully with a golden-brown croissant, two little tin cups of her amazing canned jellies, two crispy sausage patties, and a small jar of fresh honey.

"Thank you, Lila," I said, catching her around the waist and hugging her before she could get away.

The older woman wasn't one for overt affection, but I felt her soften after a tiny pause, and her arms came around my shoulders as she laid her cheek against my head. I'd had no mother, and she'd had no children, so we'd always kind of filled those spots for each other without saying it out loud.

What would happen to her if I let the bank foreclose? Of course she would come with me wherever I went.

Wouldn't she? And we'd do what? I had the tiniest little bit of a personal purse stashed away for emergencies that I hadn't touched since my father died, but it was truly minimal. I, myself, would only last maybe a year if I was frugal, but that didn't take into account finding a new place to live or giving Lila a wage.

But an honest job wasn't out there for me. A woman. With cattle ranching skills, no less. I could sew a little, thanks to Lila. She took on sewing projects in her spare time and was glorious at it. She would be able to find steady work as a seamstress, no doubt, but no one would pay me for my meager ability.

"You'll be okay, Josie," she said against my hair, as if reading my mind. "You may have to wear a dress every day if you're going to be my assistant, but you'll survive that."

I barked out a laugh and gazed up at her.

"You'd hire me and all my thumbs?"

"In a heartbeat," she said with a wink that I didn't quite believe. "You'd get better, doing it regularly. Before you know it, you'll be measuring, pinning, and threading in your sleep."

That sounded horrid.

A long pause passed between us.

"I know life would be easier if I went with—*any* of the other options," I said. "Things could carry on as normal."

"But it wouldn't be normal for you, my girl," she said, stroking my hair.

I let go of a long breath. "Martin gives me the willies," I said as Lila chuckled, then moved away to pick up a handkerchief from the back of my chair. "He's always leering at my chest, and now the oil thing . . ."

"Mr. Mason's words are weighing on you."

The sound of his name sent warm tingles down my spine.

"Everything is weighing on me," I said, gazing down at the beautiful breakfast in front of me for which I had no appetite. "Could I live with the leering and the uncertainty if it meant the ranch was secure for my employees? That I could actually hire them back?"

"With no cattle?"

I sighed. "Would he really do that?" At her shrug, I averted my eyes. "But I wouldn't have to worry about other things."

"Things that have very little to do with business, I suspect," she said, a knowing tone in her voice.

I met her gaze, shaking my head. "There was a moment," I whispered.

She chuckled. "Oh, there's no doubt about that," she said. "Any fool within five miles knew about that *moment*. It was radiating from both of you, neither of you looking at each other."

I covered my face with my hands.

"I'm such an idiot, Lila. I can't let that happen again."

"No, you can't."

I heard the reproach, but it was much less than I expected. I waited for the lamenting of impropriety, but she just opened my wardrobe.

"That's all?" I asked.

She shook her head, her back still to me. "You don't need me to tell you right from wrong anymore, Josie. You're a grown woman." She pulled out a dress, surveyed it, and put it back, where she knew it would likely stay for the next six months. "You just need to be careful."

I sighed. "I know."

"Do you?" She closed the wardrobe, looking back at me. "Because the shattered young woman I pieced back together five years ago is not someone I want to see you wearing again."

I bit down on my lip as I felt the burn begin behind my eyes.

"Protect your heart, Josie," she said. She moved her gaze around the room. "This house, this land—they are just things." She crossed the space to sit on my bed. "He's a good man, I can see that. But this thing between you is—"

"Dangerous," I finished, my voice choked.

The emotion in her face was evident. "And tempting," she said. "I know. And that's a gamble. It could be wonderful, or it could be disastrous, but that's how life is, sweet girl."

"Did you ever—"

"We aren't talking about an old woman now," she said, the mother coming back into her tone as she got up.

"We could be."

"And yet we're not," she said, fixing me with the *look*. There was a flush to her cheeks with the diversion, however, that I didn't miss.

"I don't have that luxury," I said. "Not with him." I swallowed hard. "I can't trust my judgment with him, and that's not good business."

"Business," she echoed, picking imaginary lint off the quilt. "Well, that's a choice."

I frowned. "How is it a choice?"

"Between being the strong person I know, or letting your fears rule you," she said. "If you're afraid of being broken again, Josie, then you will be. And in that case, you're right. You can find other places to live, rebuild your life, but there are only so many times you can rebuild *yourself*."

I just nodded, looking down at my tray through a haze of hot tears, willing them back. When they wouldn't be denied, I blinked them free and swiped them quickly away.

"So one, foreclose and lose everything," I said, pulling apart the croissant. "Or two, marry Martin and keep the ranch, but risk the integrity of it."

"Or three . . ."

I stuffed the flaky bread into my mouth, not even tasting the warm, buttery goodness before I swallowed, shoving everything else down with it. She was right. I was letting my fear rule me. But I couldn't put my ranch down as collateral for my heart. It wouldn't be fair to my employees to hope again and lose. That would be even more disastrous.

I can't make you trust me.

"There isn't a three," I said softly.

Chapter 13

1904

Josie

I was sweeping, pushing, and pulling wet sticks and small debris from the long, wraparound porch when option number two came to call. Martin LaDeen, in all his puffed-up glory and enclosed carriage, rolled up, straightening out his suit as he stepped down.

"Miss Josephine," he said, brushing his hands over his jacket before stepping up to hold one out to me.

I wasn't usually a fan of proper greetings, so the lack of a "Miss Bancroft" was on point, but today, for some reason, it rankled me. Perhaps because this man had no personal knowledge of me, and yet wanted me to saddle up with him in spite of it. It felt presumptuous. Then again, today *was* the day.

"Mr. LaDeen," I said, taking my time resting my broom against a railing. I turned to let him take my hand in his meatier one just in time to see the disdain color his features.

I had on my daily outfit. Breeches, riding boots, and a top shirt. Sans hat. I had rounds to make shortly, checking on any further damage to the buildings, and I needed to check the herd and double check Malcolm's estimates on fence repairs. In short, I was at work, and this was my work uniform.

Mr. LaDeen had never seen me in it, however. We'd only met twice, once when I was meeting with my accountant in town and again at the party, both times looking much more put together than now. Then again, if he'd worked here at the Lucky B once, when Ben was here, he would have. My daily wear hadn't changed in five years.

"I hope my unannounced visit doesn't offend," he said, kissing the backs of my fingers a little too long. It was all I could do not to yank them back and wipe my hand on my shirt. "Or catch you at an inopportune time," he added, gesturing toward the broom, as if it were the traitorous culprit that had me dressed so offensively.

"Not at all," I said. "I was just doing some chores."

"On your birthday?" he said, a grin pulling at his lips. "Surely one of your help could take care of chores today."

"My help." I chuckled. Maybe too harshly. "Well, one of them is feeding the animals, and the other is in town to pick up food to feed *us*, so . . ." I grabbed the broom handle, needing something in my hands. "I'm it."

He paused, as if about to say something before clearly thinking better of it, placing his other hand over mine on the handle to cover it instead.

"Well, all this will change, I assure you," he said softly. "You won't have to do such inappropriate tasks again—"

"I don't mind," I said, clenching my jaw. "Cleaning makes me feel productive."

"Understandable, understandable," he said, nodding. "But would you like to change and let me take you to lunch for your birthday?"

"Of course," I said. "After you tell me why you were fired from here several years ago."

He withdrew his hand as if I'd burned him.

"Excuse me?"

"I couldn't believe I didn't remember you," I said. "Imagine my surprise. Then again, not everyone is memorable."

His face became a mottled canvas of pinks, reds, and something resembling plum.

"I don't know what you think you've heard," he said, his Adam's apple bobbing. "But you shouldn't listen to gossip, Josephine."

"There was no gossip," I said. "I found my father's notes and ledgers. His shocking revelation right after the big storm that 'Heavy Lean Deen' was stealing from him."

It wasn't a complete lie. There *were* notes and ledgers. Maybe not about *him*, but that was inconsequential. There were also years of teaching me to call a bluff.

The plum color turned positively purple and spread down his neck.

"It was all a conspiracy because Malcolm didn't like me," he sputtered. "He spread rumors about me—"

"Actually, he told no one and fired you quietly," I said, turning to resume my sweeping. "You can go, Mr. LaDeen."

"Josephine . . ."

"Sorry you wasted your day," I added.

I heard a huff of breath behind me. "You don't understand just how profitable our relationship could be."

Profitable.

I looked back at him over my shoulder.

"I'll survive the disappointment," I said. "Goodbye."

The front door opened as his carriage jerked and sped away like his horse wanted away from him as well. Lila stepped out onto the porch.

"I take it you heard?" I asked.

"I might have," she said quietly.

I swallowed, gripping the broom handle as I watched the dirt cloud behind the carriage.

"Can you find me something appropriate to wear, please?" I asked, the words thick on my tongue as I shut my eyes tight against them. My heartbeat was loud in my ears. "For a ride into town?"

I felt the pause. "Would you like me to try to ring up Mr. Green?" she asked. "The line may be full today, but I can try."

I shook my head. "The town will know soon enough," I said. "I don't need a bunch of nosy blowhards speculating beforehand."

"Josie." I turned at her tone. Firm. Expectant. "It's okay, sweetheart. We'll be okay. All three of us. You're making the right choice."

The hot tears burned my eyes. "Am I?"

* * *

I arrived at the office of Harris Green, Accountant, at one o'clock in the afternoon, driving solo in the small buggy Malcolm used for supplies. It wasn't the best we had, but it rode smoother than the silly little carriage, and, also, I didn't care. I'd dressed appropriately feminine in a simple ankle-length dress with laced boots and conservative gloves, and that was enough. I refused to wear any of the hats Lila put out. Hats didn't belong on me unless I was riding a horse. For pleasure. Or work. Not for going into town alone on my birthday to sign my very life's work away. They didn't deserve me in a damn hat. I conceded to an updo. That was all I could stomach.

It wasn't really *town*, per se. The places we frequented—the market, the butcher, the bank, and Mr. Green's office—these were all in a small subset of Houston proper. All within a two-block radius, and not inside the city itself, which was fine by me. Much less hustle and bustle, and less pretentiousness as well.

The sound of my booted feet on the worn wood of the steps leading to his door sounded ominous. Like I was walking to my demise.

In a way, I was.

I shut my eyes tight against the burn, as I lifted my hand to the doorknob.

"I'm sorry, Daddy," I whispered. "I'm so, so sorry."

The knob squeaked as I turned it, and the door gave way to the musty smell of old paper as I walked in. The room was dimmer than the last time I'd been there, a testament to the layer of dust coating the windows.

"Josephine," Mr. Green bellowed jovially, entering from a back hallway. "Happy birthday, my dear." He crossed the room as I removed my gloves and took one of my hands in both of his. "What brings you all the way here?"

I blinked, confused. "What—what brings me?" I chuckled bitterly. "What do you think *brings* me? You said that my deadline was today."

It was Mr. Green's turn to blink and be taken aback.

"Yes," he said.

I widened my eyes. "And so here I am." I took a deep breath and forced out the words. "I'm letting the bank foreclose. I only ask for a couple of weeks' grace to get the animals placed and our furniture—"

"Josie."

The way he said my name stopped me. With fervor and curiosity. Possibly alarm.

"What?"

"The debt has been paid," he said. "Yesterday evening, before closing. I—I thought you knew."

My skin prickled with his words. "Yesterday? What—how?" My quickening breaths echoed in my ears. "Who?"

"Benjamin," he said, as if that was perfectly logical. "Mr. Mason. He—" A shake of his head preceded a worried look in his eyes as he passed a hand over his face. "Josie, I thought you and he had agreed upon this."

My chest went tight. "Agreed on *what*?" I managed to wheeze out. "Were there—are there papers? Does he own the Lucky B now? Did something transfer to—" My head went dizzy as the thoughts hit me at lightning speed. "Does he own *me*?"

I knew that last one wasn't legitimate. We'd have to marry for that. But what had he done? What did he go behind my back and do *now*?

I can't make you trust me.

Well, no damn wonder.

Turning on my heel, I ran from the room, the door swinging open behind me and Mr. Green's voice calling my name. It was all a distant haze, covered by the ringing in my ears and my blood rushing through my brain. I had one mission, and one destination.

He had tricked me with his pretty words. Again. Let me think he cared for me, when all he wanted was my property. Well, I wouldn't be obligated to someone who spent his life thinking of new ways to rip my life apart, and I would not be played for a fool. I would find a way to fix this, to get out from under him in every way. And by God, this would be the last conversation I had with Benjamin Mason.

Chapter 14

1904

Ben

"Daddy?"

The sweet little voice called my name again, breaking through the pounding in my skull. I knew I needed to haul my butt up from the chair and go to the tree and see which present she was pointing at this time. Because it would be different from the other fifteen times, and each one was vitally important to her.

"Daddy, did you hear?" she said, padding across the room in her tiny, soft little slippers, a shiny, red-wrapped box cradled in her arms. "Is this the one I get to open tonight?"

"Whichever one you want, sweetheart," I said, leaning on the arm of the chair as I massaged my right temple. "You can open one gift tonight before Santa comes. One gift from me. You decide."

"Do you get to open one, too?"

I chuckled. There wouldn't be one for me. Not yet. Not till after she went to bed and I filled our stockings with gifts from Santa Claus. Then there would be the new knife I'd been eyeing at the tannery and finally bought, and the small tin of strawberry tarts from the bakery. My favorite. Because obviously, Santa had to bring me something, too.

"I'll wait till tomorrow, bug," I said. "Tonight is all for you."

"What did you ask for, Daddy?" Abigail asked. I met her beautiful, innocent hazel gaze.

That was a good question.

Until a few days ago, the answer would have been the same as it had been for the last four years. Peace and love and happiness for her. I was just Abigail's father. I didn't need anything for myself. But now . . .

I rubbed at my eyes as I pondered the *but now*.

Now, I couldn't get a pair of dark eyes out of my head. Again. The same ones I fought so hard to forget the first time around. Opinionated, sharp words that flowed from a mouth I had devoured just yesterday. I hadn't been able to stop myself once I'd started. Her taste drove me mad, and her hands on me—God, they were intoxicating.

And not just because she had felt divine under my touch, all responsive and reactive and warm. Not just because my dick knew exactly where it wanted to be as it nestled against her hot core. But because being in her radius yanked me back in time to the twenty-two-year-old

I'd been, hanging on her every word and wanting to listen for hours. Falling hard for the one person I had no business even thinking about.

I didn't have the luxury of being that guy again. I was a father, and a rancher. I didn't have time for that. But, God, the way Josie looked at me—nothing woke up the man in me more than one glance from her. And nothing made me crazier than any of the random conversations we'd had in the last few days.

In short, she'd awakened the beast I'd buried. The damning, burning need for the love I'd found, lost, and would never have again. I'd come to terms with that, and made peace with it. I was good, wasn't I? Content. Then she'd shown up out of nowhere, and I had to go and cross that line as if no time had passed. I'd tasted heaven again, and damn if I could untaste it now.

What did I want for Christmas? Josie Bancroft. In every way.

So, what did I do? The one thing that would royally piss her off and ensure that she'd never want me back. Help her.

"Daddy?" Abigail's voice brought me back from my torturous ride through hell.

I sighed. "I'm sorry, baby, what did you say?"

"What did you ask Santa for?" she asked.

I twisted one of her blond ringlets around my finger and tugged, making her giggle.

"It's a secret," I whispered conspiratorially. "I sent him a secret wish, and I'll just have to wait till tomorrow to see if he grants it."

"Why wouldn't he?" she breathed.

"Well, those are rare," I said, gazing toward the beautiful tree that she and I had decorated together, all the ornaments clustered at her level. "So all I can do is send the wish, and not be disappointed if it doesn't happen."

I was babbling my way down an impossible hole. What the hell was wrong with me? Secret wishes? Now my daughter would grab onto that idea next year and not tell me what she wanted, thinking this secret thing was something special. *Good job, Dad.*

"Do those come wrapped in sparkly white packages that glow?" she asked.

I nodded. "Sure."

The deep sound of the heavy metal knocker landing against the hard oak of my front door rescued me from spiraling further into lunacy, and Theodore was there before I could get all the way to my feet.

I knew who it was.

It was just a matter of time.

"Miss Josie!" Abigail exclaimed, stopping Josie in her tracks as she rounded into the living room ahead of Theodore. "Did you know that today is Christmas Eve?"

I bit back a smirk. Any other time, Josie's expression at being waylaid by a four-year-old would have doubled me over with laughter, but I had to restrain myself. She looked just this side of enraged.

Everything she had on her lips, ready to throw at me, she swallowed back at the sight of Abigail, grinning hugely up at her.

"I—do," she said stiffly, gripping her coat tighter around her when Theodore caught up and offered to take it. "Hello, Abigail."

"Merry Christmas Eve!" Abigail sang, bouncing on her toes.

I should have stopped her, but her antics were both entertaining and diverting, and just laying eyes on Josie left me with the need for the extra few seconds. Even angry and windblown, Josie was breathtaking. Hell, yesterday she'd been a drowned rat, and I'd damn near taken her against a tree. I was doomed.

"Happy birthday, Josie," I said, resting my hands in the pockets of my trousers, as if I wasn't wound tighter than a drum.

Abigail sucked in a melodramatic breath.

"It's your *birthday*?" she breathed. "Happy birthday, too!"

Josie smiled gratefully, but I noticed that it didn't reach her eyes, nor did it slow the shallow rises and falls of her chest.

"Thank you, sweet girl," she said. "Can I have—"

"So, do you get double presents?" Abigail asked. "Because you have to wait all year?"

Josie's gaze met mine, and I knew her ire wasn't going to be thwarted with more questions.

"You paid my debt," she whispered under her breath, her lips barely moving.

"Happy birthday," I repeated, just as softly.

She scoffed. "I can't be indebted to you."

"You aren't indebted to anyone," I said. "It was a gift."

"A gift," she echoed.

"A present?" Abigail chimed in. Josie smiled down at her again, and reached out to stroke her cheek. My heart squeezed so painfully I had to clench my jaw.

"No," Josie said, answering her but looking at me. "It's not. I can't take a gift like that. It comes with strings."

"Like bows?" Abigail asked.

Josie's head was shaking. "No," she said. "Like reins. You can't do this, Mr. Mason."

I felt my eyebrows shoot up. "*Mr. Mason* is it again?"

"I don't care what I call you," she said, attempting in vain to keep the smile affixed. "You cannot do this—"

"I can, and I did," I said, stepping closer.

The fury in her eyes was mesmerizing.

"You are infuriating," she said through her teeth, raising her chin defiantly as I stepped closer again.

"I—" I clamped my mouth closed and flexed my fingers, knowing that what I wanted to do and what I had to do didn't match. Spinning on my heel, I knelt in front of Abigail. "Baby girl, I need to have a very grown-up conversation with Miss Josie for a minute," I said, squeezing her tiny hands in mine. "Can you go help Mrs. Shannon with the cookies?"

"Can Josie stay for Christmas, Daddy?" she whispered. Loudly.

I searched my daughter's eyes, and leaned forward so that we were head to head and nose to nose, my heartbeat thundering in my ears.

"Would you be okay with her being around for more than that?" I whispered very low, so only she could hear. "Like maybe all the time?"

Abigail nodded, her curls bouncing. She giggled as she skipped out of the room, and I took a deep breath as I pushed back to my feet. I knew my daughter only recognized the excitement of the moment and her permission wasn't weighted in anything. That I needed to think of her first and probably much more in depth—but this wasn't a fleeting thing. This wasn't someone I'd just met or hadn't already gone through this thought process about in pain-staking detail.

"Benjamin Mason," Josie said, her words heavy with impatience as I stepped closer to her. "You are by far the most—"

Whatever I was the most of, it was lost when my mouth landed on hers.

Chapter 15

1904

Josie

I couldn't breathe as the lips I'd fantasized about since yesterday claimed my mouth, cutting off my words, my thoughts, my logic. His hands framed my face, holding me as he kissed me again. And again.

But wait . . .

"Ben," I said, my voice husky, drunk on his taste.

All the reasons I'd come here danced over my head, just out of reach. Anger. I was angry. He couldn't just shut me up with—with—

I pushed against his chest, curling my fingers into his shirt at the same time.

"I love you," he said, his voice thick and gravelly.

Everything froze. My hands, my breathing, my heart.

I leaned back a fraction and peered up into eyes so fiercely passionate that goose bumps peppered my entire body.

"What did you say?" I whispered, the words barely forming.

He didn't blink, didn't flinch, didn't look for one microsecond like anything got away from him. My insides had gone rogue, my heart threatening a coup.

"You heard me," he said softly, his fingers trailing over my face as he slowly let me go and backed up a step.

Pulling free of my grip on his shirt. Instantly missing the contact, I stepped forward to follow, cursing my body's reaction to him. I forced my feet to stop, and I shook my head.

"Don't say things like that," I said, my fingers going to my lips before I yanked them away and clasped my hands in front of me. "You don't—that's not love you feel, Ben. That's chemistry."

"Oh really?" he said on a chuckle I wanted to smack right off his face.

"And guilt."

The laughter faded from his eyes. "Still, with that?"

"I'm not talking about history," I said, the blood returning to my brain, logic within touching distance again. "I'm talking about this thing you call a *gift*, that's just another pretty word for manipulation."

He crossed his arms over his chest. "Do tell."

I raised an eyebrow. "Buying out my tax debt so that I'm indebted to you. So that you can what? Win me over? Marry me so that my property goes to you?"

"Let me tell you something," he said, dropping his

arms and stepping back into the space between us. His eyes flashed. "I'm perfectly fine over here. I don't need anything of yours to complete my business or pad my land rights. I don't give a shit about your ranch, Josie. And I don't have time to win anyone's affections with money." He flung an arm in the direction Abigail had skipped away. "She's everything," he said. "My whole world. Everything with me and you might have gone to hell that day five years ago, but Winifred could have stayed in Colorado and never told me about her. I have my daughter *because* she came here and tore our world apart."

My hands shook at the palpable love that came over him at the mention of Abigail. It was a phenomenal thing to see on a man, and so beautiful. And he was right. In spite of all the drama with her mother, Abigail was no mistake or casualty of battle. She was the prize.

"Then why did you—"

"Help you?" he said incredulously. "My God, Josie, are you that jaded? That distrustful of me?"

I wanted to say yes. To call on the days and weeks and months of anger and resentment that had built up these horrible walls. But the last two days with him had made those walls weak. Made me see a different perspective.

"You apologized for not telling me what was going on back then," I said. "For keeping it from me. And then the very next minute, go and do another thing *that involves me*—without telling me. Again. How would you feel?"

He sighed wearily, nodding as he dropped his gaze to the wooden floor beneath our feet.

"I helped you because I have never stopped loving you, and I have the means to do it," he said with a slight shrug. "It's just that simple."

That simple, and yet the words falling out of his mouth stole my breath. I reached for the nearby wingback chair to ground myself and keep my knees from giving way.

"There are no complicated twists or hidden agendas." He blew out a breath. "I'm not a complicated man. But I see your point, and I'll try to do better."

I lifted my chin and gripped the chair's fabric a little tighter. "Better?"

He reached over to a nearby shelf at the same time, and plucked something from a basket, holding up a sprig of mistletoe. A bitter taste filled my mouth.

"I started a conversation back then that I never got to finish."

It was my turn to sigh wearily. "Promises made under a silly plant mean nothing, Ben. Our lives have proven that."

"I proved exactly what I said," he responded. "I promised you that I would love you for the rest of my life, and I will do exactly that. I don't want your ranch," he continued. "Yes, we can make something truly special by merging them if you ever want to, but that's inconsequential."

His gaze was intense as he stared down at me and shrugged.

"What's yours would still be yours, Josie. I'd deed it right back to you."

I blinked. "You're—talking about—"

"I want *you*," he said, so close to me again now that we were almost touching. "I want to be the one to kiss you good night every night, and wake you up every morning." He touched the mistletoe to my lips and then tossed it aside, lowering himself to one knee before me.

A gasp escaped my throat, as my eyes burned and my

mind raced back to the last time. His last proposal, also made on the fly, before his fiancée walked in.

"What are you doing?" I whispered, the déjà vu of the moment making me dizzy.

"I don't need that thing to say what I want to say," he said. "I asked you a question back then, before we were interrupted."

"Ben—"

"I love you, Josephine Bancroft," he said, looking up at me with an adoration I knew in my heart was a once-in-a-lifetime thing.

Suddenly, all that was spinning just—stopped. The noise cleared. The fog lifted. Regardless of all the heartache and chaos, I knew that nothing had ever, or would ever, be more amazing than that moment, as I gazed down at this man.

"I've loved you from the first day I watched you ride up on that horse, bringing us water," he said. "And you have owned my heart from the first time I kissed you. We may have been broken and lost, but we're being given a second chance to—"

"I love you."

The words tumbled out with no warning, no plan, as if my heart shoved them out to make room for all the emotion blowing up in there.

Ben's composure faltered, a rush of breath escaping his chest as he blinked rapidly and fought it back.

"Will you be my wife, Josephine Bancroft?" he asked, his voice breaking on my name.

A sob stole my breath, and I clapped a hand over my mouth. How had it—I came over here to blow my top and now—now my entire brain felt like it was going to explode, and yet nothing in my whole life had ever felt more right and more real than this.

"Please, Josie," he said. "Marry me. Today. On Christmas Eve."

Warm tears fell over my fingers, and a crazy bark of laughter choked out of my throat.

"Today?" I squeaked.

Because *that* was clearly the strangest part?

"I'll get the preacher here before dark—hell, I'll go pick him up myself," he said, rising to his feet, his eyes never leaving mine. Rough hands touched my cheeks and wiped away my tears. "I'll marry you this very day and make Christmas Eve a day to make you smile. For once."

My thoughts jumbled over one another, screaming resounding yeses for every no I searched for.

"But—Abigail," I began. "Replacing her mother isn't—"

"She never knew her mother," he said. "Any more than you did. She—" He spun quickly. "Abigail!"

I jumped, startled. "Oh my, I—"

Little feet bounded from the kitchen.

"Yes, Daddy?"

"Come here, bug," he said, scooping her up with one arm and letting out a deep sigh. "I never thought I'd ever find anyone to live their lives with us," he said, looking at her seriously as she matched his expression. "That anyone would ever be worthy of you. But what do you think of Miss Josie? Not just for Christmas, but in our family for real?"

"Forever?"

"Forever," he echoed.

Abigail slid her gaze to mine, full of so much personality, then back to her dad.

"She didn't know her mommy, either. She's a half orphan, like me," she said, making me dig my nails into my palms to keep it together. Oh, this girl would surely break my heart, too.

He looked at me and swallowed, hard. "Trust me, Josie," he said quietly, pleading with his eyes. "Trust this."

In front of me was what could be my future. My family. Ben looking at me so intently, my skin felt like it might catch fire.

"Will you share your secret place with me?" she asked. "In the stable?"

I chuckled and swiped under my eyes. "If I can come sit in the library with you sometimes?"

Abigail nodded, her curls making it a full-motion activity.

"Deal."

I started to laugh nervously, blinking more tears free and thinking I hadn't cried this much in years, but the anxious, expectant look on his face was priceless. I shrugged at the sheer simplicity of it.

"Deal," I whispered.

"Can I go back to the cookies, Daddy?" she whispered loudly.

He set her down and crossed the space to me in seconds as the sound of her steps pattered away, and my hands could finally go up around his neck and into his hair.

"Yes?" he breathed.

"Yes."

Chapter 16

1904

Josie

"Josephine Bancroft Mason," I whispered, testing the sound of it on my tongue. "Josie Mason. Mrs. Benjamin Mason."

It was all very bizarre and exciting. This morning, as I'd awakened on my birthday to Lila bringing me breakfast, I'd hardly expected to be married by evening.

I gazed down at my left hand, where my mother's wedding band now resided. At the still beautiful white satin and lace dress that now lay across the chaise in Ben's—in our bedroom.

Our bedroom. In Ben's house, that was my home now, too.

Married.

Me.

On Christmas Eve.

The very second I'd said yes, the day had turned into a whirlwind. Ben sent people to attend to every need. Theodore went for Lila, who then went back and forth twice more for my mother's ring and wedding dress, not allowing me to help her in the name of my birthday. Another went to find someone to marry us. Yet another brought us food to stay in and snack on all day, and Mrs. Shannon—who I could already tell was Abigail's very special version of my Lila—whipped us up a wedding cake. A simple one, granted, but in the midst of Christmas baking, I called it a miracle.

Then I'd married Benjamin Mason.

And he'd married me.

What?

I laughed out loud at the irony of it. At the crazy culmination of everything this day had ever represented. Death, birth, sadness, stress, and heartbreak, now rounded out with unspeakable joy and the love of a lifetime.

And a daughter I'd never expected, tossing rose petals at our feet.

Bizarre didn't even begin to cover it.

Now, after their Christmas Eve night tradition of opening a gift, and watching Abigail's squeals of joy and anticipation at waiting for Santa Claus . . . I was the one waiting.

For Ben.

"Wait for me in our room, love," he'd said before heading off to tuck Abigail in and read her a story.

I hadn't even been back to my house since leaving for Mr. Green's office that morning. It was like living in a dream. I didn't know how daily life was going to roll out going forward, but we would figure it out.

"Our room," I'd echoed. "That sounds so . . ."

"Delightful?" he said under his breath, dropping a kiss on my lips. "Decadent?"

"Both," I said. "Shall we wait for Santa as well?"

He raised an eyebrow. "I'm hoping to get my present early."

I laughed softly. "I do believe you already opened one under the tree. Plus gained a person."

"Well, see, there was this chat that my daughter and I had today about secret wishes and how they'd be sparkly or something," he said.

"Oh?"

"And we were just getting to the crux of that when this woman came over and started yelling at me."

I clamped my lips together and then grinned. That felt like a year ago. Now, my ranch was safe, new plans were in the works, I could hire back all the old hands to help Malcolm, and my heart—it was soaring for so many reasons.

"I see. How did you handle that?"

"I married her," he said simply. "So, I'm going off incomplete information, but I'm thinking that the sparkly stuff is still to come tonight," he said, pulling me to him and kissing me as I giggled. "I want very, very, *very* much to make love to my wife," he whispered against my lips. "Sparkles or not."

Tingles of lightning-hot heat went straight to all things south.

Wife.

God, nothing sounded better. I had been worked up into a frenzy since he'd kissed me into a proposal that morning. Watching him in action today was like an aphrodisiac.

"You know, technically, we could have made that happen while all the people scattered at your command like you were the voice of Zeus," I said to his already shaking head.

"I said *wife*," he clarified, glancing around for little ears. Pulling me to him again, he brushed his mouth against my ear. "I've loved you on a rock, in a field, and made you come against a tree," he whispered, sending shivers of desire down my neck. "The next time I touch you, love of my life, I want you in my bed, calling me your husband."

Hence . . . now I waited. Staring at his huge four-poster bed.

Because I couldn't wait to do just that.

When he finally strolled in, boots in hand, latching the lock behind him, my breath caught in my chest. Gone was the black jacket he'd worn to say his vows. Gone was the tie. His shirt was open at the neck, pulled a little loose at the waist—probably from tickling Abigail. His shirtsleeves were unbuttoned and rolled up on his forearms.

More than any of that, it was the expression he wore. A look of pure happiness mixed with a driving carnal need that intensified as his eyes raked my body.

I was dressed in *only* a dressing robe that Lila had

brought over. A long one, made of fine black silk, that I'd found in Houston years ago. My grandmother bought it for me when I'd eyed it longingly at a boutique, probably thinking she was adding to a soon-to-be-needed boudoir.

Well, she did. Just much later, and not to whom she expected.

My hair was down in waves, and the robe was wrapped tightly around me and belted, showing all my curves. It was sinful and decadent, and completely unladylike, and I didn't care. If I couldn't show up this way for my husband, what was the point of taking his name?

"You look—stunning," he said breathily.

"You look too far away," I said, crossing to him.

I didn't have a need for etiquette either.

Ben's hands went into my hair as our mouths met, moaning as I pressed myself against him.

"God, I've waited so long for you, my love," he growled against my mouth.

Pulling his shirt free from his trousers, I made quick haste with the buttons. I needed it gone. I needed him.

Yanking it off his body, he pulled away from me for a moment and dropped it on the floor. He grabbed my hand and tugged me to him, and in one quick swoop, swept me off my feet.

I squealed and wrapped my arms around his neck, laughing.

"Pretend that's a threshold," he said, walking over it and carrying me straight to his bed, looming over me as he laid me down and kissed me, deeply and thoroughly.

When my robe magically came loose, and he worshipped my body with his kisses, angels sang in my head. When my hands relieved him of his trousers and stroked his heavy length, he cursed and fisted the sheets underneath me.

"Josie," he growled as he finally slid inside me, making all my muscles tighten around him.

"I love you, Mr. Mason," I said on a gasp.

"I love you more, Mrs. Mason."

I rolled my hips and relished his quick inhale. My lips curved upward.

"Prove it."

For more from Sharla Lovelace, check out the first in her Charmed in Texas series . . .

A CHARMED LITTLE LIE

Charmed, Texas, is everything the name implies—quaint, comfortable, and as small-town friendly as they come. And when it comes to romance, there's no place quite as enchanting . . .

Lanie Barrett didn't mean to *lie*. Spinning a story of a joyous marriage to make a dying woman happy is forgivable, isn't it? Lanie thinks so, especially since her beloved Aunt Ruby would have been heartbroken to know the truth of her niece's sadly loveless, short-of-sparkling existence. Trouble is, according to the will, Ruby didn't quite buy Lanie's tale. And to inherit the only house Lanie ever really considered a home, she'll have to bring her "husband" back to Charmed for three whole months—or watch Aunt Ruby's cozy nest go to her weasel cousin, who will sell it to a condo developer.

Nick McKane is out of work, out of luck, and the spitting image of the man Lanie described. He needs money for his daughter's art school tuition, and Lanie needs a convenient spouse. It's a match made . . . well, not quite in heaven, but for a temporary arrangement, it couldn't be better. Except the longer Lanie and Nick spend as husband and wife, the more the connection between them begins to seem real. Maybe this modern fairy tale really could come true . . .

Published by Kensington Publishing Corp.

Chapter 1

"Take caution when unwrapping blessings, my girl. They're sometimes dipped in poop first."

In retrospect, I should have known the day was off. From the wee hours of the morning when I awoke to find Ralph—my neighbor's ninety-pound Rottweiler—in bed with me and hiking his leg, to waking up the second time on my crappy uncomfortable couch with a hitch in my hip. Then the coffeemaker mishap and realizing I was out of toothpaste. Pretty much all the markers were there. Aunt Ruby would have thumped me in the head and asked me where my Barrett intuition was.

But I never had her kind of intuition.

And Aunt Ruby wasn't around to thump me. Not anymore. Not even long distance.

"Ow! Shit!" I yelped as my phone rang, making me sling pancake batter across the kitchen as I burned my finger on the griddle.

I'm coordinated like that.

Cursing my way to the phone, I hit speaker when I saw the name of said neighbor.

"Hey, Tilly."

"How's my sweet boy?" she crooned.

I glared at Ralph. "He's got bladder denial," I said. "Possibly separation anxiety. Mommy issues."

"Uh-oh, why?" she asked.

"He marked three pieces of furniture, and me," I said, hearing her gasp. "While I was in the bed. With him."

I liked my neighbor Tilly. She was from two apartments down, was sweet, kinda goofy, and was always making new desserts she liked to try out on me. So when she suddenly had to bail for some family emergency with her mom and couldn't take her dog, I decided to take a page from her book and be a *giver*. Offer to dog-sit Ralph while she was gone for a few days.

"Oh wow, I'm so sorry, Lanie," she said.

"Not a problem," I lied. I'm not really cut out to be a giver. "We're bonding."

"I actually kind of hoped he'd cheer you up."

What? "Cheer me up?"

"You've been so—I don't know—forlorn?" she asked. "Since your aunt died, it's like you lost your energy source."

Damn, that was freakishly observant of her. Maybe *she* got the Barrett intuition. She nailed it in one sentence. Aunt Ruby *was* my energy source. Even from the next state over, the woman that raised me kept me buzzing with her unstoppable magical spirit. When her eyes went, the other senses jumped to the fight. When her life went, it was like someone turned out the lights. All the way to Louisiana.

I was truly alone and on my own. Realizing that at thirty-three was sobering. Realizing Aunt Ruby now knew I'd lied about everything was mortifying. Maybe that's why she was staying otherwise occupied out there in the afterlife.

Then again, *lying* was maybe too strong a word. Was there another word? Maybe a whole turn of phrase would be better. Something like *coloring the story to make an old woman happy.*

Yeah.

Coloring with crayons that turned into shovels.

No one knew the extent of the ridiculous hole I had dug myself into. The one that involved my hometown of Charmed, Texas, believing I was married and successful, living with my husband in sunny California and absorbing the good life. Why California? Because it sounded more exciting than Louisiana. And a fantasy-worthy advertising job I submitted an online resumé for *a year ago* was located there. That's about all the sane thought that went into that.

The tale was spun at first for Aunt Ruby when she got sick, diabetes taking her down quickly, with her eyesight being the first victim. I regaled her on my short visits home with funny stories from my quickie wedding in Vegas (I did go to Vegas with a guy I was sort of seeing), my successful career in advertising (I hadn't made it past promotional copy), and my hot, doting, super gorgeous husband named Michael who traveled a lot for work and therefore was never with me. You'd think I'd need pictures for that part, right? Even for a mostly blind woman? Yeah. I did.

I showed her pictures of a smoking hot, dark and

dangerous-looking guy I flirted with one night at Caesar's Palace while my boyfriend was flirting with a waitress. A guy who, incidentally, was named—Michael.

I know.

I rot.

But it made her happy to know I was happy and taken care of, when all that mattered in her entire wacky world was that I find love and *be taken care of.* That I not end up alone, with my ovaries withering in a dusty desert. Did I know that she would then relay all that information on to every mouthpiece in Charmed? Bragging about how well her Lanie had done? How I'd lived up to the Most-Likely-to-Set-the-World-on-Fire vote I'd received senior year. Including the visuals I'd sent her of me and Michael-the-Smoking-Hottie.

My phone beeped in my ear, announcing another call, from an unknown number. Unknown to the phone, maybe, but as of late I'd come to recognize it.

"Hey, Till," I said, finger hovering over the button. "The lawyer is calling. I should probably see if there's any news on the will."

"Go ahead," she said. "I'll call you in a few days and see how my Ralph is doing."

So, not coming back in a few days.

"Sounds good," I said, clicking over. "Hey, Carmen."

"Hey yourself," she said, her voice friendly but smooth and full of that lawyer professionalism they must inject them with in law school. She warmed it up for an old best friend, but it wasn't the same tone that used to prank call boys in junior high or howl at the top of her lungs as we sped drunk down Dreary Road senior year.

This Carmen Frost was polished. I saw that at the funeral. Still Carmen, but edited and Photoshopped. Even when I met her for drinks afterward and we drove over to the house to reminisce.

This Carmen felt different from the childhood best buddy that had slept in many a blanket fort in our living room. Strung of course with Christmas lights in July and blessed with incense from Aunt Ruby. That Carmen was the only person I truly let into my odd little family circle. She never made fun of Aunt Ruby or perpetuated the gossip. Coming from a single mom household where her mother had to work late often, she enjoyed the warm weirdness at our house. It wasn't uncommon for her to join us to spontaneously have dinner in the backyard under the stars or dress up in homemade togas (sheets) to celebrate Julius Caesar's birthday.

Returning for the funeral and walking into that house for the first time without Aunt Ruby in it broke me. It was full of her. She was in every cushion. Every bookcase. Every oddball knickknack. Her scent was in the curtains that had been recently washed and ironed, as if she'd known the end was near and had someone come clean the house. Couldn't leave it untidy on her exit to heaven for people to talk.

We sat in Aunt Ruby's living room and cried a little and told a few nostalgic stories, trying to bring back the old banter, but it was as if Carmen had forgotten how to relax. She was wound up on a spool of bungee rope and someone had tied the ends down. Tight and unable to yield.

Still, we had history. At one time, she was family. Which is why Aunt Ruby hired her to handle her will and estate.

A word that seemed so silly on my tongue, as I would

have never associated *estate* with my aunt or her property. But that was the word Carmen used again and again when we talked. Her *estate* involved the house and some money (she didn't elaborate), but it had to be probated and there were complications due to medical bills that had to be paid first.

Which made sense. It had taken almost two months, and I had almost written off hearing anything. Not that I was holding my breath on the money part. I was pretty sure whatever dollars there were would be used up with the medical bills, and that just left the house. I figured that would probably be left to me. I was really her only family after my mom died young. Well, except for some cousins that I barely knew from her brother she rarely talked to, but I couldn't imagine them keeping up with her enough to even know that she died.

I didn't know what on earth I'd do with the house. It was old and creaky and probably full of problems—one being it was in Charmed and I was not. But it was home. And it had character and memories and laughter soaked into the walls. Aunt Ruby was there. I felt it. If that was intuition, then okay. I felt it *there*. But only there.

So I'd probably keep it as a place to get away, and spend the next several months going back and forth on the weekends like I had right after she passed, cleaning out the fridge and things that were crucial. Mentally, I ticked off a list of the work that was about to begin. That was okay. Aunt Ruby was worth it.

"How's it going over there?" I asked.

"Good, good," Carmen said. "How's California?"

Oh yeah.

"Fine," I said. "You know. Sunshine and pretty people. All that."

I closed my eyes and shook my head. Where did I get this shit?

"Sounds wonderful," she said. "It's been raining and muggy here for three days."

"Yeah," I said, just to say something.

"So the will has been probated," Carmen said. "Everything's ready to be read. I wanted to see when you'd be able to make it back to Charmed for that?"

"Oh," I said, slightly surprised. "I have to come in person?"

"For the reading, yes," she said. "You have to sign some paperwork and so do the other parties."

"Other parties?"

"Yes—well, normally I don't disclose that but you're you, so . . ." she said on a chuckle. "The Clarks?" she said, her tone ending in question.

"As in my cousins?" Really?

"I was surprised too," she said. "I don't remember ever even hearing about them."

"Because I maybe saw them three times in my whole life," I said. "They live in Denning. Or they did. I don't think you ever met them."

"Hmm, okay." Her tone sounded like she was checking off a list. "And you'll need to bring some things with you."

"Things?"

"Two, actually," Carmen said, laughing. "Just like your aunt to make a will reading quirky. But they are easy. Just your marriage certificate—"

"My what?"

Carmen chuckled again, and I was feeling a little something in my throat too. Probably not of the same variety.

"I know," she said. "Goofy request, but I see some doozies all the time. Had a client once insist that his dog be present at the reading of the will. He left him almost everything. Knowing Aunt Ruby, there is some cosmic reason."

Uh-huh. She was messing with me.

I swallowed hard, my mind reeling and already trying to figure out how I could fake a marriage certificate.

"And the second thing?" I managed to push past the lump in my throat.

"Easy peasy," she said. "Your husband, of course."

Almost Christmas

LINDA BRODAY

Chapter 1

Blessing Falls, Texas, 1880

Almost Sinful.

Noelle Blessing frowned at the name she'd bestowed on her latest candy creation. It seemed odd that she couldn't come up with something better. All her life she was *almost* enough but never quite achieving the prize. So, the name seemed appropriate for her. Sinful, but not quite. Yes, that worked. She thought about her growing Almost List and it still brought a sting so painful it was hard to breathe.

She was almost tall and slender.

Almost Joseph's Mary in the Christmas play in the town square three years ago.

Almost a bride.

Had almost known love. Almost.

Of course, the list wasn't even half complete. As was typical when memories got the best of her, she sighed and reached for a chocolate bonbon. The candy slid over her tongue and filled her mouth with delectable sweetness. The cherry center burst open like sweet fireworks on the fourth of July and she closed her eyes, savoring the taste.

This . . . now this was sinful. She felt a little giddy.

The early morning sunshine spilled into the Sugar Spoon, Noelle's candy store, which was all decked out in festive garland, tinsel, and greenery. The wonderful fragrance mixed pleasingly with the rich, decadent chocolate hanging in the air. It was better than perfume to her way of thinking—much to the detriment of her waistline.

Her reflection caught in the large mirror behind the counter. Yes, she was . . . what was the word? Plump. Her hair was more a dishwater blond than golden and her eyes the color of mud, of all things. Therefore, if chocolate was the balm for her misfortunes, so be it. She didn't compare to Hershel, the town drunk, who guzzled whiskey to forget he lost a leg in the war.

Of course, there was a difference.

The door opened and her best friend, Mazie McKenzie, blew in with the stiff breeze, waving a handbill. "Take a look at this, Noelle."

"What is it?"

"A dance in the town square Saturday to kick off the holiday season. We need to talk about what to wear. I think I'll add new lace to my green wool and spruce up the waist with a large red flower. What about you?"

Noelle took in Mazie's vibrant auburn hair and the bloom in her cheeks. Her friend had never been an almost. She was the real thing in spades with more than anyone could imagine. She'd set her cap for the town mayor, Tom McKenzie, and got him, then added a precious baby a year later. Mazie was everything Noelle was not, but she loved her like a sister.

"I'm much too busy. I'll have to work extra to fill all the orders." Noelle ducked her head to rearrange her trays of divinity and frosted sugar cookies.

"Oh no you don't. You can't hide the truth from me." Mazie marched behind the counter and waited until Noelle straightened, then she went on the attack. "You're afraid you'll run into that worm Albert. Admit it."

Noelle's cheeks grew hot in the silence that followed. "I almost had a life," she whispered.

"You still do, honey." Mazie's soft words were a comfort as she put an arm around Noelle. "You have a chance at much more than what he could ever offer. Albert was never right for you. He made it pretty clear that he wanted to marry you because of your standing in the town as a member of the founding family, not because he loved you."

"I know." In fact, Noelle had heard the same from a number of people. She could've overlooked part of it but when it came down to it, she simply couldn't marry him.

She wouldn't marry any man who spoke ill about her, and Albert voiced plenty.

"You deserve someone who'll love you no matter who your family is, what you weigh, or how you talk. Some wonderful man is waiting for you to come along right now and love you exactly as you are." Her voice softened. "You don't want to miss him."

"Stop. You forget I'm jinxed in love." Noelle tucked a strand of hair behind her ear. "He'll be nothing but another almost-the-one again."

"That's craziness." Mazie gave her a gentle shake. "You're not jinxed. It was a blessing you didn't marry him. You would've been miserable. I never did understand what he did for a living."

"He was an investor."

"In what?" Mazie rolled her eyes. "Gossip, getting others to buy him a meal, acting like a bigwig? He just walked around town all day doing nothing."

The bell over the door jingled saving her from a reply. Albert's occupation had puzzled her also. Then came the final straw—she'd seen something she wasn't supposed to.

Mrs. Wright entered with her five-year-old twin boys and the jingling stopped.

Noelle blinked away the memory and smiled. "Hello, Mrs. Wright. Would you like to try some of my new French chocolates?"

The woman pursed her lips. "Are they from France? What's wrong with American?"

"Not one thing. Can I interest you in some Martha Washingtons? They're delectable." The sweet creamy centers surrounded by smooth melted chocolate were a favorite of many Blessing Falls residents. "I made a fresh batch this morning."

"I want a candy cane!" hollered Ben, the twin with the cowlick in front.

The only way Noelle could tell them apart was the cowlick. Both were as hard to please as their mother.

"I want a sucker!" Bob promptly hauled off and kicked his brother's leg, which resulted in a scuffling match on the floor.

Their mother grabbed each boy by an ear. "Straighten up. Two candy canes, Miss Blessing."

The transaction was swift, and the woman had no sooner left with her unruly offspring than two more customers entered. These were truly pleasant and a joy to wait on.

After a stern lecture to think about the dance, Mazie soon went on about her business. Noelle had ended up agreeing not to discount the event without a thorough consideration.

The day sped by with not a moment to herself. Her feet aching, she locked the door and trod wearily to the little house adjacent to the shop where she lived with her grandmother Pearl. She quietly let herself in, her gaze flying to the old dear asleep in the overstuffed chair next to the sofa. Noelle grabbed a soft blanket and gently covered her before going to the kitchen. A light supper would be good. She swore she'd gained extra pounds simply by inhaling the sugar and chocolate for eight hours.

Well, and eating a good portion also. A defensive rebuttal sprang to mind. The sugar gave her energy and she needed lots during the holidays to keep up.

Tired of arguing with herself, she warmed some soup she'd made the previous day and woke Gram. Afterward, they moved to the comfortable parlor with piles of their favorite things. In addition to crocheting needles and yarn were books to inspire the soul.

Gram sunk deep into her chair with a happy sigh. Although sixty-three, she didn't look a day older than fifty. Gray just barely streaked her light brown hair. She ate what she wanted and never worried about such things as her figure, which Albert would say was disgusting. The extra pounds looked good on her though, kept her young in spirit. She could probably run circles around most younger women.

After a moment's quiet, Gram sat up straight. "Dear, we need to get you a dress ready for the dance on Saturday."

"Not you too, Gram. I have no intention of going to that silly function." Noelle patted the hand that had seen too much hard work resting on the chair. "I'd rather stay home with you."

"What do you mean? I wouldn't miss this. Blessing Falls doesn't have that many occasions and I promised Lucius a few turns around the floor." Pearl's pale blue eyes sparkled. "He might even kiss me."

"Gram! Stop that. Lucius Winters is so much older than you."

"He's not as old as poor Joad Tenpenny. Have you heard that man's latest prediction?"

Noelle nodded. "Why in the world would he go around spreading that it's going to snow on Christmas? It leads me to believe Joad's lost what little mind he has."

The sweet dear shook a finger. "I love you, Noelle, but you should never discount his rattlings. A few times, he's been right."

"Ha! It hasn't snowed once in my twenty-three years and even before that. Old-timers talk about it every winter. What's the chance of it now?"

"You've forgotten about your last year in school," Gram chided.

"That didn't count. It was one almost-flake."

"We're off the subject. I want you to take me on Saturday, so get busy finding a dress."

Noelle shut her mouth. She knew better than to argue with the woman she loved more than anyone on earth. She'd escort her to the holiday affair.

Then she'd leave before Albert could spot her. She couldn't take any more of his snide comments. Why had she ever accepted his proposal in the first place? That he'd refused to get down on one knee because he'd get his trousers dirty should've been a clue.

That and the fact he couldn't pass a mirror without preening.

When she called the wedding off an hour beforehand, she'd known it would cause talk. She was a member of the town's founding family that silently endured whatever they must, even those things they didn't like. She'd brought shame to her gram and that ate at her conscience. However, her gram didn't know the real reason for canceling. No one did. It was better this way.

Yet, her actions had unleashed Albert's vengeance with no signs of it stopping. Now each time he passed near, he narrowed his eyes to slits and whispered, "I see you haven't lost an ounce. You really did me a favor. I couldn't afford to be tied to a fat wife anyway, especially one who couldn't keep her word. No man will ever want you. I'll see to that."

The memory stung to the quick as though he stood in front of her. She reached for a recipe book on candy making and held it over her face.

One day she'd show Albert Reginald Pussett III that someone did want her.

And she'd no longer be almost enough.

The week flew by and Saturday arrived before Noelle knew it. She donned last year's scarlet dress and fingered the white fur around the neckline and cuffs. It was beautiful and for a moment she nearly felt pretty with her hair framing her face and spilling across her shoulders.

"Are you ready, dear?" Gram called.

"Just finishing." Noelle stuck her tongue out at herself in the mirror and turned the gaslight low.

Wrapped in warm capes against the chill in the air, the two women strolled arm-in-arm, talking. Gay, colorful streamers and wreaths decorated businesses and street corners, heralding the coming of Christmas. Noelle took it all in with a happy sigh. This was her favorite time of the year. She loved the festive atmosphere with joyful laughter adding finishing touches to the decorations.

Blessing Falls glistened like diamonds under the gas streetlamps. She could almost imagine snow on the rooftops, then decided she needed to be admitted to an asylum along with Joad Tenpenny.

She helped Gram past the gazebo, up the steps, and onto the large wooden dance floor the men had built outside under the stars.

When she turned to go, Gram clutched her hand. "I know you don't want to be here but please stay for a bit. For me. You're beautiful in that dress, dear."

Noelle smiled and patted the wrinkled hand. Gram asked little enough of her. After Noelle's parents lost their lives in a train wreck, Gram had taken her in and given her the love and comfort she'd needed. The woman had also helped finance the candy store.

Noelle stared hard at her escape route and sighed. "Only for you, Gram."

Dashing as always with beautiful silver hair and a trim figure, Lucius appeared just then, and the elegant couple whirled off to the strains of a romantic waltz. She glanced around for someone to talk to. Farmers and ranchers were in town for the yearly event. A group of cowboys had congregated close by along the edge of the dance floor. Their conversation drifted to her.

"I don't know why I let you talk me into this," one ranch hand said, groaning.

"You want to dance with a pretty girl, don't you?"

"Well, yeah. Don't every man here?"

"Then you have to go where they are," came the matter-of-fact answer.

Noelle turned. Where was Mazie? Clusters of mothers and single women perched on hay bales, but her friend was nowhere to be seen. Old Joad Tenpenny wobbled in and collapsed on a chair. No doubt, he'd be spreading the word about snow to everyone who'd listen.

Her heart plummeted as Albert made his way toward her, a smirk on his face.

The last time he'd harassed her with an added threat. "Tell anyone what you saw, and I'll make you very, very sorry."

No one knew what Albert had done, not Gram or Mazie.

Tonight, she wouldn't let him make her feel less than a woman or make veiled threats. She tilted her chin a bit. Yet despite the self-bolstering, she felt her resolve beginning to crumble.

Heat flooded over her and she desperately moistened her lips.

Ten feet separated them. Albert's thin mouth curled in disgust and his eyes had narrowed to slits. This would be the ugliest, and likely the loudest, encounter yet.

Heaven help me! Please. Somebody. But there was no one.

Noelle grabbed a cowboy dressed in denims, boots, and a Stetson next to her and slid her arm through his. Her words were barely louder than a whisper, "You promised me a dance, darling."

Chapter 2

Dance? The word jarred Cord Dalton. He met the beautiful brown eyes staring up at him. How could he have forgotten a promise to waltz with such a pretty woman? "Beg your pardon, ma'am?"

She shot a frantic gaze toward the sullen man stalking toward them. While he didn't know the exact cause of the belligerence, he decided it didn't hurt a thing to play the game. Or help a lovely woman in distress.

"Of course. I apologize for my lapse of memory." He held out a hand and took her palm. She fell into the large, sweeping steps of the waltz as though they'd danced all their lives.

"I'm sorry for using you to get away from that man. If you'll just leave me at the other end, I'd be indebted." The words came low, her voice throaty.

"No apology needed, and I always dance an entire

waltz with my partner." He met her embarrassed gaze from under dark lashes. "I don't think I've ever met anyone with eyes the color of rich chocolate before. I'm Cord Dalton."

"Noelle Blessing. Odd that I make you think of chocolate. I own the candy shop in town."

He chuckled. "The Sugar Spoon. Love the name. By chance do you belong to the founding family?"

"I do. This was my great-grandfather's vision."

Cord stared, mesmerized at the blond beauty. Her curves seemed made to fit against him as they executed the steps. Noelle had relaxed now, her embarrassment gone. He wondered about the ill-tempered jackass intent on harassing her. He'd had his own dealings with Albert Pussett III and cut a wide path around him ever since. The nickname Slick Al fit to a tee for the man and his hair glued down with pomade.

"Isn't there a funny story about Jubal Blessing?" Cord asked.

"I was hoping you wouldn't ask that but since you saved me, I'll tell you. Jubal was wandering across the prairie one day, tripped on a rock, and fell into the stream that formed a small waterfall. He broke his leg and while he waited for the bone to heal, took a look around and decided he couldn't go a step farther so he created a town right here."

Noelle had a delightful lilting laugh and Cord couldn't help joining in. It was good she could see the bright side of things. He liked that in a woman.

"And the waterfall?" he asked.

"It's since disappeared along with the stream. Both have dried up. People never remember anything but that story."

"It is memorable all right."

They whirled around Albert and his stick-thin partner with a persimmon mouth. In hopes of provoking Pussett, he called, "Thanks for helping me get acquainted with Noelle. I owe you."

The jackass looked confused for a moment, then snorted and dragged his date off the floor, the pomade on his hair shining under the lights.

"I wish you hadn't done that, Mr. Dalton," Noelle murmured.

"Call me Cord, please. Will he make things more difficult for you?"

"This won't make it easier."

"If he bothers you, please let me know. I can handle him." Just like Cord wrestled steers. Get him on the ground, then twist Pussett's overly groomed head until he hollered.

They danced in silence a long moment until Noelle asked, "Do you work on one of the ranches around here, Cord?"

"I'm the ranch foreman for the McCready Land and Cattle Company."

"That's a big outfit and a lot of responsibility. How long have you worked for McCready?"

"Five years now." He maneuvered her around a slower couple and tightened his arm. Noelle's breasts were almost rubbing his chest. His breath hitched and his thoughts tumbled to places they shouldn't. He inhaled sharply and reined himself in. "I don't plan to always work for someone else. One day I'll own my own land, run my own cattle."

"Are you a dreamer, Cord Dalton?"

"No, ma'am. A realist. There's a difference."

She bit her bottom lip and studied him. "Care to explain?"

"A dreamer sees what can hopefully be with time and work. A realist sees what is without blinders on."

"So, you already know you'll have your own land and cattle?"

"Yes, ma'am." He grinned. "I've been buying cattle from Mr. McCready as I get the money and he lets me put them with his herd until I pay off my land."

"What an amazing man. I knew he was generous, but this beats everything I know about him."

Her brown eyes sparkled, now reminding him of rich saddle leather. The white fur collar and cuffs on her red dress set off her dark blond hair and the hem brushed seductively against his pant leg like a lonely saloon girl. Maybe one day he'd . . .

No, stop it. Dreaming would accomplish nothing. A woman belonging to the founding family wouldn't want the son of a murderer. Cord knew the stain of shame. He'd heard the slurs hundreds of times, the name-calling. Folks said the sins of the father were visited on the son. which is why he'd vowed never to marry.

The rotten bloodline of Blackie Dalton would end with him.

"In a way, I guess McCready is like a father to me." Cord said that as much for his own benefit as hers. He looked around and saw that the dance floor was empty except for them. "Let's sit for a while. It's a star-studded night if I've ever seen one."

"That sounds nice. But you don't have to. I don't see Albert—I think he left."

"Stop that. I didn't dance with you because I took pity on you." He led her to a seat. "I did it because you're the most interesting woman here and it was you who took pity on a poor lonely cowboy."

Violins and guitars played while dancers took the floor again, but Cord didn't pay them any mind. His attention was riveted on the enchanting woman beside him.

She glanced up at the sky, pulling her wrap tighter. "This night couldn't be more perfect. I've never seen so many stars. When I was a girl, I used to think they held magic and could make all my wishes come true." A smile curved her lips. "I lost both parents when a train ran off the trestle and fell five hundred feet. . . . I needed something that might make my world worth living again. Then Gram opened her arms wide and I walked in and found warmth and love."

"Little boys need magic and something to believe in too," Cord said quietly. "Only mine came in the form of a kindly rancher."

"I'm glad for both of us. Whatever happened you seem to have found a way through it,"

"The story is not for starry nights and waltzing with a beautiful lady. Much too depressing." He lifted her hand and studied it. "Your palm is so small, yet you have such strength. You're a remarkable woman, Noelle."

An older couple strolled by and stopped, seeming to know Noelle.

"Noelle, dear, I'm glad you found someone to talk to." The woman's gaze went to Cord's hand holding Noelle's, which he promptly dropped. "I don't believe we've met."

"This is Cord Dalton." Noelle introduced her grandmother and Lucius.

Cord stood and shook hands. Noelle didn't appear to shrink away or be embarrassed.

Pearl Blessing was as kind as Cord had heard. Her eyes sparkled when she talked and seemed to give the impression she had a secret. Maybe she did. Lucius Winters had been quite the lady's man in his younger days. Or so the rumors had circulated about town. Perhaps the two were more than just friends.

"I met you one day out at McCready's." A light breeze ruffled Lucius's silver hair. "He raves about your ability to handle the ranch hands. Said you're a natural-born leader and cowhand to boot."

"I love my work." Cord smiled. "Are you enjoying the dance?"

"We certainly are," Pearl answered. "Noelle, you don't have to wait for me."

"I'll walk her home when we finish dancing," Lucius quickly added.

"Thank you for that, Lucius" Noelle kissed her grandmother's cheek. "Enjoy yourself."

"I intend to." Pearl slipped an arm through her elegant partner's and they walked on.

"That was interesting," Noelle murmured.

"Your grandmother is nice." Cord leaned closer. "Do you mind if I walk you home tonight? The dance has brought all kinds of people into town."

"I would love that."

"Let's waltz. I love this song." He extended his hand.

Just then two of the McCready cowboys exchanged punches and the fight was on.

"Excuse me for a moment. Don't go anywhere." Cord hurried away to quell the tempers before the men got thrown out.

It didn't take long to separate the two men and send them back to the ranch. When Cord returned, Noelle was nowhere to be seen.

His Christmas angel had flown away.

Noelle let herself into the house. Her thoughts were tumbling like a pair of river rocks swept along in floodwaters. What had just happened?

Cord's compliments swept through her brain. He didn't seem to notice her weight or any of her shortcomings.

She sighed and leaned against the door. He'd said she was pretty. Her heart sang as she sat down to wait for Gram. Could he mean it? Cord didn't appear to be the kind of man to lie, with his earnest amber eyes with those golden glints.

A pang of remorse hit her. She hadn't waited for him to settle the fight.

No, she'd run like a frightened deer. It seemed safe to say that he'd think less of her now. Her one *almost* had turned into a *maybe* and she hadn't stuck around. She released a loud groan.

She was sitting with her hands over her face when Gram entered looking radiant. The dance had been good for her and seemed to shave off a few years.

"I'm gathering that Lucius kissed you. You have that look, Gram."

The old dear hung up her cape and patted her hair arranged in an artful swirl against the nape of her neck. "A woman never tells. But I had the most wonderful night." She turned. "Why were you sitting with your hands over your face when I came in?"

"Cord Dalton had to go break up a fight between his men and asked me to wait." Noelle made a face. "I didn't."

"I see. What do you think you ought to do about that?"

"Find him and apologize. Only, I don't know when I'll have time to go out to the ranch."

"Some things are worth missing a few hours. Besides, won't Mazie help you out in the candy store?"

"Yes, I'm sure." Noelle rose and kissed Gram's cheek. "Why are you so smart?"

"Life experience, my dear. I learned a lot in my sixty-three years. Want some hot tea?"

"That sounds good." Noelle put her arm around Gram's waist, and they went into the kitchen. "I'm so lucky to have you."

"That goes for double for me. Tell me about your handsome cowboy."

"He's not mine. But he did say I was pretty." Noelle's face grew warm. She still couldn't believe it.

"Sounds like he has good eyesight to me. You looked like you were enjoying his company."

"I was. Cord is so easy to talk to. And then I ruined everything."

Gram patted her shoulder and put the water on the stove. "Nothing that can't be fixed."

"Maybe." Noelle got down two cups and added softly, "He was really nice, Gram."

"There are some nice ones out there. But you have to get out and mingle. You won't find anyone holed up here or in the Sugar Spoon. It's time to put the past behind you. Life does go on and you can find more happiness than you've ever known." Gram pulled out two chairs at the table. "Sit down. Let me tell you about your grandfather."

"I'd like to hear more about him." All she knew was that he died before her sixth birthday, so the only recollection she had was of a big bear of a man in a sea captain's hat, a curved pipe clenched in big strong teeth.

"Your grandfather loved the sea, probably more than he loved me and that's saying a lot because he worshipped the ground I walked on. He was aboard a sailing vessel when a storm came up. All but four sailors perished. Your grandfather went down to a watery grave."

"My parents always spoke about him in hushed tones and I knew something bad had happened. They just told me that my grandfather had gone to heaven."

Gram ran her fingertips over the tablecloth. "I was crushed. I was only forty-five, too young to go through life alone. I had a choice to make—either roll over and slowly die or pick myself up. One day I decided that I wanted to live and not just a half-life. So, I got a job in the mercantile and began to count each day as a blessing." Her lovely pale blue gaze bore into Noelle. "We can't control most of what happens to us, but we can make a new path forward. We're like salamanders, you and me. If those creatures lose a tail, they can regrow it. You can make the best of the life God's given you."

Later, as they drank their tea, Noelle thought about that. After church tomorrow, she'd make a point to go find Cord Dalton and apologize for running away.

Chapter 3

As fate would have it, the minister came to their home for lunch after his Sunday sermon, so Noelle didn't have an opportunity to ride out to McCready's ranch. She believed everything happened for a reason and maybe she wasn't meant to ever see Cord Dalton again.

Another almost. Story of her life.

Monday morning, she was busy coating bonbons for an exclusive order when the bell above the door jingled announcing the first customer of the day.

"I'll be right with you," she said, not looking up. "Go ahead and make your selection."

Boot heels sounded on the wood floor, and then a deep voice said, "I have a yearning for a dozen of your peppermint sticks and a few of those chocolate doodads you're making."

She looked up, swiping chocolate across her cheek.

There stood Cord Dalton. The tall, lean cowboy sucked up all the air in the shop and filled the candy store with his large presence. Every word she knew flew from her head.

After several moments, she finally got her tongue unstuck. "You found me."

His crooked grin sent her heart fluttering. "Yes, ma'am. You weren't that hard to find."

"I was meaning to ride out to the ranch later and apologize for running out on you Saturday night."

"You didn't leave a glass slipper but thankfully I have a good memory. You don't owe me an apology."

"You asked me to wait only I got the jitters and hightailed it."

His soft chuckle filled the empty shop. He propped his elbow on the counter, leaning toward her. "Ah, so it wasn't that your coach was on the verge of turning into a pumpkin."

Noelle couldn't resist playing the game. "Actually, my dress was about to switch back to its sackcloth and ashes."

"Aha! I knew it was something like that."

"I do apologize for not sticking around. Not any way to repay you."

"Like I said, apology not necessary."

His deep voice set her pulse racing. She grasped the first thing that came to mind. "I have to say you don't look like a Cinderella man." With his worn Stetson, tight denims, and boots he didn't even come close to a dapper fairy-tale character.

He laughed and straightened to his full height. "Blame it on my two little nieces. I've read that story to them until I have it memorized."

"They live nearby then?"

"They're here in town so I see them and my sister Alice regularly."

"So, the candy is for them?"

"Nope." His grin spread wide. "It's for me. I have a pretty serious sweet tooth."

"I never would've guessed." The sugar hadn't affected his teeth any. They were straight and awfully white in contrast to his tanned face. Noelle couldn't help but stare.

Her cowboy prince was not even close to an almost anything. He seemed perfect thus far.

"Actually, I want to invite you to the ranch for a hayride this Saturday. Just picture a sleigh ride among the mesquites laden with snow and hold that picture. I know it's a stretch." He took a breath and added, "Please say you will. I'll pick you up about two o'clock."

Who could resist that smile, his dark good looks, and those twinkling golden irises rimmed with a dark circle?

"I'll be happy to. Thank you for the invitation." She reached for a sack and filled it with a dozen peppermint sticks and a handful of chocolate bonbons, holding it out. "This is on the house."

"Sorry, but I can't accept." He stuck a hand into his pocket for some coins.

She shook her finger. "I'm not taking your money. I want to do this. Really."

What he'd done at the dance, keeping Albert away from her, deserved a lot more than a little candy.

"Then I have to accept, don't I?"

When their hands touched, a thrill went up her arm. Of all the hands she touched day in and day out, none had caused this reaction. She pulled back and stuffed her sweaty palms into her pocket.

"I look forward to Saturday." Looking a bit rakish, he stuck a peppermint stick in his mouth. "You won't forget?"

"Not a chance." Hidden in the apron pocket, Noelle crossed her fingers for good luck.

He still didn't move.

"Do you know how beautiful you are standing there with the sun framing you, and that streak of chocolate across your cheek?"

His soft words were like a caress whispering across her skin. Flustered, she reached for a dish towel and tried to erase the chocolate.

"You didn't get it. Here, let me." He took the cloth and dipped the edge into a bowl of water sitting on the counter where she'd been working. Very gently, he wiped the smudge.

An awareness of something deeper set her insides fluttering and she wondered if he felt it too.

"There." He laid the dish towel down. "Perfect."

She released a nervous laugh. "Just trying to play the part of Cinderella except with something more palatable than dirt." What an odd thing for her to say. He must think her daft.

"It didn't detract from your lovely face, Noelle. Trust me."

A spell had fallen over her and stolen every word for a second time. She struggled for a clear thought and would've paid a year's income for something meaningful to say. The silence grew.

As luck would have it, the bell over the door jingled, breaking her trance. Two customers entered followed by Mazie.

"I should be going." Cord shifted the candy stick to the other side of his mouth. "See you Saturday."

"I'll look forward to the fun. It's been a while."

Once he left, she turned to help the two ladies who'd entered the shop. An hour later she sat with Mazie in the quiet.

Her friend grinned. "I see your cowboy found you."

"And with a streak of chocolate on my face." Noelle groaned, growing warm. The feel of his touch on her skin had remained through the morning. "He invited me to a hayride Saturday."

"And?"

"I accepted. What does one wear to something like that?"

"A casual dress. What you have on would be good."

Noelle glanced down, pulling her apron aside. The blue shade was pretty but the dress well worn. "He's already seen me in this."

"Just tie your hair back with a blue ribbon and you'll look fetching." Mazie's eyes crinkled with laughter. "The way he was staring at you, he didn't even notice what you were wearing. It appeared to me that he was about to eat you up."

Noelle gave her a gentle push. "Hush with that silliness. He was not. We were discussing Cinderella if you must know."

"Cinderella, huh? Whatever you say. Just remember I told you someone nice was waiting for you." Mazie snapped her fingers. "And here you are with a date."

"Cord Dalton is really nice," Noelle said dreamily.

"Don't forget pleasing to the eye as well."

The cowboy wasn't bad-looking. A scar marred one

cheek and his nose had been broken at one time. But a light shone from inside, from his heart, and that made him the handsomest man in the world.

Her stomach quickened. Maybe this was the one to break her almost curse.

The week passed in a blur for Cord, and as he drove into Blessing Falls on Saturday a low hum vibrated under his skin. He couldn't wait to see Noelle again. The sensitive woman had stirred something and it made him mad as hell that Pussett wouldn't leave her alone.

His boss had related the circumstances of the wedding that Noelle had broken off at the last minute. That couldn't have been easy for someone like her to do. Plus, the vicious things Pussett was now saying that she wasn't good enough for him only added to Cord's distaste of her former fiancé.

One day, he prayed he'd get a chance to teach Pussett a lesson he'd not soon forget.

When he arrived at the house next door to the candy shop, his breath caught as Noelle emerged, looking like a breath of fresh air in blue. Although the day was pretty warm and she might not use it, she carried a light wrap. This far south, it rarely got very cold.

He hopped down from the wagon. "I'm a little early. Hope you don't mind."

The fragrance of vanilla and cinnamon wafted around him.

"I don't mind being early." Her brown gaze tangled with his amber and she laughed. "It's such a pretty day and the drive will send my spirits soaring. I can't believe Christmas is just two weeks away."

"Me either." He helped her into the wagon and got her settled, then climbed in beside her. "Is old man Joad still predicting snow?"

"That he is. We're all shaking our heads at the ridiculous notion."

Cord grinned. "I don't know. I've seen the weather do some strange things. Guess we'll wait and see."

"Well, he has been right about a few things I suppose," Noelle admitted. "We did get that gully washer last year and the lightning struck the church steeple like he said. And way before that he predicted the horrible drought that lasted five years."

"Joad Tenpenny isn't as loony as folks think. His Apache ancestors are said to talk to him."

"I've heard that. My ancestors don't bother to speak. I don't think they knew much when they were alive." Noelle folded her hands in her lap. "We weren't the brightest bunch."

They rode in comfortable silence enjoying the countryside. Cord cast a sideways glance at Noelle. The slight breeze ruffled her hair and occasionally lifted a blond strand, laying it across her eyes. She wore a look of contentment. But then she had a most pleasant nature.

"How did you get your name? It's pretty unusual."

She faced him. "My mother thought it appropriate since I was born on Christmas Day."

"Really? I love the name. It reminds me of Christmas bells."

"When I was younger, I hated having a December birthday because I only got one combined Christmas and birthday gift."

"I suppose you did get cheated. I was born on my brother's third birthday, so I always had to share my day with him which I never liked. Kinda wish I'd had my own special day."

"Does he live around here?"

"No, Harlan's in Wyoming."

"And your father?" she asked softly.

"He uh . . ." There was the question he'd been dreading. Hoping to distract her focus, Cord pointed off to the right. "There's a nice underwater spring over in those rocks. Would you like to stop? The water bubbles up from deep underground and is the sweetest I've ever tasted."

"I'd love to."

Cord pulled to a stop and helped her down, then grabbed a cup from the bed of the wagon. He led her over to the spring and filled the cup. She drank first and released a contented sigh.

"This is wonderfully refreshing. It's so clear and crisp. Thank you for stopping." She handed the cup back to him.

"I've never seen a bluer sky," she said. "It's especially pretty today. The fluffy clouds remind me of my divinity candy." She opened her arms wide as though embracing it all. "I used to dream of living in the mountains with tall trees, but I've come to love the sheer beauty of the rugged landscape here in South Texas."

"Me too. Not far from here are barren mountains that rise from the desert floor like God's shoulders, wide and high and usually have a mesa nearby as flat as a tabletop." He turned. "I often ride over the land and marvel at the sparse beauty, especially at night. I've not found anything that compares to bedding down under the stars beside a campfire."

"I'd love to experience that just once." Her words were barely louder than a whisper.

One day, God willing, he'd see that she did. But today, he'd make sure she had a good time on the ranch. That would fit into his plans of spending more time with the pretty lady born on Christmas Day.

Chapter 4

McCready's ranch was the largest operation Noelle had ever seen. That wasn't saying a whole lot since she rarely had the opportunity to get out of Blessing Falls. Buildings and barns of all shapes and sizes ringed a huge compound full of bustling cowhands and animals.

Cord pulled the rig to a stop in front of a sprawling two-story building that appeared to be ranch headquarters.

She waited for him to come around to her side. "This is amazing. How many acres comprise this ranch?"

"We're nine thousand six hundred and forty acres." He grinned up at her. "Give or take a few hundred. We run approximately three thousand head of cattle and somewhere in the vicinity of nine hundred horses."

"And you're the foreman. That's a lot of ground to cover."

Noelle expected him to offer her a hand and was surprised when he put his large hands on each side of her waist and swung her to the ground.

"Oh, my goodness." Out of breath and a tad light-headed, she clutched his arm to keep from falling. "I could've managed but thank you."

"My way is faster. Hope you didn't mind." His deep voice further stirred the chaos in her brain.

"I'm used to doing things for myself." Her gentle words weren't meant as a rebuke and the warmth of an added smile came easy. "Give a girl some warning before you do that."

"Yes, ma'am, I'll try to remember that. Let's go inside. Mr. and Mrs. McCready want to meet you and you can mingle with the rest of our guests. Besides you, there are seven others." He lifted her wrap from the seat, handing it to her.

She grew warm as his palm nestled at the small of her back. "It'll be a fun time."

"We have a surprise for everyone at the turning around place." He pierced her with his gaze, his voice low. "I hope you'll like it."

"I'm sure I shall." She prayed he wasn't going to have to take care of the other guests and forget about her. She wanted him all to herself.

But when she met the obvious interest in his eyes, fear paralyzed her. No, she'd surround herself with the other guests. That might be the only protection for her heart.

She smiled brightly and took his arm. But the moment she touched him that same kind of sizzle ran through her as though she'd stuck her hand in a gaslight.

"Are you okay?" he asked.

"Couldn't be better."

Why his touch was so different from others baffled

her, but she put her musing aside and went through the door he held for her. The babble of voices led them to a pretty room dressed up for Christmas. The enormous tree must've been shipped in by train and miles of garland, silver tinsel, and handblown ornaments created a breathtaking picture. A long table was set up the length of the room laden with all sorts of cheeses, fruit, and assorted delicacies.

"Grab a plate and help yourself." Cord glanced across the room. "I need to speak to Mr. McCready for a moment to make sure everything is ready."

"Sure, don't worry about me." But inside she was trembling. She'd never been comfortable in a room full of strangers.

However, when she turned toward the guests, she found a friend she'd gone to school with—Gwen Pemberton. They'd drifted apart after graduation.

The thin, perfectly proportioned girl turned and gave her a genuine smile. "Noelle! I'm so happy to see you. How have you been?"

"Pretty busy with the candy shop but I'm having fun." Except when Albert crossed her path. "I'm glad you came so I'd know someone."

Soon they were sitting at a small table and remembering old times. Gwen's raven hair and eyes sparkled as she related that she'd attended a Boston university for four years.

"I studied medicine. It was hard but it's what I think I was meant to do."

Noelle squeezed her hand. "You were always the smartest one in our class. So, are you a doctor now?"

"Not yet. I have to complete my residency at a hospital back East before I can practice."

"I'm so proud of you, Gwen."

"Like I said, it's a difficult path but a rewarding one. What about you, Noelle?"

She cringed inside. "I own a business—the Sugar Spoon. Not nearly as prestigious as being a doctor but I'm happy putting smiles on my customers' faces. I really am." And she realized she truly meant it. It meant the world to her to make the people around her happier.

"I noticed that when I came into Blessing Falls. Congratulations! Owning a business shows gumption and pure passion. I say we've done all right for ourselves."

Her old friend glanced around. "I'm supposed to meet my date, but he seems to be late."

"Anyone I know?"

Before Gwen could answer, Cord appeared with a plate of his own in hand. "Sorry about that, Noelle. Everything is all taken care of."

"Wonderful. Meet my friend Gwen Pemberton. We went to school together and we're having fun catching up on each other's lives."

Cord's smile stretched wide. "Nice to meet you, Miss Pemberton." He turned back to Noelle. "Could I have a private word?"

"Of course." Noelle excused herself and rose.

As Cord led her to the side, Albert strode into the room as though he owned it in a suit and pair of snakeskin boots that must have cost the equivalent of six months' candy sales. Noelle's heart sank. Why was the despicable show-off here? She was barely able to breathe, and her gaze followed him to the table where Gwen was still sitting.

"That's what I was going to warn you about." Cord spoke just above a whisper to keep from being overheard.

"I'm sorry. I didn't know he was going to be here. Boss added him at the last minute as a personal favor."

As though sensing himself to be the subject of their conversation, Albert looked at her and his mouth curled in disgust.

Noelle's stomach clenched. "I don't know if I can do this."

"Do you want me to take you home? I will."

A deep breath steadied her nerves. She did not want to let Albert Pussett III ruin her time with Cord. "No. I'll stay far away from him and it'll be fine."

Cord shot her an admiring glance and winked. "I can guarantee you won't have to worry about him." He muttered under his breath, "Even if I have to hog-tie him and stuff a sock in his mouth. Let's revive our little game of pretend."

Naughty tinges raced up her spine as images filled her head of all the possible touches, hugs . . . kisses.

"I'm for it if you are. Thank you." Aware of Albert's eyes returning to them, she pasted a smile on her face and gave a tinkling laugh that carried to the sour-faced man. "The fun is about to begin, Cord."

"We'll play it to the hilt, pretty lady. How's this for starters?" He dropped a lingering kiss on her cheek and captured her hand.

The moment his mouth touched her skin her heart raced like a herd of wild horses. She didn't even think to see if Albert was watching. Nor did she care. All that mattered was Cord's nearness, his warm breath fluttering across her face.

When she could get her tongue to move, she whispered, "If that was only the start, I can't wait to see what follows."

His eyes smoldered. Strange that it seemed so genuine. He was really good at this pretend stuff.

"Just you wait," he murmured at her ear. "Put your feet in the stirrups and hang on tight, Christmas lady." He threaded his fingers through hers and warmth spread through her.

She shot Albert a glance from under her lashes and saw the surprise on his face. Good. Maybe now he would leave her alone.

Cord murmured, "I think we have his attention. Let's rejoin the group."

With his hand around hers, they headed back to the table. Her head was spinning.

"Sorry to step away. It was urgent." Cord smiled and reached for their plates, then carried them to a table by themselves. Setting their food down, he pulled out her chair. The perfect gentleman with impeccable manners. He could be dining with the queen instead of a lowly shop owner.

"This is fun." She loved knocking Albert back on his heels. Although most likely his appearance here had little to do with her and everything to do with Gwen being here.

Now that made sense. Gwen would be quite a catch.

Everyone finished eating and they climbed up on a flatbed trailer that was loaded with hay bales. Instead of Cord driving the team of horses as she'd half expected, another cowboy got into place on the seat. Cord sat back with her, making sure Albert was too far away to be bothersome.

"Ready to sing Christmas carols?" Cord asked.

After an enthusiastic chorus of affirmatives, their voices lifted in unison to "Jingle Bells." From there it was one song after another with much laughter in between. So engrossed was Noelle in having fun she almost forgot about Albert.

Somehow, in all the revelry, he moved forward next to her. “You’re making a spectacle of yourself,” he chided with a sneer. “Dalton will be the laughingstock of Blessing Falls.”

“What do you care? This is none of your affair.” She scooted closer to Cord. “Once and for all, leave me alone.”

“It’s my duty to warn him and every other man that you’re a liar and you renege on promises.”

Cord put an arm around her and drew her close. He kept his steely voice just loud enough for Albert to hear. “Pussett, if you don’t go back where I put you, I’m going to knock you off this flatbed and make you walk back. That suit won’t look too good full of cactus thorns and dirt.”

“If that’s all the thanks I get, good riddance.”

Noelle smothered a snort as red-faced Albert hurried back to his former seat. Gwen had now moved forward to sit with a nice-looking gentleman wearing faded denims, leaving Albert on his own. Served him right. Whatever his reason for coming, he wasn’t going to ruin her day. For a change.

They sang more songs as they bounced along the winding road. Noelle had never enjoyed herself more. She wondered if Cord had forgotten that he still had his arm around her. She leaned her head against his wide shoulder and dreamed of the impossible. This was only a game, a fun one at that, but she knew that chances were, once it ended, he’d disappear.

And she’d call it her almost Christmas affair.

The sun was beginning to set and it'd be dark soon. She wondered what the surprise was at the turning around place. Whatever it was, she knew that this day would linger in her memory for the rest of her life.

Even if it had just been a game of pretend. Even if it hadn't mattered. And even if Cord Dalton hadn't meant those words.

For a few hours, she'd known what it felt like to be held and cherished.

Chapter 5

The flatbed trailer full of Christmas guests rumbled through the darkness toward a large campfire ahead. Cord glanced at Noelle's face, the dainty curve of a cheek, the strong jaw, the shape of a shell-like ear—all completed the pretty profile. He was happy, really happy, for the first time in a long while.

Maybe life was supposed to be made up of thousands of little moments that added up to something meaningful in the end. And sometimes a man didn't even know it until he grew old. It just happened.

His gaze took in Pussett sitting alone. The imbecile hadn't sense enough to know when to give up. No doubt he had no idea why Noelle had broken off their engagement. He was too swelled with his own self-importance. Cord didn't know either, but what he did know was that Noelle must have had a darn good reason.

Playing the game of pretend with Noelle had been fun. Cord chuckled softly and draped an arm around *his lady*. If all went well, he had more planned before the night was over.

"Look at the moon, Cord." Noelle pointed low in the sky where it was just rising.

The orb that guided ships and set the flow of oceans was large and full.

"The Comanche call this the *wahi mua* or evergreen moon. It seems to suggest Christmas." He adjusted her wrap snug around her shoulders. "Are you cold?"

She looked up at him, her brown eyes shining in the lanterns hanging up front. "No. It's a beautiful night with only a bit of a chill in the air. I'm perfectly fine."

"We're almost there." His gaze wandered again to Pussett and his sour expression. The man would still make trouble if given half an inch. Cord meant to keep an eye on him.

The women were giving the disagreeable man a wide berth and Pussett likely blamed that on Noelle, which seemed to be true to form. He'd met a few people like him who never seemed to see their own faults. Instead, they lashed out at others, blaming someone else for everything that went wrong.

Well, enough was enough for this night.

The horse-drawn trailer pulled up to a nice warm fire that was tended by some of Cord's men. He jumped down and while the men helped the other guests he reached up for Noelle.

Remembering her plea to give her a warning, he asked, "Want me to lift you down?"

Excitement glittered in her eyes. "Please lift me."

With a nod, he placed his hands around her waist and swung her to the ground. But instead of releasing her, he held her against him for a long moment. Her heart beat wildly against his chest.

"I want to kiss you, Noelle Blessing." Damn his husky voice.

"Yes, Cord. Yes."

Setting her on her feet in the shadows, he anchored her with a palm under each jaw, then gently lowered his lips. He had no concept of time as everyone else melted away and it was just the two of them on a beautiful winter night with Christmas two weeks away.

His hand wandered to the soft curve of her waist and tugged her closer. Soft sounds sprang from her throat as he deepened the kiss.

"Hey, Dalton!" one of his men hollered. "Did you get lost?"

Noelle stiffened and stepped back, her hand flying to her throat.

"It's okay. No one can see us. You're safe." He raised his voice, aiming it toward the fire. "Hold your horses. I'm coming."

But just as he turned to go around the flatbed of the trailer, there stood Pussett. "I see she's put a hex on you too. Don't trust her. Or maybe there's no reason to buy the cow when the milk is free."

Noelle gasped. "How dare you insinuate such a thing!"

Anger raced up the back of Cord's neck. He leaped forward, grabbed the man by the throat, and held him against the flatbed. "Apologize to the lady."

Albert released a growl and tried to free himself, but Cord tightened his grip. "As I said, it's a long way back to town and unless you apologize, you'll walk. If you're lucky you might make it by suppertime tomorrow."

The others began to gather around. Noelle must hate this. And possibly him too.

A slight breeze delivered her plea. "Please, Cord. Just let him go and forget what he said. I'm used to it."

Cord took in her distraught features. "I'm sorry but I'm not. He'll show some common decency or else."

"Just wait until McCready hears about this. You won't have a job," Albert choked out.

One of Cord's men, Max Dolby, chuckled. "Better do it, Pussett. Dalton ain't bluffin'."

"We've all had it with you," Gwen Pemberton said. "Frankly, I wouldn't mind seeing you walk back to town. You're nothing but an insufferable ass."

Pussett's gaze swept over the group and found no sympathy. He spoke low. "I'm sorry, Noelle."

"For?" Cord pressed. The man wasn't going to get off this easy.

"For uh . . . for saying what I did."

Though not wholly satisfied, Cord released his hold. "I hear anything else come out of your mouth, you *will* get left behind. And I might even take your boots."

The man gave a sullen nod and stomped past the group. Cord waited until they'd all returned to the fire before pulling Noelle close. He found her shaking. "I'm sorry. I wish I could've spared you that." He was silent a moment, then asked, "Why is he so hell-bent on making your life miserable?"

She sighed and laid her head on his shoulder. "I saw

something I wasn't supposed to, and he's afraid I'll tell. I think . . . he wants to discredit me so that no one would ever believe me. But I won't tell . . . So please don't ask me to."

"I never will." He took her hand. "Let's join the others at the fire."

A few minutes later, everyone was laughing again and singing. In the midst of the joyful atmosphere, Cord's men served cups of hot chocolate. Cord was glad to see Noelle begin to relax. She made such a pretty picture he couldn't take his eyes off her.

The blue and orange flames of the fire turned her blond hair to gold and the strands curled around her face and shoulders. Gentle and wise, Noelle Blessing had the sweetest spirit of any woman he'd ever seen. Plus, she could kiss like an angel. He studied her lush mouth, the soft curve of her full breasts, her shapely hips, and he knew that he wanted her. He'd found everything he'd sought one magic night on a dance floor.

If only he could ask for her hand . . .

Still, as long as they were playing this game, what would it hurt to pretend she was his?

Peace settled over him and everything melted away except for the woman next to him. He lifted her soft hand and brought her fingers to his mouth, kissing them.

"Cord, not that I care, but I think we've become a distraction," she murmured.

"Our plan is working."

Movement came from the corner of his eye. Pussett had changed seats, picking one closer to Noelle. The piece of cow dung was anything if not persistent. It seemed nothing Cord said was going to make any difference.

He placed his mouth next to Noelle's ear. "Are you up for taking the game to a new level? One that will really set Pussett back on his heels?"

"Yes. I think so."

"Watch and wait." He stood and called for silence. "What's Christmas without gifts? We're going to play a little game now. Scattered around within view of the fire are hidden gifts with each of your names on them. Search until you find yours. If you find someone else's, leave it where it is."

One of the women clapped her hands. "Oh, how fun!"

As everyone scattered, Noelle stood next to Cord. "Is this the surprise you were just now talking about?"

"Nope. This one was set a week ago by Mr. McCready. The next one will be spontaneous." He took her hand. "Trust me."

"I do. Totally."

He met her glistening brown eyes. Someone once said the eyes were the windows of the soul and all he could say was that they must've known Noelle. He could see intelligence, warmth, and love of life. Fury rose anew at Pussett that he wished to destroy this beautiful creature. The bastard.

"Let's search for your gift." He drew her toward some large boulders at the edge of the camp. "This looks like a likely place."

"Hey, no fair. You know where they are."

Cord raised a hand. "I swear I had no part in this. My men hid the gifts."

Noelle threw her head back and tinkling laughter sprang forth. "In any event, I'll find my own. You go sit, mister."

"If that's the way you want it, Miss Independence."

"It is."

Pretending to pout, he moved back a few steps and watched her poke around between the rocks. She pulled out a gaily wrapped box and went to the fire to read the name. She shook her head and put it back.

Slowly, she moved around the camp's circle. Twice more she found a gift that wasn't hers.

Finally, she spotted one next to a small evergreen bush, read the name, and squealed. "It's mine."

She hurried back to him, sat down, and carefully removed the red ribbon from the little square box. "I can't imagine what's in here."

"It'll be New Year's before you get it open."

"Hush, I want to savor this." She took her time and opened the box at last. A soft gasp sprang from her mouth. "They're exquisite, Cord."

Nestled on cotton were a pair of Christmas earrings with silver bells dangling from them.

"They'll look beautiful on you."

"I've never had anything quite so pretty." She put them on her ears by touch. "How do I look?"

The words, bruised and hoarse, left his mouth before he could stop them. "Like an angel."

"Oh, Cord. You've made this night one I'll never forget. For the first time in I can't remember when, I feel like I matter, really matter to someone."

"You matter to me. And that has nothing to with pretending."

His gaze swept the group and found everyone seated with their gifts. Rising to his feet, he pulled Noelle up beside him and addressed the guests. "I hope you don't mind a little extra." He turned to face her questioning eyes. "I've found a most extraordinary woman who fills my dreams, and I can think of no better time for this. I'd like to ask her something with you all bearing witness."

Cord knelt on one knee, took her hand, and gazed up. "Noelle Blessing, would you be my wife?"

Chapter 6

Shocked silence hung over the group of revelers like thick, black smoke.

Noelle couldn't believe her ears. Surely, she'd misunderstood the question. The quiet grew and Cord pleaded with eyes that were like summer lightning. *Think.* The fire crackled and snapped in the hush.

"Will you marry me, Noelle?" Cord repeated.

Then she recalled what he'd said earlier about taking their game to a new level. This must be what he meant. But still, she had only one answer for him.

She moistened her dry lips. "Yes. Yes, I'll marry you, Cord Dalton."

When her cowboy again stood tall, she took his face in her hands and kissed him. His strong arms folded around her and he deepened the kiss.

The moon winked down at them, seeming to say it was a night made for lovers.

Noelle pushed away the thought that they were far from that.

Everyone gathered around except Albert Pussett. He stood by himself, glaring. "This might fool the others, but it doesn't fool me," he spat. "We'll see how long the charade lasts."

A sense of dread washed over Noelle. Their attempt to discourage Albert's nastiness had failed. And now what? She'd accepted Cord's proposal without thinking out the potentially disastrous consequences when they revealed that it had all been in fun. A make-believe engagement.

Albert would make sure that this didn't play well in the public opinion.

What had Cord been thinking? Of course she'd release him, that wasn't an issue.

Once all the well-wishers had sat back down, she slipped from Cord's embrace and hurried from the firelight. There hidden by the darkness, she covered her face and let the tears come.

She should've known any fleeting happiness would come at a hefty price. How had she forgotten that hers was the almost-life, the almost-romance, the almost-prince?

Footsteps sounded behind her. "There you are." Cord turned her around and pulled her against him. He silently held her until she'd exhausted her tears.

"What's wrong, Noelle?" He pulled a handkerchief from his pocket and wiped her eyes.

"We've just made things worse and maybe to the point I'll lose everything I own. Albert will be sure to spread it far and wide that you didn't really want me either, that marriage to me is a fate worse than death. Business will drop and I'll be forced to close."

He tilted her chin back with a thumb. "Only if we break it off," he said softly.

"I won't hold you to the pretend proposal."

"I know because that's the kind of woman you are." Sadness sat in his eyes, on his face.

"We played a game that we had no chance of winning, Cord. I knew nothing could come of it, but I played along anyway. I'm such a fool." She lowered her lashes to hide the immense disappointment that had to be lodged there. "Yet, even as we pretended to care for each other, I wanted to believe at least some of it was real. How crazy is that?"

The fragrance of the wild Texas land drifted around them as Cord pushed back her hair with his big hands, staring into her eyes. "It seemed that way because I felt it too. Believe me, if I could marry you, I would in a heartbeat."

"See? The situation is hopeless." She narrowed her gaze. "Answer me this, do you already have a wife?"

"No, nothing is farther from the truth. This is my fault, so I'll think of a way out of this that saves your reputation."

"How? What will you say? I see no story good enough to fix this." Laughter rose behind them. It was almost time to head back. "I don't know how I can face them."

"Don't worry. I'll borrow one of my men's horses and he can ride on the trailer. I'll get you back to town. No one will give our absence a thought."

Noelle sighed. "You think of everything. Thank you."

They went back to camp and Cord spoke to his men. A

short time later, Cord climbed into the saddle with Noelle in front of him and they started back to the ranch.

Exhausted, she tried to ignore the sound of his breathing, the feel of his chest against her back, muscles, and sinew that tightened with each movement. Her jumbled thoughts refused to settle. Every piece of the evening replayed in her mind. Cord talked very little and she didn't push him, telling herself it was best. Her heart heavy, she felt no need for words herself.

Midnight had approached by the time they reached Blessing Falls. A small light shone from a parlor window of the little house she shared with Gram.

Cord dismounted and helped her down. "Despite everything I enjoyed your company. Will you be all right?"

Someday. Noelle pulled her wrap tighter. "I'll be fine. Thank you for seeing me home."

"You still look like an angel with the moon's rays shining on you."

She forced a laugh. "Are you sure you don't see horns?"

"Positive." He placed his hands on her shoulders and kissed her cheek. "Good night."

"Sleep well, Cord."

The awkwardness was thick. He shifted and twirled his hat. "I'll be seeing you."

She nodded and let herself into the house. She rested her head against the door and whispered, "I almost had my cowboy, almost had the life I've dreamed for so long. But it evaporated like everything else."

Five days flew past in a dizzying whirl for Cord. He worked hard during the days but nights were devoted to thinking. The only solution he could arrive at was to marry Noelle for real. Except that she would never want to marry him if she knew the truth about his past.

He'd vowed never to take a wife. The Dalton bloodline had to stop with him.

And he wasn't sure he could ever explain this to Noelle. She would never look at him the same way again.

On Saturday, he saddled his chestnut gelding and rode into town. He took time for a haircut and shave before heading to the Sugar Spoon.

The candy shop was hopping with customers. Noelle's gram was working the counter. She called a greeting and waved when he squeezed through the door. "Noelle is in back."

He sauntered closer. "What's going on, Mrs. Blessing?"

"Everyone in town is having a Christmas party and we're overrun with orders that have to be out today. Go on back. We can use your help."

"I don't know about that. I've never made candy." He pushed through the door and found Noelle and another young woman pouring fudge, dipping chocolates, and laughing.

Noelle glanced up, her laughter freezing. "What are you doing here?"

"Your grandmother insisted that I come on back but maybe it's not a good idea. I'll just leave." He turned to back out.

"Wait," the other woman called. "You're the answer to a prayer. I'm Mazie McKenzie and I desperately have to see about my sick child, but I didn't want to leave Noelle in a lurch."

She rushed forward, whipped off her apron, and had it on him before he could blink.

"In that case, I guess I have little choice in the matter. By the way, I'm Cord Dalton."

"Nice to meet you, Cord Dalton. Indeed, you do not have a choice." Mazie blew Noelle a kiss. "Later, dear. I'll try to come back tomorrow after Sunday worship. It depends on how the baby is."

"No, absolutely not." Noelle laid down her dipping fork. "I don't want to see you until that sweet child is well. If these orders don't get filled so be it. There are more important things."

Mazie paused with a hand on the back door. "Watch out, Cord. She's a tyrant, that one."

He met Noelle's brown gaze and held it. "I'll take my chances. Maybe she won't be too hard on a beginner."

With the red-haired dynamo gone, the small room fell silent.

"Look, Noelle, I'm sorry I barged in, but I wanted to see you. Can we talk?"

She sighed and held out a stack of orders. "I really don't have a moment. Another time?"

"Let me help. I don't know much about candy making but maybe I'm better than nothing. I will do my best and that's a promise."

Her brow knitted as she seemed to weigh her options. "Okay. You'll do. Come here."

Happy that she relented, he went to the high table filled with round sugary balls and a pan of melted chocolate and stood next to her. He glanced around the messy room that had spilled sugar, chocolate, pecans, and dried fruit on every surface. A creator must not worry about keeping things tidy.

"Take each one of these balls and dip them into the chocolate, giving them a good coating. Then, place them on this sheet of parchment paper to cool without them touching."

"Sounds simple enough. What will you be doing?" He shot her another glance, relieved that her knitted brow had smoothed. He took that as a good sign she wasn't ready to bash his head in with a skillet.

"I'm going to cook batches of divinity and fudge." Her voice lowered an octave. "Thank you for offering to help. I'm glad to see you."

"You were on my mind all week and I had to find out how you were. Any proposal repercussions?"

"Everyone still thinks we're engaged." She glanced away. "I couldn't tell them it—"

"Was all pretend," he supplied. That she struggled with the words told him their ruse bothered her greatly. "Will you do me a favor?"

"If I can."

"Hold off until after Christmas. That's all I'm asking. Can you do that?"

"Of course but why?"

"There's no use ruining the holidays. Let yourself be happy for a little while. Once Christmas is over, I'll come clean about the whole affair. You won't have to say a word. The fault all belongs to me and will remain with me. Not you."

She shook her head. "Stop. I agreed to your plan so I'm just as guilty."

A noise at the back door interrupted them. Noelle opened it to find a small girl and boy standing there holding hands. Their clothes were ragged but they looked fairly clean.

"Can we have a candy stick," the boy asked softly. "I can pay." He held out a marble.

Cord was touched by Noelle's gentle hand on their shoulders.

"Of course you can. Please come in while I get your order." Noelle took the marble and went into the front of the store.

The kids tiptoed inside, their worn shoes making little noise. They stared at Cord and the boy spoke again. "Howdy, mister."

"How are you doing?" Cord knelt in front of them.

"Oh, we're making it."

"That's good. Bet you're anxious for Christmas."

The girl, who looked to be about five, nodded, her eyes twinkling. "Gonna snow."

"It is?" Amazing that what she wanted most was snow, not toys. He hated to tell them that the odds were against it. "Are you sure?"

The boy, probably no older than nine, wiped his nose on his sleeve. "Yes sir. Mr. Tenpenny said we'll have snow. We ain't never seen it but Mama says it's real pretty. We can build a snow fort and it'll be the best Christmas ever."

"Can I come and play in your fort?"

The girl giggled. "You're too big."

"Lily, Mama said we hafta be chari . . . charib . . ." Her brother stumbled over the word.

"Charitable?" Cord asked.

"Yeah. That's it. She said it's important to be nice to everyone."

"Your mama sounds like a special lady. What if I help build a real big fort?" If it didn't snow, Cord would take some of the men over to build them a wooden play fort. That is if he found out where they live.

"Yeah, and we could play in it."

Noelle bustled back inside with a small sack of peppermint sticks. "Now ask your mama if you can have these, Jimmy. All right?"

Jimmy took the sack. "Yes, ma'am."

"Is your mama still sick?"

It sounded as if Noelle knew them. Cord pricked his ears.

"Her in bed," Lily said softly.

"Tell her I'll be by tonight with some food."

"Okay." Jimmy took Lily's hand. "Let's go home."

"Bye, kids." Cord held the door for them, then turned to Noelle. "Sounds like you know where they live."

"I do. They've been coming by now and again for the last six months. Their father worked on one of the ranches around here and got hurt. I help the family with food. It's a sad situation."

"How long has the mother been sick?"

"I'm not sure . . . a few weeks, maybe. She has trouble breathing but they couldn't afford a doctor so he hasn't been around." Sadness filled Noelle's eyes as she went back to the stove.

Cord resumed his candy dipping, memories thick inside his head when his life careened out of control with violence. Two scared boys not quite men and their baby sister with a raging drunk for a father.

He rubbed his eyes, his mother's screams resounding

inside his head as though it had been yesterday. He still smelled the pool of blood. His trembles now were the same as that night when he feared he and his siblings might be next.

And Christmas carolers stood outside in the snow, lifting their voices in joyful song where there was no hope to be found.

Chapter 7

The quiet inside the small kitchen of the Sugar Spoon grew loud in Noelle's ears. She turned from the stove and found Cord unmoving, staring into space. "Are you all right?"

Her question jarred him to life, and he picked up the dipping fork. "I'm fine. Why?"

"For a moment there, I thought the chocolate fumes had gone to your brain."

His lopsided grin set her pulse galloping. Noelle reined herself in. *Stop that.*

"No such luck, Miss Blessing. Were you worried I'd pass out on the job and you'd have to revive me?"

She rolled her eyes to cover the reaction to the image in her head of placing her mouth firmly to his and breathing gently, forcing her air inside him.

Oh, my dear Lord! Stop.

Tingles swept the length of her body and she picked up a page from her recipe book and fanned herself. She was done with pretending, but the genuine thing . . . yes, the real thing would go beyond her wildest dreams. Even while playing the fake girlfriend, part of what she'd felt had sprung right from the deepest corner of her heart. She shot Cord a glance from beneath lowered lashes. If she was granted one wish it would be that he would love her.

He was making a mess with the chocolate and strewing it all over the raised table.

"Here, let me show you how to dip the centers." She hurried to his side and took the dipping fork.

When she did, chocolate flew off and landed on his nose. She froze and clapped a hand over her mouth, trying not to laugh. "I'm so sorry. I didn't mean to do that. I really didn't."

The somber lines of his face cut deep. Was he annoyed, or just pretending?

She tried to suppress laughter, but it slipped out. "If you could see yourself."

Without a word, he dipped his fingers in the warm chocolate and smeared it down Noelle's cheek.

"Why you!" She took the fork in her hand, plunged it into the pan, and flicked it at him.

He ducked. The war was on. They kept up the back and forth until chocolate coated the kitchen. Cord lifted the pan to dump the remainder on her. Noelle squealed and barely sidestepped in time.

A happiness she'd never known before settled over her. She calmly wiped each eye and licked her fingers. "You look like a very large piece of candy."

"Ha, ha! Very funny!" He took a step that brought him inches from her. "You look like a chocolate snow angel. The only thing that remains untouched are your silver bell earrings."

Before she could move, he stuck out his tongue and licked her cheek. "Taste like one too."

Delicious quivers danced up her spine and made her breathless. "Is this another game?"

"No."

She fidgeted under his unwavering stare, but she meant to get to the truth. "Then why?"

"Haven't you ever done anything because it was fun and made you happy? Maybe a pillow fight or a game of chase. Or tickling someone until they cried for mercy."

"I honestly can't remember doing something for no reason."

Cord chuckled and licked a finger. "Then it's time you did. Time you discovered life."

"I already know plenty about life. . . . As you know, I lost my parents in that terrible accident. . . ." She waved a chocolate hand around the room. "This shop provides me with an income. I know it looks fun, but it's very hard work. This is the reality of my life. And now, look at this mess that I have to clean up! And the candy centers that have to be dipped. You were supposed to be helping me!"

The smile left Cord's face. "I'd better leave you to it then. I apologize for . . . for making your life harder. I just thought . . . well, it's Christmas."

"Christmas just means a great deal of extra work." She picked up the pan.

Tension between them stretched to the breaking point. She shouldn't have spoken to him that way. His golden eyes held sorrow—plus a good deal of anger. He'd only meant to give her some laughter.

"I'm sorry," she whispered.

The door separating the room from the front of the shop swung open. Gram stood in shock. "What happened in here?"

"A chocolate explosion apparently." Cord took off his apron.

"This is the first I've heard of that." Gram turned to Noelle. "Joad Tenpenny is out front and won't buy his two pieces of chocolate from anyone but you."

"Give me a minute and I'll see to him." She washed her face and hands. Deciding the large spots on her apron would be all right, she pushed through the door. "Glad you stopped in, Mr. Tenpenny. How may I help you?"

"What's that?" The words came out just shy of a shout.

"I said I'm happy to see you. The usual?"

The old man wobbled and steadied himself with a long staff. Most of the children and dogs in town were afraid of him, and indeed he did look a bit frightening with a long white beard that hung past his waist and bony features. He'd turned ninety on his last birthday, and she'd once heard how he bought a little girl's overabundance of warts for one penny. They vanished and were still gone to this day and she'd recently turned twenty.

His mouth worked before he opened it to reveal toothless gums. "Child, I need two pieces of that candy I like. My Christmas treat." Again, his loud voice filled the shop.

The chocolate washed off, Cord Dalton came through

the door behind her and stood silently. Guilt rose for her anger, not because of the chocolate fight but because he'd reminded her of the sparse life she'd had.

Noelle reached for the Chocolate Cherry Delights and slipped them into a small sack. She went around the counter and gave Joad a hug, telling him how excited the two children who'd just visited were at the prospect of snow. She shook her finger. "Mr. Tenpenny, you know the odds. You shouldn't go around spreading false hope."

His faded gray eyes sparkled. "Everyone's gotta have something to believe in. It'll snow or my name ain't Joad."

What did she have to believe in? When had she ever believed that she deserved a life of happiness? What hope had lain in years and years of almosts?

She blinked back the hotness behind her eyes and patted his shoulder. "Mr. Tenpenny, I pray you're right. I really do."

Clutching his sack of sweets, the odd man shuffled out the door.

"I should go as well." Cord came forward, his worn hat in hand. "I've caused enough extra work for you."

Gram made no attempt to hide the fact she was watching.

"Please stay." Noelle laid a light palm on his arm. The anger that had been in his eyes vanished. "I've never had anyone quit before the job was done."

"If you're sure, I reckon I could finish and help you clean up."

"I'd like that."

"I wonder if another chocolate explosion will be in the works," Gram mused aloud.

Noelle shook a finger at the old dear, who shrugged her shoulders innocently.

The lines of Cord's face eased, and he shifted his stance. "Then I should get busy."

A black cloud lifted, and Noelle's heart sang. Her smile was probably too bright, but she couldn't help it. She followed him back to the kitchen and melted another pan of chocolate. He seemed interested in every step and asked umpteen questions.

She punched his arm. "Hey, are you planning to open your own candy shop and steal my business?"

"Not on your life. I simply enjoy knowing what I'm doing."

"I'm really glad you stayed." She met his golden eyes and grew warm.

"Me too. There's nowhere else I'd rather be, pretty lady."

"About earlier, I will confess that you hit on a sensitive subject. Fun has been glaringly absent from my life. Other than Mazie, I never had a best friend, a pillow fight, or played any games. You made me face that emptiness."

"I'm truly sorry. Growing up, my life was hard, too, but us kids loved play-fighting, a game of tag, marbles, and other things." He pointed with the dipping fork. "Your problem is you didn't have any brothers or sisters."

"I always envied other kids who did and wondered what that would be like."

Cord grimaced. "Noisy. We had to grow up . . ." Suddenly a cold hardness settled over him. "You know, forget it." He shook his head and forced a thin smile. "I don't want to bore you about the Daltons."

What had he been about to say? The sudden flip-flop of emotions was odd and puzzled her but she didn't press. Some things were better left unsaid. She knew quite a bit about that.

They lapsed into silence as they went about their work.

Joad Tenpenny's visit crossed her mind. "Did you hear that old man earlier?"

"That everyone needs something to believe in?"

"Yes."

"He's right you know. At the end of the day, what else is left? Hope keeps you going and turns storms into sunshine. Believing carries magic." Cord laughed. "Joad has convinced me."

"Lily and her brother sure believe." Noelle swung around and collided with him. The solid muscle and bone, those piercing amber eyes . . . A firestorm of flutters beat inside Noelle.

"Steady, girl." His husky voice washed over her as his gentle touch kept her upright.

"Thanks." She brushed back her hair, immediately realizing she was probably putting more chocolate into the strands, but not caring. They stood inches apart, his breath feathering across her cheek then up to the short tendrils of hair at her temple.

Barely able to breathe, she slightly parted her lips. In the next moment, he was pressing his lips to hers and heat flowed through her. His kiss drove out every thought from her head and weakened her knees. This was quite different from the pretend ones—much more potent . . . much more dangerous.

Noelle clutched the front of his apron, pressing herself farther into the warm circle of his arms.

An awakening came from deep within and whispered through her veins. A multitude of emotions swept her along toward something beautiful and real.

For the first time in her life, Noelle Blessing began to believe in something she couldn't see or touch.

Chapter 8

After finishing for the day, Cord helped Noelle clean up the candy shop. It was only right. He'd certainly helped destroy it.

A smile formed as he remembered how she'd looked with chocolate all over her pretty face.

And that kiss . . . How was he ever going to stop thinking about her now? As it was, she was there when he woke and there at night when he closed his eyes. Sometimes he dreamed of her and once or twice he'd called out her name, which had led to his men ribbing him unmercifully.

God in heaven! He was about to go out of his mind.

The words Blackie Dalton had cursed and screamed at him as the marshal had led him away echoed inside his head. "You're as worthless as me, boy! You got my blood."

He shook himself to silence that hate, focusing on the task at hand. He gave the mop a last pass in front of the candy counter. "Did we get all the orders made today?"

"Yes, we did, thanks to you." Noelle rinsed out the mop and hung it up, removing her apron. "Would you like to go with me to the Reeses'? I'm taking Jimmy and Lily a toy as well as food and checking on Mrs. Reese."

"Sure, I'll go. I told the kids I'll help them build a snow fort so I sorta need to know where they live."

"A snow fort?" She threw a shawl around her shoulders.

Cord adjusted his hat on his head. "That's right. And if the snow doesn't materialize, I'll build it out of wood."

She wagged a finger at him. "You're such a sucker."

"I know." He opened the back door for her and stepped out into the darkness. "Did we forget the box of goodies?"

"No, we'll pick it up at my house." She locked the door and took his arm. "I'm glad you're coming along."

"Not sick of me yet?"

Tinkling laughter filled the night. "You grow on a lady."

The blanket of stars overhead lit up the night sky like millions of sparkling diamonds. Not a cloud in sight. So much for snow. Damn it, he had really wanted Joad to be right.

The moon's silvery rays shone on an ornate carved bench in the back of the house next door. Looked to be made from pecan wood that was plentiful in the area. "That's a beautiful piece of wood," he remarked.

"Gram loves to sit out here and watch the birds. Sometimes store customers stop and chat with her."

"It's peaceful." Often a man looked the world over

never finding such a place. Cord held the door for Noelle, and they stepped into a warm kitchen that seemed to fold welcoming arms around him.

Gram paused in stirring a pot of something that gave off a mouthwatering aroma. "You two look mighty bedraggled. Cord Dalton, I hope you'll stay to supper. Lucius Winters will join us as well."

"I look forward to seeing him. Thank you for taking pity on me, ma'am." He kissed her smooth cheek. "After inhaling sugar all day, I'm hungry enough to eat a horse. Your granddaughter is a hard taskmaster."

Noelle feigned shock. "I am not! I let you sit down when you whined about your poor feet."

He draped a casual arm around her neck. "But did I get a bite to eat? No, I did not."

"Maybe you should file a complaint."

She glanced up, her gaze tangling with his, her moist lips that seemed to be begging for a kiss inches away. For a moment, he forgot he stood in Gram's kitchen. Forgot his vow to remain a bachelor. Forgot everything except the beautiful woman next to him. He caught himself just before he lowered his head.

Cord stepped back. "Show me the box and we'll be going."

Noelle appeared in a fog as well. It took a minute for the words to register. "Oh yes, the Reeses'. Yes, we should go."

"Don't forget the chicken and dumplings for them and don't take too long," Gram called. "Supper is almost ready."

They gathered everything and promised to be back in short order. Cord hoisted the box on his shoulder and ushered her outside.

A block later on foot they had arrived at the Reeses', and Noelle knocked on the door.

Jimmy opened the door. "They're here, Papa!" he yelled.

Lily came running, clutching a ragdoll to her chest. "Oh boy!"

The one-room house had nothing much to recommend it. Cord's gaze swept over the tiny kitchen area, parlor, and upstairs loft where the children slept. Movement drew his attention to a bed in the corner where a woman was sitting up.

A thick nightgown hung on her thin body. "Miss Noelle, you're gonna earn another gold star in your crown for this. I truly am grateful for your generosity."

"This is the least I can do, Mrs. Reese." Noelle turned to Mr. Reese and introduced Cord. "He works over on the McCready ranch, but I was happy to steal him away today to help me in the Sugar Spoon." Her eyes sparkled. "He turned out to be a fair hand."

The lilt in her voice might've come from memories of the chocolate fight and their closeness. He liked to think so anyway.

"Nice to meet you, Mr. Reese." Cord shook his palm. The man tried to stand but had to hold on to a chair.

"Sorry, I hurt my back and it hasn't healed." A forlorn look filled the man's eyes. "I'm not used to being idle. Plays with a man's spirit. Please call me Stuart."

"Stuart, there's no shame in needing help. I'm sure you've done your share of pitching in for others."

The man shook his head. "This is no role I want to play."

His wife came forward and Cord took her thin hand, shocked by the petite woman's frail body. He guided her to a chair that Jimmy dragged from the table. He winked at the boy who stood in a man's shoes. "Thank you, son."

Noelle knelt in front of Mrs. Reese and took her hands. "What I brought is little enough. It's mostly things the kids can fix by themselves."

Jimmy and Lily peered into the box, their curiosity getting the best of them.

Cord reached in and brought out the two gifts, handing them to the grinning kids. "Here you go. Tear right into 'em."

"They don't need any encouragement, Mr. Dalton." Mrs. Reese's weary smile didn't quite form before it faded completely. She hadn't the energy. "What do you say, children?" she prodded.

"Thank you, Miss Blessing. Thank you, Mr. Dalton," they replied in unison.

Noelle laid a hand on Lily's head. "You're very welcome."

"Hey, none of this was my doing," Cord protested. He'd make sure to get them something though by Christmas.

Jimmy's happiness at finding a yo-yo was apparent and Lily beamed at a jack-in-the-box.

After playing with his yo-yo for a bit, he brought it to Cord. "Do you know how to make it do tricks?"

"Let's see. I used to know Walk the Dog, Rock the Cradle, and make the yo-yo go backward, but it's been a long time." Cord slipped the string on his finger and did a few easy passes.

Soon he and Jimmy were competing with each other in the more difficult tricks. Everyone gathered around, clapping, including their mother and father.

The boy wore a look of admiration. “You’re sure good with a yo-yo, Mr. Dalton.”

“You’re not so bad yourself, Jimmy. Who taught you those?”

Sorrow filled Jimmy’s face and he glanced at his father. “My papa. He can do all sorts of things.”

“I used to, son,” his father said. “I will again. Just give me time.”

Stuart’s voice already sounded more hopeful and Cord was happy to hear it.

Cord laid a hand on the boy’s thin shoulder. “I predict he’ll be teaching you new tricks in no time.”

“Yep.” Jimmy sniffed and wiped his nose on his sleeve.

Lily tugged on Noelle’s arm. “Play with me.”

Cord’s breath caught as he waited praying she would relent and learn to have fun.

Finally, Noelle smiled. “I’d love to.” She sat on the floor with the girl and wound the jack-in-the-box over and over until she said it was time to set the table and eat.

Once they had the family eating the hot meal and satisfied they could do no more, Cord escorted Noelle home. “Thank you for letting me go with you. That’s such a sad situation. Jimmy especially needs his father in his life.”

“Yes, he does. Lily is still so young yet but both kids need their parents to be whole and hearty.” Noelle glanced up at him and though her face was shadowed he noticed her trembling chin. “I was about Jimmy’s age when I lost my parents and I guess that’s why I can relate to him having to step up and fill in the gap. I wish I had the power to take away sadness from all children.”

"That would be quite a gift," Cord said quietly, putting an arm around her.

He thought of the frightening days following the end of his family. How they'd moved around quietly in a thick haze, speaking in whispers. And the yawning emptiness that had tried to swallow Cord whole.

"Cord, I watched you back there with Jimmy and I saw how sweet you were in making him feel special." Noelle stopped. "You've never answered any of my questions about your family except for your sister, Alice," she prodded gently.

"I see no reason to speak of things in the past that have no bearing on the future." He hated the stiffness of his words, knowing it might hurt Noelle's feelings.

"When you get ready to talk about it, I'm ready to listen."

"What makes you think I have something that needs saying?"

"A lady knows." She laid a hand on the side of his jaw and the warmth spread over his skin. "Cord, I listen to customers in the shop all day long. To most, I'm invisible so they speak freely. I've heard wives discussing their husbands, husbands buying candy to smooth over a transgression, sons and daughters wanting to make their mother happy. I hear it all." Her brown eyes stared deep inside him. "I get the feeling you're holding everything in and that's not good. Have you ever told a single soul about your past?"

He looked away. "No."

Telling her would change nothing. It wouldn't make him forget the horror. Or his vow.

The moonlight shone on a bench outside the house she

shared with Gram. It seemed to draw him. Before he knew it, he took her hand and led her to it.

They sat in silence, Cord's mind tumbling end over end. Finally, he spoke. "You're right. There is something and you deserve to know in order to understand."

Clutching her hand, he told of growing up and his father's drunken rages. "As kids, we would run and hide when he came home until we grew older and realized we were leaving Mama to face him alone." He scrubbed his face with his hands. "My brother, Harlan, was older than me by three years and big. He started standing up to Blackie Dalton and that really made Blackie see red."

"I'm so sorry, Cord. That must've been terrible," Noelle murmured.

"Fights were a commonplace occurrence at our house. All the neighbors heard the ruckus. Sometimes they tried to stop Blackie but mostly they just watched the show and took care of Alice."

The scenes raced through Cord's mind, at times tripping over each other. Now that he'd started, he hurried to get through—while he could.

"Didn't the sheriff do anything?"

"Nope. He was Blackie's brother, our uncle. Besides, him and a lot of other people consider a wife her husband's property."

"That's horrible."

Animals moving about in the darkness and a baby's pitiful cries broke the silence. In the distance came the rumble of a train, then a few seconds later, the blast of its horn.

A glance at Noelle found her still, her expression one of anguish.

"Everything led up to one huge explosion one night under a winter moon. I was sprawled on the floor playing with my brother when Blackie came home." Cord ran his tongue across his lips to moisten them. "He slammed the door and kicked us boys, then started in on Mama. Harlan jumped on his back and hung on, screaming for Mama to run but she just stood there. Blackie had a . . . he had a gun and . . ." A sharp breath whistled through Cord's teeth. He bit his lip to stop the tremble and tasted blood. "He shot her."

Noelle clapped a hand over her mouth and released a cry.

"Then Blackie turned the gun on Harlan and my brother fell on top of Mama. Blood was everywhere. I was afraid to move, knowing I was going to be next and I probably would've been if by some miracle, the marshal from a neighboring town hadn't chosen that moment to come looking for Blackie about rustling."

"Thank heavens!"

"The marshal was big and muscular. He heard the gunshots, came crashing through the front door, and hauled off and hit Blackie square in the face before Blackie could even understand what was happening. The marshal dragged him to jail by his feet."

"What about Harlan?" Her breathless voice hung in the air.

"He still carries a bullet next to his spine and walks with a limp. But he's in a good place inside his head now and has a pretty wife."

"I'm so glad. It must've taken a while to rid yourselves of the nightmares. What happened to Blackie?"

"He's in prison and will hopefully rot there for the rest of his godforsaken life."

"Where did you and your siblings go after losing both parents?"

"An aunt and uncle took us in for which I'll always be grateful." He faced Noelle. "I'm the son of a murderer. That night I made a vow . . ." His voice broke and he cleared his throat. "I can never marry. I won't give the blood that's running through my veins to innocent children. The injury left Harlan unable to father any. The Dalton line stops with me. And I had no business even pretending to ask you to marry me."

Chapter 9

Cord's words hung in the air like an open trapdoor of a hangman's gallows. Noelle shivered and drew her shawl tighter. Now she understood everything. Why he wouldn't marry her, why he'd saved her from Albert Pussett, and why he'd formed such an attachment to little Jimmy and Lily.

She took his hand and wasn't surprised to find the palm sweaty. Reliving that nightmare had taken a lot out of him.

Her gentle voice cut through the night. "I understand you better now and how brave you were to experience that at such a young age. But if you truly intend to live life unencumbered by a wife, I have a question for you."

"What's that?"

A quick lick of her lips moistened them. "Why do you keep kissing me?"

The night sounds surrounded them in the quiet and wrinkles formed on Cord's brow.

Finally, he spoke. "I admit I was selfish. Pure and simple I like the taste of your lips." He pulled his hand from hers. "I gave you false hope and that's unfair. I apologize. It just felt so good being with you and I got carried away."

"I'm not complaining, mind you, Mr. Dalton." The use of "mister" was meant to put some space between them, and he appeared to get the message for he shifted away where they didn't touch.

Her heart cried out with yet another almost. When would she get the prize? Any prize?

Biting her lip, she asked, "Do you honestly think your blood is bad and that it might make you do horrendous things?"

"I have no way to be sure."

"Have you ever lost control of your temper or experienced the overwhelming desire to murder anyone?"

"I can't say that I have."

"Wouldn't it be a pure shame to miss out on love and a family when you don't need to?" Her words were soft and meant to make him take a long, hard look at himself. "You don't have to answer. Just promise to think about it."

The expression on his face was dark and puzzled. She didn't know the direction of his thoughts, but the fact he was still sitting there next to her was at least something. She felt sadness washing through her like a muddy river.

Miserable, she looked at the Sugar Spoon across the way, where they had had such memorable moments today. A light winked on in one of the windows. A few seconds later, it oddly moved to another.

What was going on? Was it her imagination?

Noelle sat up straighter, waiting. She'd almost decided her eyes were playing tricks on her when the light shone in yet a third window.

"Cord, something's wrong in the candy shop. Look. Someone's going from room to room with a light."

He got to his feet. "Stay here."

"I'm coming with you." She stood also and put her hands on her hips. "It's my store."

After an exasperated stare, he relented. "Fine. Just stay behind me."

"Of course. I'm not crazy."

As they set out across the space, Noelle's thoughts were spinning. She couldn't think of a single good reason for someone to be in the store.

Cord reached the back door and paused. "Key," he whispered.

She felt around in her pocket, pulled it out, and handed it to him. The door swung open soundlessly, thanks to the oil Noelle had recently put on the hinges.

The dark interior of the kitchen revealed no one. Noelle barely breathed, her hand gripping Cord's heavy belt as they went around the large worktable. A noise sounded in the front portion and she started, her grip on Cord tightening. *Darn her nerves*.

Was someone robbing her? Was money what they wanted?

Of course, you ninny! They didn't break in because of a hankering for candy. Stop it.

Cord paused at the door separating the two rooms, a hand on the knob. She readied for the explosion of a gun or the rush of a startled intruder wielding a club.

The faint scent of kerosene reached her. How odd.

Midway through a deep, shaky breath, Noelle fought

the urge to run. Before she could talk her feet into obeying, Cord jerked the door open.

There at the counter stood Albert Pussett III, his face illuminated by a candle flame, stuffing chocolates into his mouth. He jerked his head up, guilt written all over him. He froze, trying to swallow.

Hot anger rose. Forgetting her promise to stay behind Cord, she rushed to him, her fists clenched. "What in God's name are you doing? I worked hard making those for my customers." She hauled off and kicked his shin. "And you berating me each chance you got. Shaming *me* for a few extra pounds. How dare you!" She kicked him again.

"Ow! Stop it!" Albert hopped on one foot, holding the other.

Cord's voice interrupted her. "Noelle, you better look at this."

Keeping Albert in her sights, she half turned to see Cord pointing to a can of kerosene and soaked rags on the floor. Her stomach twisted to see Albert's intentions fully exposed.

"You sack of horseshit! You were going to burn my business! But before you did what you came for, you had to get your fill of candy." She doubled a fist and shot it into his stomach. "I don't know which makes me madder."

Albert groaned, but didn't dare defend himself with Cord right behind her.

"And I thought stealing the church's collection plate was about as low as a man could go," she spat, blood boiling. "Stealing money that goes to help the poor." She pointed a finger. "You took food from those people's mouths, clothes from their backs. What you did was unconscionable. I thought you had learned your lesson, but I see now that you'll never change."

Cord grabbed Albert's arms and tied them behind his back with a piece of cord from a burlap bag the man had carried the rags and kerosene in. "I'm marching you to the sheriff. Your days in this town have ended."

"It's all Noelle's fault," Albert sneered. "If she hadn't broken her promise to marry me, none of this would ever have happened. I needed what she could give me and she snatched it away."

"Do you hear yourself?" Cord snorted and grabbed the front of Albert's shirt. "That's twisted thinking. You and you alone are responsible for your own crimes."

Noelle stared at the man she'd once wanted to marry. What had she ever seen in him? Mazie was right. He was nothing but a self-centered, arrogant worm.

Gram burst through the door with Lucius. "What's going on? We kept waiting supper on you but finally saw the door open over here."

"Albert was going to burn me out if we hadn't stopped him." Now that the excitement was over, Noelle felt like a puppet with her strings broken. Her legs didn't want to support her. "Cord, if you don't get him out of my sight, I think I'll throw up."

"I wouldn't want that. He's not worth it." He jerked Albert's arm. "Come on."

Looking rather dignified in a gray felt hat and silk vest, Lucius gathered the kerosene and rags, stuffing them back into the burlap sack. "I'll go with you, Dalton. I have a thing or two to add myself."

"Shut up, Lucius," Albert growled. "You have no proof."

Noelle wondered what else Albert had gotten caught doing. Better yet, what no one had seen him do. She wasn't sure she wanted to get the full list. What she had seen was revolting enough.

Lucius faced him. "I know I saw you sneaking buck naked from a certain house early one morning carrying your clothes, just as the woman's husband was opening the front door."

Noelle smothered a giggle. She'd love to have seen that.

An angry red flush washed over Albert's features. "I don't have to explain anything to you."

"That's right, you don't. But the husband might drag you to the town square and whip the daylights out of you." Lucius smiled.

Cord shook his head. "All your secrets are coming out now, Pussett."

Albert struggled to free himself before collapsing in vain against the candy counter. The men each took a side and marched him out of the Sugar Spoon.

Gram put a bracing arm around Noelle. "You look beat. Let's go home."

They locked up and were soon sitting at the kitchen table with a bowl of chicken and dumplings and cornbread.

"Yum, this is your best yet, Gram." Noelle met her grandmother's steady gaze. "Each time in my life when I've needed bolstering, you've always been there with a hot bowl of soup or a cup of tea and soon everything seemed better." She let out a long breath. "A lot happened tonight."

"It does seem so."

"What appeared like a sure thing turned into an almost and this one not so bad. The Sugar Spoon seemed destined to turn to ashes but it wasn't."

Gram nodded. "An *almost* can be a very good thing. You came close to marrying Albert."

"Too close. I feel immensely blessed at how my life's turned out. I'm alive, well, and reasonably happy." She had little to complain about.

"What would make you totally beyond doubt happy, dear?"

Should she put words to her pipe dream?

Why not? Noelle kept her gaze on the tablecloth. "I would be deliriously happy if Cord Dalton would say he can't live without me and would love me forever if I'd be his wife."

"Any chance of that?" Gram reached for her glass of milk and took a sip.

"I don't think so." Noelle dipped her spoon into the chicken and dumplings. "Cord and I had a long talk tonight and it seems he made a vow long ago to never marry." She told her gram about Blackie and the fact Cord harbored fears he was like his father.

"I can understand that in a way. Some claim a son carries the sins of the father and maybe Cord thinks he does, whether consciously or not."

Noelle rose to look out the window. "We'll see, I guess. I gave him something to think about."

"You like him a lot. I can tell."

"More than anyone I've ever known." She turned from the window. "He sees me as I am and is happy with it. Albert saw me as someone lacking and needing a lot of work to change. I still can't understand why I didn't see the real him until it was almost too late. I think I must've been blind."

"He kept his real self hidden for the most part. Lots of

men do that." Gram rose and put an arm around her. "Come and eat. It's getting cold."

She didn't have the heart to tell her she wasn't hungry, so she sat down and picked up her spoon.

"I didn't tell you that the mayor came by today and asked for our help in getting the children together to sing Christmas carols on the square. I thought of Jimmy and Lily. Those kids are hurting and need something fun to do."

"I agree. Does the mayor have a date in mind for this?"

"Christmas Eve I think."

Five days. That was doable. "I'll make time, Gram."

A tap sounded at the door and Lucius let himself in. "We got the prisoner in a cell. The sheriff said he'll be by tomorrow to ask a few questions."

"Thank you for taking care of that." Noelle glanced at the door, expecting Cord to walk through.

Lucius sat down. "Dalton stopped by the doctor's office and gave him some money to check on Mrs. Reese. He said he'd let you know what the verdict is tomorrow."

Deep disappointment wound through her that she wouldn't spend any more time with him this night. Pain shot through her heart.

The cowboy who couldn't save himself was trying to save everyone else.

Chapter 10

Noelle didn't sleep much that night and kept having disturbing dreams of Albert. But there was one with Cord in which he was pushing her away each time she got close.

By morning, her stomach was tied in knots and she feared the worst. Cord Dalton definitely appeared to be putting distance between them.

Around noon, Jimmy showed up with a note from Cord saying Mrs. Reese had pleurisy but would get better soon with medicine the doc had left.

She smiled at the boy. "Your mama's going to be all right."

"Yep." Jimmy grinned. "Guess what?"

"I have no idea. Tell me."

"Mr. Dalton slept at our house last night. And made pancakes for breakfast."

A current of surprise shot through her. Just when she

thought she had Cord Dalton figured out, he did something totally unexpected.

"Well, I'll be. I think he must have a big heart."

"Yep. And my papa's back and legs are stronger."

Noelle clapped. "Hallelujah! That's wonderful!"

Jimmy shook the hair from his eyes and looked up. "Would you have a candy cane for me and Lily? We can share."

"You won't have to share. I'll give you both one and some gumdrops just because I'm happy about your mama and papa." She reached into the jar and handed him the treats. "I want to see you and Lily on Saturday in the square to sing Christmas carols."

"Oh boy! But it'll be snowing, Miz Blessing."

There was that again and she couldn't burst the boy's bubble. She rested an arm across his shoulders. "Then we shall sing in the snow. Won't that be fun?"

"Yep. I'm gonna tell Lily." He said goodbye and ran out to go spread the news.

The sheriff came by to ask some questions and investigate. "Attempted arson is a serious crime, Miss Blessing. He's going to remain in jail for a while."

"I think that might be exactly what he needs."

Except that she didn't want his fingers all over her candy, she had a mind to take rolled sugar balls and melted chocolate over and make him re-create the sweets he'd stuffed in his big mouth. That still burned her up. It just showed that a man reaped what he sowed, and in this case, Albert would be reaping briars and weeds for many years.

By the close of day, she still had yet to see Cord.

The same thing in subsequent days.

An ache sat in her chest. She had no choice but believe she'd pushed him away. Immersing herself in the holidays, she bought Gram and the Reese kids some things for Christmas and wrapped them. When she went over to take food and check on the family, she found that Cord had brought them a small juniper bush, which the children had decorated. He appeared to think of everything.

Why hadn't he stopped to see her since he'd come down the street?

Noelle tried to work up a temper but found it too much work. The only conclusion she arrived at was that everything was over between them. Including friendship. He wanted nothing from her.

Another almost for her list and this was the most devastating of all of them combined.

Not even his sweet tooth drew him to the Sugar Spoon.

With a heavy heart, she filled the week of Christmas with work, stuffing benevolent boxes for the poor, and spending time with Gram. Yet, when she allowed her thoughts a moment of free rein, memories of the dark-haired cowboy with a heated touch and ready smile rushed over her. She wondered if he ever thought of her.

Gray clouds hung low in the sky as they drew closer to Christmas. Each day the weather grew colder and customers would say it looked more and more like snow. Noelle smiled and nodded but inside thought the notion totally ridiculous. Joad Tenpenny needed his head examined. False hope was worse than no hope at all to her way of thinking.

On Friday, she opened the door to find a juniper bush on their doorstep. Whoever left it had planted it in a five-gallon bucket painted bright green with red berries around the top and bottom.

Gram beamed. "It's so pretty. If you'll put a sign on the store to come over here if customers need something, we'll decorate it. Is there a note with the tree?"

"No, but my bet is on Lucius. He wanted to surprise us."

"Well, I'm not going to look a gift horse in the mouth."

The colors really did brighten Noelle's mood. Between the two of them, they carried the greenery into the parlor and set it on a table. With few customer interruptions, they filled the morning making and decorating what served as a Christmas tree. In areas of Texas like theirs where few trees grew, folks were known to use whatever was at their disposal. Including tumbleweeds. In their case, juniper and mesquite were plentiful.

Noelle tied the last red bow on a branch and stood back to admire their handiwork. In addition to red bows, popcorn strings, candy canes, and homemade ornaments, they carefully unwrapped a fragile angel that had belonged to Gram as a child and secured it to the top.

"It's beautiful, Gram." Noelle's eyes misted at the angel's sweet face and gossamer wings. "The tree just needs one more thing to be perfect."

She went out to scoop up a vacant bird nest from the porch rafter and placed it on a juniper branch.

Gram clasped her hands together over her heart and beamed. "That completes it, dear. I love the rustic beauty of bird nests."

"Me too." Noelle hugged Gram, grateful for God's blessings.

Lucius dropped by and declared it the prettiest tree he'd ever seen, denying any part in delivering it to their doorstep. "Don't look at me. Juniper makes me sneeze."

And with his denial, the matter was dropped. Yes, Cord had taken juniper to the Reese's . . . But Noelle had given up watching for a certain cowboy with kisses that had once heated her blood.

All she could hope for was that he'd think of her once in a while and remember one magical night by a campfire, silvery moonlight around them, Christmas carols in the air. Two hearts beating in perfect rhythm.

Christmas Eve arrived with much anticipation. Even Noelle hurried to the window to look out.

"Joad said it would snow on Christmas, not the day before," Gram admonished.

"Mark my words, tomorrow will be no different," she muttered darkly.

"Have you seen how cold it's gotten? And the sky has turned dark. It looks like snow."

"The sky is dark gray." Noelle opened the door. Cold air swirled around her, bringing a shiver, and sending her scurrying inside. "Brrr. We'll have to bundle up."

With the shop closed until the coming week, she had little to do until collecting the kids to go sing in the square. She'd already selected the songs, washed and fixed her hair in a becoming style, and laid out a vibrant green dress to wear.

"Why don't you make us some hot tea?" Gram suggested. "I could use a cup."

That sounded good even though she saw through her grandmother's attempt to give her something to do.

A bit later, they sipped on the tea and Gram asked, "Do you think Cord Dalton will come to town today?"

Her heart beat faster at his name, but she gave a nonchalant shrug. "I really couldn't say what that man will or won't do."

"It would be nice to see him." Gram sighed. "I always thought he looked a bit like your grandfather when he was young. Cord is a nice-looking man."

"Yeah, well, that bridge is washed out I'm afraid."

Gram took a drink of her tea. "I heard the sheriff moved Albert to San Antonio until his trial."

"Good riddance. The town's better off."

Finally, it was time to collect the kids. Wearing her silver bell earrings, Noelle first picked up Jimmy and Lily, who did nothing to hide their excitement, then went to ten other houses. She ended up with quite a gaggle of children.

Then . . .

Wonder of wonders, it began to snow. Happy shouts accompanied them to the square.

At noon, bustling shoppers stopped to gather around amid huge flakes of snow. Old Joad had almost been right. He was only off a day. Wearing a toothless grin, he hobbled to the square. "My knees told me this would be on Christmas Day, but we'll take it a day early."

Noelle nodded. "Indeed, we will, Mr. Tenpenny."

The kids stood in the decorated gazebo and began lifting up their voices. With the exception of one older boy hollering the verses instead of singing them, their sweet voices blended in harmony, bringing tears to Noelle's eyes. Nothing had ever been so rewarding.

They sang the first eight songs, then she turned the page to "It Came Upon a Midnight Clear." She readied to give the opening note when a deep voice sounded from behind.

"You sing like an angel, Noelle."

She turned and her tongue glued to the roof of her mouth. Cord stood there looking as handsome as ever in a new black Stetson, his waist trim in a pair of thigh-hugging denims. He held two wrapped gifts.

"Thank you," she finally managed, her palms sweating. "Christmas shopping?"

"For my nieces." He widened his stance. "Any chance you'd talk to me? I've been thinking a lot about what you said."

What was it she'd said? Panic rose. Which part did he refer to? The way he stood there smiling like Cinderella's prince was quite disconcerting. Her thoughts scurried like naughty schoolchildren evading her grasp.

Expectation was in his eyes. She had to say something. "Ahh, I see. We're about to perform the last song if you'd like to wait."

"Sure."

"Miz Blessing, maybe you oughta talk now," Jimmy said, grinning. "It might be important."

"Please," Lily pleaded.

The older boy piped up. "Here's the thing, Miz Blessing. We ain't in no hurry 'cause all we gotta do is chores when we get home anyway. Here, we get to enjoy the snow."

Noelle hid a grin with a palm. She met Cord's golden eyes and felt herself falling for him all over again. Darn the man for reawakening everything she'd buried.

Cord shrugged. "The kids have spoken. What do you say?"

"All right. Keep this low." She turned her back to the children, hoping they wouldn't hear. "But first, did you plant a juniper in a green bucket and leave it at our house?"

"I don't know if this'll get me hugged or shot but yes, I did."

"Thank you. I just wish you'd have stuck around."

"I didn't know how you'd feel about seeing me." He touched one of her silver bell earrings and listened to the tinkle. "You make a lot of sense for a candy maker."

"I do?"

"I spent the last week looking back over my life and . . . if you're willing to take a chance on me, I'm ready to forget my vow. The past has no place in my . . . our . . . future." He set his packages down and took her hands. "I've wasted part of my life already and don't want to let another second go by. I want you, Noelle Blessing. No pretending either." He paused. "That is if I'm not too late."

Her chin quivered as tears filled her eyes. A snowflake rested on her lashes, momentarily blinding her. "Oh, Cord. I think I love you."

"That's good because I love you more than I've ever loved anyone." He lowered his head and pressed his lips to hers.

Noelle didn't care that half the town was watching. She tilted her face, accepting the kiss, the little bells on her ears tinkling merrily. Her knees weakened with love for this cowboy who'd saved her on a moonlit night with waltz music playing around her. Slipping her arms around his waist, she clung to him as a drowning woman did a piece of driftwood.

Breaking the kiss, he whispered, "No more almosts."

There with the miracle snowflakes falling gently to the ground, he knelt on one knee and held her hand. "This time is for real, sweetheart. Will you please be my wife forever and always?"

She swallowed the lump of emotion in her throat. "Yes, I'd be truly honored."

Much to her amazement, he stood, produced a silver ring from his pocket, and slipped it on her finger, meeting her questioning gaze. “I’m a gambling man and believe in being prepared.”

“Can I expect more of that in the future, my soon-to-be husband?”

He winked. “I’ll never tell.”

While the children ran around trying to catch snowflakes on their tongues, the snow-draped crowd erupted with eager clapping and loud shouts of excitement. Gram, her face shining with joy, was front and center.

With happiness bursting inside, Noelle snuggled against Cord’s broad chest. “It’s almost Christmas.”

“No, sweetheart, it *is* Christmas. Happy Birthday.”

“Did I say I love you?”

He kissed the tip of her nose. “Yes, but repeat it as often as you wish. I’ll never get tired of hearing the words. I love you too.” He paused, his golden eyes twinkling. “Oh, there is one more thing. Can we celebrate with another chocolate fight?”

“Yes,” Noelle said, her eyes brimming with laughter and love. “Every day for the rest of our lives, if you like.”